Praise for Cynthia Baxter and

MURDER WITH A CHERRY ON TOP

"*Murder with a Cherry on Top* is a sweet treat. I
loved everything about the Hudson Valley setting,
from the small-town ice cream shop to the organic cows.
Cynthia Baxter's characters feel real enough to touch and
her descriptions are mouthwatering. This book is best read
with a spoon and a tub of ice cream nearby."

—Laurien Berenson, author of *Ruff Justice*

"Ice cream lovers and mystery fans alike will gobble
up this charming cozy featuring ice cream store owner
and aficionado Kate McKay. Chock full of mouthwatering ice cream treats, a clever plot twist, and a
dollop of romance, *Murder with a Cherry on Top*
is an absolutely yummy read!"

—Laura Levine, author of *Death of a Bachelorette*

"Wake up, Rip Van Winkle! Kate McKay's returned to
the Hudson Valley and is mixing up sweet ice cream
treats, rekindling an old romance, and solving a
sticky murder. Cynthia Baxter's *Murder with a Cherry
on Top* is every bit as delicious as a hot fudge sundae,
and I can't wait for a second helping!"

—Leslie Meier, author of *Turkey Trot Murder*

Books by Cynthia Baxter

MURDER WITH A CHERRY ON TOP

HOT FUDGE MURDER

Published by Kensington Publishing Corporation

Murder with a Cherry on Top

Cynthia Baxter

KENSINGTON BOOKS

www.kensingtonbooks.com

KENSINGTON BOOKS are published by

Kensington Publishing Corp.
119 West 40th Street
New York, NY 10018

All Kensington titles, imprints and distributed lines are available at special quantity discounts for bulk purchases for sales promotion, premiums, fund-raising, educational or institutional use.

Special book excerpts or customized printings can also be created to fit specific needs. For details, write or phone the office of the Kensington Sales Manager: Kensington Publishing Corp., 119 West 40th Street, New York, NY 10018. Attn. Sales Department. Phone: 1-800-221-2647.

Kensington and the K logo Reg. U.S. Pat. & TM Off.

First Kensington Hardcover Edition: April 2018

ISBN-13: 978-1-4967-1414-5 (ebook)
ISBN-10: 1-4967-1414-8 (ebook)

ISBN-13: 978-1-4967-1413-8
ISBN-10: 1-4967-1413-X
First Kensington Trade Paperback Edition: January 2019

10 9 8 7 6 5 4 3 2

Printed in the United States of America

To Nicole

Chapter 1

87% of Americans have ice cream in their
freezer at any given time.

—www.IceCream.com

"I don't believe it! I do not be-*lieve* what I am seeing with my very own eyes!"

I blinked, then blinked again, hoping I was simply imagining it. Yet there it was, staring at me as boldly as the bright red cherry on top of a hot fudge sundae.

I stood frozen to the spot, poised like a mannequin over the real-life hot fudge creation I was concocting with all the passion that Michelangelo must have felt as he painted the Sistine Chapel.

For this ingenious creation, I'd lovingly arranged baseball-size scoops of three delectable flavors of ice cream into an old-fashioned tulip-shaped ice cream sundae dish: a scoop of creamy Classic Tahitian Vanilla, a scoop of sinfully rich Chocolate Almond Fudge, and a scoop of an invention of my own, Berry Blizzard, a tangy strawberry ice cream dotted with bits of fresh strawberry, raspberry, and blueberry and delicately spiced with just a hint of cardamom and cinnamon.

Over it I'd dripped about a quart of wonderfully gooey chocolate syrup, handmade by me just a few hours earlier. It was a specialty of the house, a recipe I'd created myself: a rich chocolate syrup dotted with pieces of bacon that had been glazed with brown sugar. I called it Salty 'n Sweet Chocolate Syrup with Bacon. I expected my customers at Lickety Splits, my brand new ice cream shop, to call it Heaven on Earth.

Next came the generous dollop of whipped cream, also hand whipped by *moi*, followed by an avalanche of chopped almonds, hazelnuts, and pecans.

In fact, I was just about to add the perfect finishing touch, a plump red maraschino cherry, when the bright, hot pink sign about thirty feet away from where I was standing caught my eye.

The sign, taped in the window of the shop directly across the street from Lickety Splits, had been neatly hand lettered with a black Sharpie. The sign was right below the pink-and-white striped awning that was edged with swirly letters, spelling out SWEET THINGS PASTRY PALACE. Directly below, in letters that were smaller but even swirlier, were the words HOME OF THE MILE-HIGH CUPCAKE.

The new sign in the bakery's window read: NOW SELLING HOMEMADE ICE CREAM!

"How *dare* she?" I sputtered, barely glancing at my best friend, Willow Baines, who was helping me out in the shop for the afternoon. "This is absolutely the last straw! It's bad enough that Ashley Winthrop practically destroyed my entire childhood! That she turned my middle school and high school years into the sequel of *Mean Girls*! But now that we're grown up and she *still* thinks she can just go ahead and ruin my life—"

"Calm down!" Willow said, sounding annoyingly calm herself. "Take deep, cleansing breaths, Kate. In, out. In, out . . . Somehow we'll figure out what to do about this."

"I know *exactly* what to do about this," I shot back. "And it involves a heavy, blunt object. Something along the lines of a . . . a three-gallon tub of Cappuccino Crunch!"

It wasn't surprising that Ashley Winthrop's sudden foray into the world of ice cream had me so upset. Not only had the two of us been enemies practically our whole lives. But fifteen years after graduation—after I'd gone to college, moved to New York City, developed a successful career in public relations, and just three months ago, come back to my hometown to start a new chapter in my life—she threatened to start up our rivalry all over again.

I'd just become the proud owner, operator, chef, sales force, marketing director, and janitor of the Lickety Splits Ice Cream Shoppe. At the risk of sounding melodramatic, opening my own business truly was nothing less than the realization of a lifelong dream. And the fact that my brand new shop featured my absolute favorite food in the entire universe made the whole experience even sweeter.

Thanks to the randomness of real estate markets, it just happened that my store was located right across the street from the bakery that Ashley had been operating for a little over five years. I learned that because right after I'd moved back, the local paper, the *Daily Roost*, had run a big article about Sweet Things celebrating its five-year anniversary, complete with photos. Still, the shop I'd rented had a great location—and everyone knows the number one rule of real estate is Location, Location, Location. It was on Wolfert's Roost's main thoroughfare, Hudson Street. And it was less than a hundred feet away from the charming town's busiest intersection.

The front of my building was incredibly cute. It had a Victorian look, with ornate wooden columns framing the door and window boxes along the display window. Inside, it had a shiny tin ceiling and a black-and-white tiled floor. It even had an exposed brick wall that gave the place a touch of old-world charm.

The space also happened to be the perfect size. In the front section, there was enough room for two glass freezer cases displaying the eighteen flavors of ice cream that I intended to change from day to day, as well as the line of eager customers I'd hoped to regularly attract. But there was also room for six small, marble-topped tables, three along each wall. Each table accommodated two black wrought-iron chairs with pink vinyl seats.

And in back, there was plenty of space for the two industrial-size ice cream makers I'd installed, along with a gigantic ice cream freezer, six feet wide and six feet high, that provided enough storage space for at least two dozen giant tubs of ice cream. I'd also squeezed in a big counter for chopping chocolate and shredding coconut.

The moment the real estate agent took me inside the empty storefront, I'd seen its potential. And as soon as I'd signed the lease, I jumped into realizing that potential. I'd had the exterior of the shop painted a soft shade of pink, then personally painted the wooden columns and the window boxes lime green. Next I'd put a wooden bench in underneath the big display window, painting the slats pink and green. As a finishing touch, I'd filled the window boxes with pink and white petunias that spilled over the front and sides, the green of the leaves picking up the building's lime-colored accents.

Inside, I'd hung paintings of ice cream concoctions along the brick wall. My BFF, Willow, had made them, since in addition to being the most phenomenal yoga instructor in the Hudson Valley, she also happened to be an amazingly talented artist. On one, Willow had painted a gigantic ice cream cone; on the second, a banana split; and on the third, a huge ice cream sandwich.

The colorful, almost cartoonish artwork was the perfect accompaniment to the glass display counters, technically called dipping cabinets, that ran across the opposite wall, showing off the vats of ice cream I whipped up in back. To me, Willow's paintings were a symbol of her confidence in me to succeed at creating a business based on one of the things I loved most in the world.

But even better than the paintings of ice cream on Lickety Splits' walls was the *real* ice cream. That, of course, was what it was all about.

I planned to offer three basic types of ice cream flavors. The first type was the classics, like chocolate, vanilla, strawberry, and coffee, but I was going to make them so rich and so flavorful that they were guaranteed to be the best version anyone had ever tasted. My Classic Tahitian Vanilla served as the perfect example, since it truly was made with vanilla that had come all the way from Polynesia.

The second type reflected my own take on the slightly more adventuresome flavors that were popping up everywhere. Hawaiian Coconut that was made with actual strands of fresh coconut and big chunks of macadamia nut. Caramel Sea Salt that had ribbons of luscious caramel running through. Peanut Butter on the Playground, consisting of peanut butter ice cream made with freshly ground peanuts and sweetened with generous globs of grape jelly.

The third type, which I was most excited about, consisted of my very own creations. The idea of being able to express my love of ice cream in unique ways was what made my heart pound and my head spin as I lay awake nights, thinking up fun and delicious new flavors. Strawberry Rhubarb? I couldn't wait to make it, especially since I intended to add bits of piecrust pastry to make it just like the ever-popular pie. S'mores? Chocolate ice cream dotted with chocolate chips, little chocolate marshmallows, and broken-up pieces of graham cracker. Cashew ice cream? Kahlua and Chocolate? Cheddar cheese? *Goat* cheese?

Why not?

The shop I was lucky enough to rent was ideal, with every

feature I could possibly want. The place was so perfect, in fact, that I figured I could learn to live with having the despicable Ashley Winthrop and her bakery right across the street.

In a flash, all that had changed. The fact that once again, Ashley had found a way to wedge herself between me and my latest dream was making my head feel as if it were about to explode.

I was still staring at that sign, thinking that there was probably so much steam coming out of my ears that it was going to melt all the ice cream, when the customer who'd ordered the Hudson's Hottest Hot Fudge Sundae I'd been in the midst of concocting cleared his throat. Loudly.

"Uh, excuse me?" he said. "Is that sundae about ready?"

"I'm so, so sorry," I said, snapping back into the moment. I glanced over at the young man standing on the other side of the counter, wearing a loud tie-dye T-shirt and sporting a long ponytail. He looked as if he was on the verge of experiencing severe chocolate withdrawal.

"Let me just add the cherry," I told him, then proceeded to do exactly that.

At the moment, there were no other customers in line. Not that the place wasn't buzzing. Five out of my six tables had customers at them, making a total of ten customers. Six were devouring ice cream cones, sampling a variety of flavors that ranged from simple Divine Chocolate to one of my more exotic offerings for the day, Honey Lavender.

Three of the customers had gone for more complex ice cream treats. A teenage girl with very cool purple eyeglasses was wolfing down a Bananafana Split, made with slices of frozen chocolate-covered bananas piled up on top. Her friend, sitting across the table from her, was alternating between slowly sipping the ice-cold soda in her Rootin'-Tootin' Root Beer Float and sucking up small spoonfuls of the baseball-size chunk of Classic Tahitian Vanilla ice cream floating in it.

From the looks of things, she was savoring every mouthful with such deliberation that she was going to make it last for at least another half hour. And number ten, well, he was the happy recipient of the hot fudge sundae I'd just concocted, now sitting at a table by himself. From what I could see, he'd already snarfed down a good third of it, dribbling just a tiny bit of Salty 'n Sweet Chocolate Syrup with Bacon onto his tie-dye shirt. Fortunately, it blended right in.

The fact that there were no other customers for me to serve at the moment gave me a chance to concentrate on my hatred of Ashley Winthrop.

"Do you know what I'm going to do?" I said, turning to Willow. "I'm going to march right over there and tell that stupid Ashley that—"

"Don't do it," Willow said, grabbing my arm as if to demonstrate that she was prepared to use physical force to stop me if necessary. And trust me, yoga instructors have a surprising amount of upper body strength. "Kate, this is not the time to confront Ashley. You'd be better off waiting until you've had a chance to put all this into perspective."

"Perspective?" I repeated. "*Perspective?* Honestly, Willow, when is it going to *end?*"

Surely nearly three decades of enduring Ashley Winthrop was enough. And she really had been tormenting me for that long.

It had all started back in kindergarten. It was probably early October when my teacher, Ms. Trautman, invited us five-year-olds to delve into the exciting new world of finger paints. Even then I was a sucker for bright colors, and I could hardly wait to get my hands on those big plastic jars of paint— in particular, the yellow.

So as soon as we donned our smocks, I made a beeline for the jar that was the color of daffodils. But Ashley, barely out of Huggies, beat me to it. She appeared from out of nowhere, her pale blond ponytail bobbing behind her as she darted in front of me and grabbed the last jar of yellow before I'd even reached the art supplies table.

That was just the beginning. In second grade, she stole away my very first boyfriend ever, Skippy Nolan, an impressive young gentleman who'd risen to instant popularity the moment he'd demonstrated his ability to turn his eyelids inside out. Ashley had beaten me in our fifth grade's annual Spelling Bee Extravaganza, looking infuriatingly smug as she stepped up to the podium to correctly spell the word "ignominious" right after I'd foolishly misspelled "enemy," a word I could spell in my sleep but that for some ridiculous reason I'd begun by saying "*E-M* . . ." and sealing my fate.

By high school, Ashley had graduated to Most Popular. She was homecoming queen, captain of the cheerleading squad, class president both our junior and senior years . . . you get the picture. And she never passed up a single opportunity to use the power she got from being queen bee to make my life more difficult. She would make a cutting joke about my outfit in front of a group of giggling girls, go out of her way to flirt with a boy I had a crush on, and snatch away anything I wanted, from the best seat at the Class Talent Show to the highly coveted position of chair of the junior prom decorating committee.

None of those gotchas compared to this.

"But I have to do something," I insisted. "This is a new low, even for Ashley."

"That's certainly true," Willow agreed. "She's been jealous of you since day one, since she knows as well as any of us that the one thing she's always lacked was a brain that's half as good as yours." She ran her hand through her pale blond hair in a short pixie cut, a style that was as practical as her outfit: a loose white T-shirt and stretchy black yoga pants.

"But I have to admit that good old Ashcan has really outdone herself this time."

I appreciated my best friend's use of our middle school nickname for my nemesis. But even that didn't do much to improve my mood.

"I mean, this goes beyond unethical," I continued. "Not that it's the first business decision she's made that shows her true character. Look at her claim about the Mile-High Cupcake! The woman is guilty of false advertising! How can a cupcake be a mile high? It wouldn't even be a cupcake anymore! It would be a—a *tower* cake! A *spindly* cake! A cupcake out of Ripley's Believe It or Not! A monstrosity that would require *cranes* to build, and some kind of major support system to hold up—"

"Deep, cleansing breaths," Willow said in a soft, calming voice. "In, out . . ."

But my breaths were coming too fast and furiously for me to control. In fact, they were more like snorts. And that steam was coming out of my ears again.

"I don't care what you say," I announced to Willow. "I'm going over there right now." As if to show how serious I was, I yanked out the ponytail band I'd been wearing to hold back my shoulder-length straight brown hair and tore off my black-and-white checked apron emblazoned in pink letters with "Lickety Splits Ice Cream Shoppe."

"Kate, she's probably not even there," Willow said, her tone pleading. "On a beautiful May afternoon like this one, she's probably off . . . I don't know, getting her nails done or something. At some fancy spa. In a gorgeous pastoral setting."

Just then, as if on cue, a sleek red Corvette pulled up in front of Sweet Things Pastry Palace and slid into the big parking space that happened to be free. The door opened, and who climbed out but Ashley Winthrop, Princess of the Pastry Palace, herself.

I hurried over to the shop window to get a better look. Willow was a few feet behind me.

While I hadn't seen Ashley since high school—graduation day, in fact—I immediately saw that she'd barely changed in the past fifteen years. She was still tall, slim, and graceful, although the easy way she moved had always had as much to do with her extreme level of self-confidence as it did with any innate quality that a ballerina would envy. And she still had long blond hair. But she wasn't wearing it the way she used to—in a long ponytail that she annoyingly let swing from side to side whenever she walked. Instead, it now hung down her back, straight but with just a hint of curl at the end. The woman was clearly no stranger to a curling iron.

At least as impressive as her fancy car was her outfit. She was wearing a simple white dress that, from the way it fluttered in the light breeze, was undoubtedly silk. From the way it was cut, and the way it draped over her obnoxiously thin Gwyneth Paltrow frame, it just oozed expensiveness. Her shoes looked as if they'd cost a lot, too, since they had bunches of bling attached to them. As if that weren't enough to make me imagine a triple-digit price tag, the heels were so high they had obviously been made for someone who spent a lot of time sitting at a desk, making important decisions.

Perched on her nose was a pair of sunglasses, the gold insignia of the designer glinting in the bright afternoon sun. And even from this distance, I could tell that her robin's-egg-blue leather purse was Kate Spade. Not one of the outlet store ones, either. This was the real deal.

Ashley had clearly done well for herself, making me wonder, just for a fraction of a second, whether I'd been wrong to go into ice cream rather than baked goods.

But that fleeting thought left my head in a flash. Instead, fury curdled in my stomach as I watched her position herself in front of her despicable hand-lettered sign, pull out her phone, and take a bunch of photos. Even more annoyingly, she then stepped in front of the sign, plastered a big phony smile on her face, and snapped a few selfies.

"Grrrr!" I growled. "I bet nasty old Ashcan is going to find a way to get that picture on the front page of the *Daily Roost*," I muttered. "She's such a manipulator that she's going to make sure that the fact that her shop is now selling ice cream is the biggest news in town. The next thing you know, this new sideline of hers is going to drive me out of business!"

By this point, Ashley had tossed her cell phone back into her Kate Spade purse. She slithered in front of her car, checked for traffic, and strutted across the street.

Making a beeline for my shop.

"O-M-G," Willow muttered under her breath. "Kate, do you believe this? She's heading our way!"

"No! She wouldn't . . . she *couldn't* . . . !" I leaned closer to the window, wanting to see for myself.

But she would. And she could. She was getting closer and closer. She stepped up to Lickety Splits' front door, pulled it open, and strode inside.

Even in my frenzied state, I couldn't help noticing the smirk her bright pink lipsticked mouth was drawn into. She paused, pulling off her designer sunglasses and surveying my shop appraisingly.

Instinctively I glanced around the store. The customers who were sitting at the marble tables appeared to be completely oblivious to the drama unfolding before them. They were too absorbed in devouring their mounds of Melty Chocolate Malt (a particular favorite of mine, especially since I made it with chopped-up pieces of chocolate malted milk balls) or my amazing Better Butterscotch or refreshingly tart Lucky Lemon Raspberry Swirl.

Just then, a group of three middle-aged women also wandered into the shop, so close behind Ashley that they nearly tripped on her. Two of them were carrying shopping bags from Stitchin' Time, a quilting shop a half a block away from mine.

"I'll help these customers," Willow said. In a whisper, she added, "Kate, behave yourself."

I decided to do just that.

"Ashley! What a pleasant surprise!" I greeted the she-devil as the group of quilters headed toward the ice cream display cases, leaving Ashley and me to ourselves.

"Hardly," Ashley replied. She eyed me up and down before adding, "Goodness, time certainly has taken its toll, hasn't it!"

I gritted my teeth, wishing that that morning I'd styled my lank brown hair instead of simply washing it, put on some makeup, and worn anything but jeans and a white cotton shirt that had lost its crispness hours earlier.

And taken off the eight pounds I'd put on since high school. Well, ten.

And hating myself for caring.

As politely as I could, I asked, "Is there anything I can get you?"

Ashley glanced over at the display of ice cream, then pretended to shudder. "Heavens, no. We're not *all* in such a hurry to let ourselves go."

"Interesting comment from a bakery owner," I commented. "I wonder how your customers would feel about it."

"My customers are positively addicted to the goodies I sell," she retorted. "They don't care about anything or anyone but getting their fix of my Chocolate Coconut Dream Bars or my Apricot Almond Muffins."

I had a few ideas about what she could do with her muffins, but I kept them to myself.

But I noticed that while I was doing an admirable job of restraining myself, Ashley's voice was getting louder.

Willow noticed, too. "Excuse me, Kate," she called across the shop, her voice as sweet as the Earl Grey Tea with Shortbread ice cream she was scooping into a waffle cone for one of the quilters. "It might not be a bad idea for you and Ashley to continue your conversation outside."

Of course, I would have been perfectly happy not to continue our conversation at all. But as I glanced over at my customers, I realized they could hear every word we were saying. The girl in the purple glasses and her root-beer-loving pal were suddenly eating much faster than before, and a couple of the ice-cream-cone eaters were gathering up their things, acting as if they couldn't wait to get themselves and their portable treats out of there.

Once Ashley and I were out on the sidewalk, all bets were off.

"Okay, Ashcan," I said, "what do you think you're doing, suddenly deciding that your true calling in life is going into the ice cream business—and doing it the very same week I open *my* shop?"

She waved her hand in the air. "It's a free country," she said, sounding like a seven-year-old. "Chalk it up to free enterprise. The spirit of capitalism. Pursuing the American Dream."

"American Dream?" I cried. I was really seething by that point. "Given the fact that you're driving a Corvette—in a color that clashes horribly with your lipstick, I might add—it looks like pursuing the American Dream has already done you enough good. It seems to me that you don't exactly need to start stomping all over my business just to make yourself feel like you can do anything I can do!"

"But of course I can do anything you can do, and so much better!" Ashley replied. "I already know that." She sighed. "It's just that it's so much fun seeing you squirm. It always has been. And I guess some things never change."

"You're not going to get away with this!" I insisted. "Just because you make a decent coconut bar—"

"Chocolate Coconut Dream Bar," she corrected me haughtily. "Made with seventy percent dark chocolate. From the Amazon!"

"Amazon, my foot!" I returned.

By this point, my voice had gotten louder. In fact, it was loud enough that several people turned to look at us. Not in a good way, either.

But I wasn't about to retreat.

"Ashley Winthrop, you're a complete phony!" I yelled. "I bet the ice cream you're selling isn't even homemade!"

A sly smile crossed her face. "Prove it!"

Her response only made me even more furious. "I'll call the board of health! The truth in advertising squad! I'll—I'll call *Consumer Reports*!"

Ashley just laughed. "Good luck with that. I doubt anyone will care." Sweeping her blond hair back over one shoulder, she added, "And if they do, I'll just find a different adjective. 'Artisanal,' maybe. Or 'totally natural.' Or here's one: 'gluten free!' "

"Ice cream is *always* gluten free!" I exclaimed.

"In that case, I really will be telling the truth," she replied.

I suddenly noticed that right behind us, a small crowd had gathered. Three or four people, anyway, including one dog walker. But everyone on the street—quite a large number, given what a lovely day it was—seemed to have stopped in their tracks and turned their head to get a better view of the dramatic scene unfolding on Hudson Street. And that was probably a few dozen people or so.

I was suddenly mortified.

"Look, Ashley," I said. "I'm not going to waste my time arguing with you. Why should I, when you haven't been even close to reasonable since you were five years old? You've gotten so used to getting your way that it's never even occurred to you that anyone could stop you. But this time is different. This time, it's not about Skippy or the prom or—or yellow paint! This time, *I'm* different! And I will now leave you with this promise: *This isn't over!*"

With that, I turned, let out a huge "*Hrmph!*" and stalked back to my shop. As I strode by the onlookers, I did my best to hold my head high, acting as if I'd actually won.

I sure didn't feel that way.

"Welcome back," Willow said as I slunk back into Lickety Splits, my shoulders slumped and my mood even slumpier. "Who won?"

"Ashley always wins," I returned. "It's as if the universe is punishing me for something I did in a previous life."

"You don't believe in previous lives," Willow pointed out. "Besides, if the universe was out to get you, I have a feeling it could come up with something worse than having some full-of-herself competitor selling second-rate chocolate ice cream across the street from you."

At the moment, I was unable to imagine anything worse.

Still, as I glanced around, I got more than a little pleasure from seeing what I'd already accomplished—and in just a few short weeks. My brand-new ice cream shop was already running smoothly, even though it had only been open for a few days. A few happy ice cream eaters were sitting at the tables, and a new bunch of customers had gathered in front of the display cases, oohing and aahing over my beautiful creations. A few were studying the menu posted on the wall above, no doubt trying to decide which irresistible concoction to choose.

I only hoped Ashley wouldn't mess it all up.

I suddenly wanted to get away. My ugly interaction with the pastry princess had left me feeling shaken, and I couldn't stand being so close to her or her shop for another minute.

Turning to Willow, I said, "I have an errand I've been meaning to run, and this seems like the perfect time to do it. Would you mind looking after the shop for me, just for an hour or so?"

"No problem," she replied. "In fact, I've got nothing on my schedule for the rest of the day, so why don't you go take care of whatever you have to do and then just go home?"

"Really? You wouldn't mind?"

"Not at all," she said, already pushing me toward the door. "It's gotten pretty hot today, and you could probably use some time to cool off."

I knew perfectly well she wasn't talking about the weather.

Chapter 2

New York is the nation's fourth largest dairy
producing state, with 5,000 farms and
600,000 cows.

—New York Times, *August 31, 2016*

I was still steaming as I drove my shiny red pickup truck along Route 9, a winding highway that runs along the Hudson River. Usually I love taking that road, since it passes through both breathtaking forested areas and, as a wonderful contrast, some of the ever-more-trendy towns dotting the valley. The route also offers amazing views of the water that always have a calming effect on me.

Not today.

Today, I felt like I was a child again, and not in a good way.

In fact, my street fight with Ashley Winthrop made me feel like that five-year-old kindergartener who'd just had the daffodil yellow paint grabbed away.

And Willow's deep breaths weren't going to take care of it.

Think of something positive, I told myself. Something happy, something that will make you feel better.

As was so often the case, I decided to focus on ice cream.

Ah, ice cream. My favorite food for as long as I can remember. Whenever I think about my childhood, my fondest memories are of walking into the luncheonette in town with the handful of change I'd just earned by doing some chore and treating myself to a double dip cone of Chocolate Mint Chip and Vanilla Fudge Swirl. When my mother took my two older sisters and me to an amusement park, my favorite part wasn't the whirligig or the Ferris wheel or the merry-go-round. It was the ice cream pops we bought at a vending machine, hard, frozen bars of vanilla ice cream slathered in coconut or chopped nuts or a crisp chocolate shell that would break into smaller pieces when you bit down on it.

The summer I was nine years old, Mom and Grams and my sisters and I spent a week in New Jersey, visiting relatives. I still have fond memories of a day trip we took to Atlantic City. But even though I loved the beach and the boardwalk's entertaining sideshows, that wasn't what impressed me the most. Instead, it was all about the smooth, luscious, soft-serve frozen custard sold at a stand called Kohr's that had started in 1919. The ice cream and custard at Kohr's came in flavors unlike any I had ever seen, flavors like Bubblegum and Cotton Candy and Black Raspberry and Orange Cream. Deciding which to choose seemed like the hardest thing I'd ever had to do.

But there was even more behind my passion for ice cream. Aside from the euphoric experience of something creamy and sweet and icy cold dissolving on my tongue, filling my mouth with a burst of flavor that seemed almost too good to be real, at least as meaningful to me was my father's love of ice cream.

I don't have that many memories of him, since he died when I was just five years old. But I do remember that we both were committed to marking each and every important event in our lives with our favorite frozen treat.

For my third birthday, my dad took me to an ice cream emporium in a nearby town and set before me the biggest banana split I had ever seen. Believe it or not, I can still remember those three mounds of ice cream—a scoop each of chocolate, vanilla, and strawberry, since this particular shop liked to stick with the classics—smothered in slices of banana and chocolate syrup and whipped cream. And not one but three cherries sat on top, commemorating the specialness of turning three. I seem to recall that I wasn't able to finish the whole thing, but my partner in culinary crime was more than happy to help me out.

On my fourth birthday, Daddy surprised both my mother and me by announcing that that year he wanted to take charge of the birthday cake. But instead of whipping up a Duncan Hines cake mix or trotting off to a local bakery, he concocted his own version of an ice cream cake. I watched in awe as he stuffed a layer of Chocolate Marshmallow ice cream into the bottom of a springform pan, then added a layer of chocolate cookies. Next came a layer of Vanilla Fudge ice cream, followed by a layer of vanilla wafers. On top he squished in a third layer of ice cream—Chocolate Mint Chip, my absolute favorite at the time. He covered the top with sprinkles in every color of the rainbow, stuck in four candles plus one in the center for good luck, and as a final touch added a handwritten sign that said, HAPPY BIRTHDAY, KATE!

I still treasure the photographs I have of that cake. My dad had never exactly displayed any Martha Stewart capabilities, so in the pictures, his creation looks kind of like a throw pillow that somebody sat on for too long. But to me it's a work of art. To this day I have never had such a magnificent birthday cake.

Once my dad passed away, Mom, my sisters, and I moved in with Grams. I felt as if my entire world had shifted, but there was one important thing that didn't change: the starring role that ice cream played in my life. On hot summer evenings, the five of us would sit at the kitchen table, laughing over fun card games like old maid and gin rummy. At least as important as our hilarious rivalries were the bowls of Grams's favorite ice cream, Cherry Vanilla, that were a part of every evening.

But Cherry Vanilla ice cream wasn't the only frozen treat that was available for celebrating summer. The freezer was always stocked with Eskimo Pies or chocolate and vanilla ice cream cups or whatever other ice cream novelty had just been invented. Grams loved to experiment trying different foods, and since she knew how much I loved ice cream, she was happy to indulge me.

Then Mom passed away the summer I turned ten. Grams suddenly found herself playing the role of mother. She knew how devastated my sisters and I were, and to help us all cope with our confusion, our anger, and our intense feelings of loneliness, she did her best to keep our lives as much the same as they had been before. A big part of that was to keep our family ice cream addiction going, since it was one of the easiest and most obvious ways of linking us to the past and moving ahead with our lives.

When I grew up and moved to New York City, my strong and happy relationship with ice cream continued. It was my comfort food in a brand-new place, a link to my past even as I struggled to create a new present and future for myself.

My studio apartment in the East Eighties was tiny, but there was always room in the refrigerator for a pint or two of Häagen-Dazs or Ben & Jerry's or one of the newer brands that was always springing up. Something new was happening in the world of ice cream. As was the case with so many other foods, ice cream was rising to an art form. New flavors were being developed all the time. Ingredients whose names had never before been used in the same sentence as the words "ice cream" were suddenly popping up in shops and supermarket freezers all over the city, ingredients like cornflakes, chili powder, bacon, cardamom, avocado, gingerbread, lavender, and rose.

And then, a few months earlier, everything changed. The increasingly debilitating arthritis in Grams's knees caused her to fall, sliding down three steps at the bottom of the staircase that connected the front hallway with the second floor. Thank goodness for the Wolfert's Roost Fire Department and their topnotch EMTs. But once the immediate crisis was over, a new normal took over. The tasks of day-to-day living that had been becoming more and more difficult for Grams were suddenly impossible. She needed someone to take care of her. Making the decision to take on that role took me all of three seconds.

The first couple of weeks after I'd moved back to Wolfert's Roost were intense, since even though she fortunately hadn't broken any bones, she was still pretty bruised. I took over running the entire household: shopping, cooking, doing the laundry, paying bills, and keeping the house reasonably neat.

But Grams quickly got stronger and soon became able to do more things. As my duties lessened and my new schedule became more routine, I began wondering what would come next.

And then, one evening as I sat in front of the TV, watching silly pet videos and eating a huge dish of green tea ice cream, I had a brainstorm.

Opening my own ice cream emporium in Wolfert's Roost suddenly seemed like the best and most obvious idea in the world. I loved ice cream, my town didn't already have an ice cream shop, and I desperately needed something to do—not to mention a new source of income.

Eleven weeks later, I opened Lickety Splits.

And it looked as if opening my own business couldn't possibly go any more smoothly. At least, until that afternoon.

Which brought me right back to my miserable mood.

By that point, I'd reached the turnoff that the GPS on my phone told me would take me to my destination: the Juniper Hill Organic Dairy.

I drove along a side road that became bumpier and bumpier, finally disintegrating into a dirt road pitted with potholes. I was beginning to wonder if my GPS had failed me when I caught sight of a hand-painted sign reading, You're almost there! Only 1,000 feet to Juniper Hill.

At least the owner had a sense of humor, I thought, forging ahead.

I'd never dealt with this dairy before. In fact, I'd worked out a deal with my local supermarket to buy the milk and cream I needed to make the ice cream I sold at Lickety Splits.

But I was someone who listened to my customers. And since opening four days before, at least a dozen times someone had asked me, "Is your ice cream made with organic ingredients?"

I decided to investigate whether or not that was even a possibility. So I Googled "Organic Dairy Hudson Valley." Sure enough, Juniper Hill popped right up. And when it turned out to be located only a few miles away, I was convinced I'd found the perfect supplier.

I'd been anxious to check it out, and after Willow had shooed me out of the shop, it seemed like the perfect way to distract myself.

I finally reached the end of the road, where I found an unimpressive wooden building with another hand-painted sign. You're here! it read. Welcome to Juniper Hill!

Frankly, the place looked more like a shack than a place of business. But the sign convinced me that I was in the right place. And right behind there was a huge field in which happy-looking cows grazed in the bright June sunshine. Beyond that was a huge barn, several outbuildings, and a couple of silver silos glinting in the summer sun.

Given how contented the cows looked, I was already certain they could make my customers feel equally contented.

I went inside. The interior of the small building was just as rustic, with a wooden floor strewn with pieces of hay, a counter, and a single employee. He looked as if he was a teenager, especially since he was wearing earphones and bopping his head up and down. I only hoped there was music coming out of those earphones that would explain all the head bopping.

The young man—a boy, really—had straight black hair that was so long in front I could barely see his eyes. Between him not being able to hear me and possibly not being able to see me, I was already nervous about how this interaction was going to go.

"Hi!" I said brightly, hoping he'd be able to hear me.

Whether he had extraordinary hearing or could lip-read, I don't know. But he focused his attention on me and said, "Hey. What's up?"

So far, this was going much better than I'd expected.

"What's up is that I'd like to place an order," I replied. "I'd like to buy twenty gallons of milk and forty gallons of cream."

"For when?"

"For now," I said. "I'd like to get that to go."

"Whoa," the boy said. "That's a lot of stuff."

I sighed impatiently. "This is a dairy, isn't it?"

"Well, yeah. Sure." Frowning, he added, "But that's kind of a big order for a walk-in. I mean, we have regular customers who have a standing order, but that's something we plan for, so—"

I was getting impatient. You can take the girl out of the big city, but—well, you know the rest.

"Look," I interrupted, doing my best to remain calm even though I'd been in a terrible mood even before I walked in.

"I'm just trying to place a simple order. Can I talk to whoever it is who runs this place?"

"Sure," the boy replied with a shrug. "He's right back there."

I turned in the direction he was pointing. Through an open back door, I could see a tall man with broad shoulders and a trim frame standing with his back to me. Just then, he turned his head slightly, just enough that I got a view of his jawline and the bridge of his nose.

"Oh no," I whispered. "No. It can't be."

But it was. The sinking feeling in the middle of my chest told me that my hunch was correct. The boy's boss wasn't just another cowhand. There was no doubt about it: that was Jake Pratt.

My Jake Pratt.

My heart was pounding so hard that the floor was practically vibrating. The entire room seemed to be swirling around. My mouth was dry; my whole body was covered in sweat. . . .

Part of me hoped I had just begun experiencing early onset menopause.

The rest of me knew better.

"You know, on second thought . . ." I started to say.

But it was too late.

"Hey, Jake?" the boy called over his shoulder. "This lady wants to talk to you."

"No, really," I said, backing away. "It's—it's not that important."

Way too late. Jake was already heading into the building. And now—even now, fifteen years since the last time I'd seen him—my heart was doing flip-flops. And while I knew perfectly well that they had nothing to do with menopause, there was absolutely no doubt in my mind that they were definitely related to my hormones.

Jake was smiling as he came inside, but his eyes, which were as blue as ever, had a faraway look. I could see that his mind was still elsewhere, and that what was happening here hadn't yet registered with him the way it had with me.

"How can I help—" He froze. Our eyes had just locked and I saw that he was experiencing exactly the same shock that I was experiencing.

Suddenly he was speechless.

For what seemed like hours, the two of us just stared at each other, unable to speak, struggling to process what we were experiencing.

Breathe, I instructed myself, remembering Willow's advice.

"Hey, are you guys okay?" the boy asked. I was vaguely aware that he was looking from one of us to the other, trying to figure out what could possibly be going on.

"We're fine," Jake suddenly said, distractedly running one hand through his light brown hair. His voice sounded calm, but I knew him well enough—even now—to hear the strain he was trying so hard to mask. "Absolutely fine."

"Do you two know each other?" the boy asked. He didn't seem to be hearing my silent plea to just keep quiet.

"We used to know each other," Jake replied. His eyes were still locked in mine and his voice had a strange calmness. "A long, long time ago."

"Very long," I added. Unlike Jake, my voice was breathless and overflowing with emotion. "Like fifteen years ago."

"Fifteen years!" the boy exclaimed. "Wow, that's like a whole lifetime, practically!"

Yet it feels like only yesterday, I thought.

By now, the deep breaths I had been taking were starting to pay off. My heartbeat was slowing down enough that I no longer felt as if I was about to pass out. The room didn't seem to be spinning around quite as fast, either.

Jake suddenly broke up our staring contest by glancing over at the boy. "Ethan," he said, "why don't you go out back and check on Elsa? She was acting a little funny this morning and I'm wondering if I should call in the vet."

Ethan shrugged. "Sure. Whatever."

He headed out the back door, but not before casting us a puzzled look, then shaking his head.

"So," Jake said once we were alone. "Katy McKay has returned."

"*I've* returned!" I cried. "*Me? I'm* the one who's returned?" The shock of only a minute or two before had vanished. In its place was a rage unlike any I'd felt since—well, since prom night, fifteen years before.

I could practically see Jake's defenses snap into place. His blue eyes instantly grew distant, and every single muscle in his face seemed to harden. Even his position changed—barely discernible, but to me, as easy to read as a comic book.

That ability of mine, to know what he was feeling as well as I knew what was going on with me, was apparently still there, as fresh as it had always been.

"It's true, I'm back," Jake said, sounding annoyingly matter-of-fact. "I came back to the area a couple of years ago."

"Couldn't resist the lure of the Hudson Valley, after all?" I asked dryly.

He hesitated. "It's more like there was a death in the family."

I immediately felt like a jerk. "I'm so sorry," I said.

"Thanks. It was my uncle." Glancing around the wooden shack, he added, "I came back to run the family business."

The wheels in my head were turning. Family dairy . . . I suddenly remembered that Jake's family had, indeed, run a farm back when I was in high school. At least I'd thought it was a farm. Whatever it was, it certainly wasn't an organic dairy.

But none of that mattered. I was still trying to process running into Jake like this, with no warning, no chance to prepare. . . .

Just then, another customer walked in, a man in jeans and a plaid flannel shirt holding a list in his hand.

The timing couldn't have been better.

The mood really shifted this time. Jake and I were suddenly as distant as—well, as the owner of an ice cream shop and one of her suppliers.

"What can I help you with today?" Jake asked me, his tone now formal.

"I'd like twenty gallons of milk and forty gallons of cream. To take with me right now, as opposed to having it delivered."

Jake's eyebrows shot up. "That's quite an order for a walk-in."

"It's an emergency," I replied sarcastically. "My doctor told me I have a calcium deficiency."

"You look pretty healthy to me." Jake eyed me appraisingly. I could feel my cheeks turning as red as . . . well, as that proverbial cherry on top. "In fact, I'd say you look pretty—"

"Can you fill my order or not?" I snapped.

He held my gaze for a few seconds. "I can do that," he said, back to being all business again. "But I'll need about twenty minutes to get it packed up. I'll get Ethan on it right away. In the future, if you plan on placing a big order like that, it'd be a good idea to call first and—"

"It's for ice cream," I suddenly said. "I've just opened an ice cream shop in town."

Jake looked shocked. "This town? Our town?"

"That's right. It's on Hudson Street, right near the big intersection."

"So . . . you're back?"

I jutted my chin a little higher in the air, as if to say, "What's it to ya?" But aloud I said, "That's right. I've come back home to help Grams out. She's been having some health issues lately."

"That's nice of you." There was no warmth in his tone, though. I noticed that right away.

I also noticed all the things he *didn't* say. Things like, "Wow, you're back? That's great!"

Or "Hey, we should get together for coffee some time. You know, to talk about old times."

Or—a truly wild fantasy—"I missed you."

Whoa, said a voice in my head. The sensible voice, the one that tried its best to keep me out of trouble. You do *not* want Jake Pratt saying he missed you.

You don't want anything at all to do with Jake Pratt. For goodness sake, hasn't having had your heart broken by him once already taught you anything?

Besides, that voice added, at this stage of your life, your main goal is becoming an ice cream magnate.

"So-o-o," I said curtly, "can I get that order filled?"

"Sure. No problem." He kept his eyes locked in mine for another second or two, then turned away and yelled, "Ethan? Come back in here. I need you to fill an order."

And then he pointedly turned his attention to the customer who had just come in. "And what can I do for you?"

Chapter 3

The average American consumes more than 23
pounds of ice cream each year.

—*International Dairy Foods Association*

My heart was still pounding and my head was still spinning as I drove away from the Juniper Hill dairy as fast as I could. The wheels of my pickup truck kicked up the pebbles along the dirt road, making it sound as if the skies had opened up and started pelting me with sleet. The gallons of milk and cream stashed in back sloshed around loudly, adding to the feeling that I'd gotten caught in a storm.

And that's exactly what had just happened.

And Hurricane Katrina and Super Storm Sandy were nothing compared to Super Duper Hurricane Jake.

Darn! I thought as I swerved along the narrow road. Why did Jake Pratt have to end up back here in Wolfert's Roost?

As is so often the case with me, I suddenly had an acute craving for ice cream. An ice cream sandwich, to be specific. A full-octane one: chocolate cookies with nuts, any kind of nuts, and a thick slab of Pistachio Almond ice cream.

After all, there are some things that only ice cream can fix.

But part of me realized that even an ice cream sandwich the size of a pizza wouldn't be enough to calm me down.

"Honestly, could this day have been any *worse?*" I moaned, forcing myself to loosen my grip on the steering wheel since

I'd just realized my hands were starting to hurt. "First a close encounter with Ashley Winthrop, the Wicked Witch of the Northeast. Then, as if that wasn't enough to ruin my day, running into Jake Pratt, of all people—and without even the slightest bit of warning . . ."

I was beginning to wonder if coming back to Wolfert's Roost had been such a great idea after all.

Like a lot of kids who grow up in small towns, I couldn't wait to get away from mine. Sure, when I was a little kid, I thought that it was the best place in the entire universe.

And in a lot of ways, the place where I spent most of my childhood was pretty idyllic, almost like something out of a Norman Rockwell painting. It offered a charming main street lined with shops, enough parks and playgrounds and bike trails to keep me busy for entire summers, and of course, the magnificent views of the Hudson River. If Norman had ever caught sight of those views, I'm sure he would have incorporated them into his work.

But by the time I was a teenager, I was convinced it was the dullest.

True, the hustle and bustle of New York City was only a two-hour train ride away. I adored the Saturday outings I took with Grams and my sisters, then later on my friends, to see the Rockettes at Radio City Music Hall, the giant Christmas tree in Rockefeller Center, and the countless works of art at the Metropolitan Museum of Art.

But trips into the big city were generally reserved for special occasions like Christmas and birthdays. The rest of the time, I was dealing with the inevitable angst of adolescence. Agonizing over Who I Was and Where I Wanted My Life to Go, struggling to get good grades, and of course, maneuvering my way around my ongoing rivalry with Ashley Winthrop . . . It was no wonder that the arrival of Jake Pratt on the scene when I was a junior was so monumental.

And we all know how *that* turned out.

But at that time the town was pretty sleepy. There was no movie theater, no fun places to shop aside from the mall, which was far enough away that it required a willing parent to drive my friends and me there. There was a cast of local characters that, to me, seemed about as interesting as—well, as a piece of apple pie without the à la mode part.

After my eighteenth summer, spending half my time working at the local shopping mall, folding sweaters at a clothing store, and the other half holed up in my room—missing Jake, hating Jake, plotting ways to get back at Jake—I couldn't wait to go off to college. Then, after four relatively happy years at the state university in nearby New Paltz, it was time to embark upon life as a grown-up. I immediately headed off to the place that I'd always yearned for more of.

After traveling to quite a few big cities, I found that the Big Apple was my favorite city in the world. Not one of them, from London to Sydney to Hong Kong, came close to matching the sheer energy of Manhattan. The streets and sidewalks positively vibrated with it. I loved the noise of the traffic, including the honking horns, or at least most of the time. I loved the sea of faces everywhere you look. I loved the endless avenues lined with coffee shops and boutiques and department stores and restaurants with cuisine from all over the world and street vendors selling everything from kids' books to cupcakes. . . .

I could go on and on. I loved the city, and I always will.

And I'll always think of those ten years as one of the happiest periods of my life. But then Grams had a health crisis, and it was clear that she needed me more than I needed my life in the big city.

Yet here I was, trying on other possible scenarios for the first time in the three months I'd been back. Such as, maybe I should have had Grams move in with me.

I immediately dismissed that one. While my one-bedroom apartment was spacious by Manhattan standards, adding another person would have been like moving a herd of cattle into my bedroom. Not as smelly, of course, and not as noisy, but just as crowded.

Maybe just moving Grams *closer* to where I lived before, in a place of her own?

That wouldn't have worked, either. I'd still have a heck of a time dealing with the day-to-day logistics if I had to take a train or even a subway to get to wherever she was.

And in both those scenarios, there would be the problem of forcing her to relocate. Grams loved Wolfert's Roost. She'd lived there for five decades, ever since she'd married my grandfather, the love of her life, and become my true life example of Living Happily Ever After. I didn't remember him well, since I'd been pretty young when he'd passed away. But I did remember him as a kind, gentle man who always had a smile and a hug for his granddaughters.

Of course, in those days, the town didn't have the colorful name Wolfert's Roost. When Grams moved there—and, in fact, the whole time I was growing up—it had had the same name it had since it was founded in 1699: Modderplaatz. That's right, Modderplaatz.

If you think it's bad in English, it's even worse in Dutch. *Modder* means "mud" and *plaatz* means "place." That's right, my hometown's original name means "muddy place."

My high school yearbook was called Modderplaatz Memories. Our football team was the Modderplaatz Monsters. And even though we all got teased by kids from places with more normal names, it never occurred to anyone to change any of it.

At least, not until 1996 when the residents of another Hudson Valley town, about an hour's drive south, voted to change the name of their village from the workaday North Tarrytown to Sleepy Hollow. Making the name cuter was an attempt at improving its economy, mainly by attracting tourists.

The cute new name came from a story by Washington Irving called "The Legend of Sleepy Hollow." Irving, who also wrote the famous short story "Rip Van Winkle," lived in Tarrytown. He used the place he called home as the setting for his famous tale about Sleepy Hollow, which featured the terrifying Headless Horseman as well as a considerably more sympathetic character, the nerdy schoolmaster Ichabod Crane.

It's hard to know if changing the name helped North Tarrytown in any way besides creating a boom in the map-making industry, not to mention the local folks who were lucky enough to print up business cards and personalized stationery. But it sure put a bee in the bonnet of the residents of Modderplaatz, who suddenly decided that their own town's name could use some improving, too.

And taking advantage of the Hudson Valley's most famous writer seemed like the way to go. (The second most famous is probably James Fenimore Cooper, author of *The Last of the Mohicans,* a great work of literature that these days is commonly used to torture schoolchildren.) A bit of research revealed that another one of Irving's great works, a collection of short stories, had the charming title *Wolfert's Roost, and Miscellanies.*

Wolfert Acker was a real person from the colonial period. He was born in Brooklyn but moved to Irvington. During his life he worked in government, serving as an advisor to Peter Stuyvesant, who was head of the Dutch colony of New Netherland until it became British and was renamed New York. Acker named his Hudson Valley homestead Wolfert's Roost, which, in Dutch, actually means "Wolfert's Rest."

Washington Irving clearly liked the name, since he called

his own home Wolfert's Roost and used that name in the title of his story collection. I guess the powers that be in Modderplaatz decided that if the name was good enough for both an advisor to Peter Stuyvesant and the area's best-known writer, it was good enough for them. In 2005, Modderplaatz became Wolfert's Roost. And no one seemed the least bit bothered by the fact that the real Wolfert's Roost was more than an hour away.

It's hard to know how much of an impact the name change actually had. A couple of months after the name change, a major arts center opened on the edge of town. I have a feeling that that had an even bigger influence on the town. The arts center was what started bringing in the tourists . . . and, not far behind the day-trippers, the upscale restaurants, the browse-able shops, and irresistible enticements like Annoying Ashley's bakery, and of course, Lickety Splits.

But even with the inevitable changes that force their way into every town, bringing about the demise of favorite hardware stores and run-down but convenient little grocery stores, this one was still the place Grams loved the best. The place she belonged. It was her *home*.

Which meant that once again it had to become *my* home.

I'd just begun fantasizing about pretending I was in the Witness Protection Program—changing my name, dyeing my hair a different color, acting as if I didn't recognize Ashley or Jake or even Willow—as I pulled into the driveway of 59 Sugar Maple Way after dropping the milk and cream off at my shop. My stomach was in knots from thinking about creative ways to make my homecoming more palatable.

But then the front door of the house opened and Grams stepped out onto the porch, wearing a big welcoming smile. She was dressed in her usual at-home attire, a pair of black sweatpants and a bright, flowered, cotton blouse. Her hair, which she'd only let go gray about eight years ago, hung in a sharply cut pageboy, neatly framing her face.

The knots in my stomach instantly turned into limp pieces of rope. They got even droopier when, seconds later, I got another warm greeting as Digger, Grams's half-crazed but infinitely lovable terrier mix, came racing across the front lawn toward me. His dark brown eyes were so bright and his tail was wagging so furiously that you'd think I was a real-life version of Rip Van Winkle, showing up after having slept for twenty years, suddenly up and around and badly in need of a very large latte.

Okay, I told myself. So maybe it really isn't *that* bad being back in Wolfert's Roost.

"Hey, Digger!" I cried, crouching down to scratch the sides of his head, knowing it was something he absolutely adored. "How's my favorite doggie?" And then, giving in to the irresistible urge to resort to baby talk, I added, "Whooza sweetest doggie in the world? Who? Oh, yes, it's Digger. Digger's the sweetest doggie in the world!"

He was in a state of complete ecstasy, first struggling to jump up and lick my face, then lying on his back, hoping for a tummy scratching. All in all, it was quite a scene.

I glanced up and grinned at Grams, who stood poised atop the three long stairs that led up to the porch and were cut in half by a wooden ramp we'd had installed right after her fall.

"I thought I heard your car pulling up, Katydid," Grams said. "Of course, Digger's endless barking was another clue that you'd come home."

Home. There was that word again. The stressors of the day were seeming more and more remote. Being back here at Grams's house, the place I'd called home ever since I was five years old and my father passed away, felt as good as climbing into a king-size bed and pulling a huge, fluffy comforter over my entire body—with a dish piled high with macaroni and cheese and a big bowl of Triple Chocolate Chaos ice cream sitting on the night table.

The house even looked like the perfect place to grow up in. Who wouldn't instantly fall in love with such a grand, three-story Victorian?

At least it used to be grand. It was built in the late 1880s, a time when the brand new inventions of Alexander Graham Bell and Thomas Edison were starting to seep into day-to-day life, playing croquet was all the rage, and the Wild West was still pretty darned wild. Coca-Cola, elevators, and ball-point pens were all brand new phenomena, helping to create modern life as we still know it.

And the house at 59 Sugar Maple Way reflected all the romance and promise of that era. It had a lovely porch running along the entire front, perfect for wiling away long, lazy summer afternoons with lemonade and a good book. A charming turret jutted out of the center, with a conical roof that, to me, had always looked like a giant ice cream cone. And according to family legend, the house had always been painted bright yellow. The story went that my great-great-great-grandfather, who'd had it built, had insisted to the builder that it be made a color that was "mellow." The builder had misheard, and . . . well, the rest is history.

These days, the house at 59 Sugar Maple Way still had a dignified presence, but it was definitely showing its age. The porch sagged so badly that it looked as if it might simply collapse anytime it felt like it. The yellow paint was chipped in some spots, and the window frames were cracked. They seemed to be crying, "Strip me! Repaint me! Or better yet, replace me!" The front yard was a patchwork of scraggly grass and weeds. I always hoped that if people didn't look too closely it would simply look green.

Yet even in its somewhat dilapidated state, the house had plenty of homey touches. There were three mismatched rocking chairs on the porch—one wicker with a tear in the back, one with peeling blue paint, and one that was just plain old wood. I'd spent hours rocking in those chairs as a kid, reading or playing word games with my sisters or just staring up at the clouds and daydreaming. Each rocker was adorned with a needlepoint pillow of a different type of flower, all of them made by Grams. They all showed signs of wear and were faded by the sun. "Just like me," Grams liked to joke.

Flowerpots of different sizes and vintages were lined up along the banister, housing a colorful profusion of flowers. Gauzy curtains peeked out from the windows and there was a wreath of dried flowers hanging on the front door, another creation of Grams's. The welcome mat lying outside the door featured a black silhouette of a cat with the words "Wipe Your Paws."

As soon as I walked inside, the feline who was the inspiration for the clever welcome mat predictably came running over to me. Chloe may have been aging, but she hadn't lost her need for connection with humans. Unlike some cats, she thrived on companionship. In fact, I used to joke to Grams that Chloe had obviously been receiving instruction from Digger.

As for that other furry little being, he was still at my side, clearly not ready for me to shift my attention away from him—especially to a cat, even though if there was an actual showdown, he would invariably be the one to back down.

"Hey, you two!" I cried. I crouched down to return their greeting with as much enthusiasm as they'd shown me.

"How nice that you're home early so I get to spend more time with you," Grams said. "Besides, on most nights, when you get home you're so worn out from the long day that you can barely talk."

I couldn't disagree. Starting my new business had required me to work, work, work every waking hour. Some nonwaking hours, as well, since I often dreamed about possible new flavors or better ways to arrange things in the shop. So I was really looking forward to a quiet evening at home.

I let out a deep sigh as I walked inside, following Grams. I loved every inch of that house, just as I had since I was small. It felt so cozy, as if it were wrapping its big arms around you from the moment you stepped inside.

The front faced south, which meant that bright sunlight streamed through all day, even in winter. It had large windows, too, curved bay windows in both the living room and dining room that started about waist high and ran all the way up, almost to the ceiling.

The furnishings were old-fashioned, comfortably worn, and always inviting. The dark red velvet couch with the gold carved feet, the dusty overstuffed chairs, the huge, heavy dining room table with six tall chairs . . . everything in it was designed to feel welcoming.

And Grams's signature was present in every room, just as it was on the house's exterior. In fact, that's what I'd always loved most about the place. Draped along the back of the velvet couch was an afghan that Grams had crocheted decades earlier, a startling combination of orange, lime green, and gold that screamed, "This was the seventies!" Four more needlepoint pillows were crowded along the back.

In front of the living room's overstuffed easy chair was a footstool she'd created, using the rug-hooking technique. On it was a picture of a house, complete with a green lawn and a bright yellow sun. Hanging on the walls were half a dozen of Grams's patchwork quilts, all of them reflecting her love of color and eye-pleasing geometric design.

And sprinkled throughout the house were the partially

completed craft projects that Grams seemed to work on non-stop. Lying on the couch was a stack of patchwork squares in pastel shades, soft pinks and pale blues and apple greens that would eventually be combined to make a full-size quilt. Her latest knitting project, a purple scarf that looked as if it were made of pieces of popcorn, sat on the dining room table, sealed up in a bag to keep curious cats away. A shoe box on an end table contained antique buttons that waited to be turned into a necklace, using a new technique she'd read about in a craft magazine.

In addition to all the signs of Grams's creativity, there were also three curio cabinets that displayed the souvenirs she had picked up during her many travels. A tiki God from Tahiti, colorful hand-painted wooden animals from Mexico, ceramic pitchers and vases from Greece and Portugal and Turkey . . . In fact, her love of travel was what inspired me to do as much globe-trotting as I could, once I had the time and the money.

Even though it was early, I was already hungry. I set about making dinner as Grams sat at the kitchen table, peeling vegetables and slicing cheese.

"How was your day?" Grams asked as she attacked a carrot. "And how did you ever manage to get away so early, even though this is still Lickety Splits' first week?"

"Willow took over for me," I explained, glancing over from the stove. "She's turned out to be such a great help."

"It was certainly nice of her to give you the rest of the day off," Grams commented. "I'm sure you're exhausted. This has been some week!"

I was silent for a few seconds, wondering if I should tell her about the return of Ashley Winthrop in my life, suddenly showing up the way she did, as welcome and as unexpected as a canker sore. After all, Grams had been hearing about Ashcan my entire life—and offering soothing words and promises that one day, that girl would get what she deserved.

Instead, I launched into a report of all the good things that had happened at the shop that day. The customer who had ordered a Peanut Butter on the Playground ice cream cone and liked it so much she'd ordered two quarts to bring home so her kids could try it. The young man who'd ordered a Bananafana Split, mumbling something about how he was celebrating, then stuck a twenty-dollar bill in the tip jar after explaining that what he was celebrating was that he'd just proposed to his girlfriend and she'd said yes.

It wasn't until Grams and I had sat down to dessert that I brought up the other noteworthy encounter I'd had that day. Somehow, in order to get the words out, I needed to be seated in front of a big bowl of Cappuccino Crunch ice cream slathered with Bittersweet Chocolate Syrup that had been laced with espresso, a new topping I was experimenting with.

"So here's something else interesting that happened today," I said, trying to sound casual. "Guess who's living back in Wolfert's Roost again."

"I can't begin to imagine, Katydid," Grams replied. She seemed much more focused on licking her spoon, which was coated with my newly concocted chocolate-with-espresso syrup. I had a feeling I'd come up with a winner. "An old friend, I hope?"

I screwed up my face, not sure if the person I was speaking of would exactly fall into that category.

"Jake Pratt," I replied.

"*Really.*"

Grams knew the whole story, of course. After all, she'd been the primary witness to my two-year romance with Jake. Every day of my junior and senior years, I bounded home from school. Over milk and cookies, usually homemade cookies she'd just taken out of the oven, she'd listen to every detail of what had happened with Jake that day. The clever thing he'd said in history class, the funny poster he'd put on his locker, the way he'd won the baseball game against Rhinebeck High by hitting the ball out of the park.

She'd heard about the bad stuff, too. The occasional quarrels, the disappointment when he'd forgotten our six-month anniversary, the time I got crazy-jealous when Ashley started making comments, extremely loudly, about what a hunk Jake Pratt had become now that he was almost six feet tall.

And of course, Grams had been right at my side on prom night.

I still remembered every detail of that evening in May. The spring air had wafted through the screens on the windows, a sure sign that the school year was almost over and summer was coming. I'd spent hours getting dressed. My primping had started with a mani-pedi and a haircut with styling at Lotsa Locks. Then came a long bubble bath. Finally, I'd spent enough time putting on makeup that you'd have thought I was getting ready for the opening night of *Cats*.

Most important of all, of course, was The Dress. I'd spent weeks shopping for it, certain that it had to be the perfect dress for the perfect night. When I'd finally found The Dress, after my hundredth shopping spree with Willow, I put it on in my bedroom and came out to model it for Grams.

It was long and flowing, but cut so well that it expertly accented the gentle curves of my seventeen-year-old body. It was strapless, my first and last strapless dress. And I adored the color, a pale blue that was the same shade as the sky on a perfect day. I liked to think of it as the color of Jake's eyes.

I already knew how special that dress was. But even so, I needed to hear it from Grams.

"Katydid, it's absolutely lovely!" she had cooed. "It looks like it was made for you!" She had actually gotten tears in her eyes.

"Grams, why are you crying?" I'd demanded.

"Because my little Katydid is all grown up," she had replied.

At age seventeen, that was exactly what I wanted to hear.

The night of the prom, I put the dress on again, and Grams teared up all over again. But an hour later, I was shedding tears of my own. And they had nothing to do with the dress or being happy.

Jake never showed.

Not only did he stand me up on prom night. He vanished.

That's right, he vanished. He'd left town. No one ever saw him again. No phone call, no note, not even a Hallmark card.

Not a single word of explanation, much less an apology for ruining what was supposed to be the best night of my high school career.

No apology for ruining my entire life, either.

Of course I was devastated. Also, angry and hurt and confused and a whole bunch of other things, not one of them positive.

I hadn't heard a single word from Jake since that night, fifteen years ago. I had heard, through the grapevine, that while he'd left Wolfert's Roost, he hadn't left the planet. He was alive and well. He was just alive and well somewhere else.

Which was why running into him again, back here in the Hudson Valley no less, had been such a big deal. And why I expected some kind of reaction from Grams.

Instead, she was being annoyingly noncommittal.

Was it possible she couldn't see what a big deal this was for me? I wondered. Or was it simply something she didn't want to touch with the proverbial ten-foot pole?

I realized quickly it was the latter.

"And how was that for you, Katydid?" she asked gently. "Running into him again after all this time?"

"It was fine," I replied brusquely. "All that was a long time ago. I just thought I'd mention that he was back in Wolfert's Roost so if you ran into him, you wouldn't be surprised. He's now running his uncle's dairy, which has a new name: Juniper Hill."

With that, I stood up and began clearing the table. Fortunately, I'd finished my ice cream before I'd brought up Jake. For some strange reason, I'd suddenly lost my appetite.

As I bustled around the kitchen, cleaning up, I felt bad that I'd cut Grams off that way. I knew she was surprised by my reaction, and I hoped she wasn't angry.

But it wasn't that I didn't want Grams to know what I thought and felt—not only about seeing Jake again, but also about knowing he was back in town.

It was that I didn't know myself.

Bang, bang, bang . . .

The relentless banging, coming from somewhere downstairs, slowly dragged me out of what felt like a very deep sleep. I know I was dreaming, but aside from weird appearances by both Jake Pratt and Ashley Winthrop, the plot line vanished the moment I opened my eyes.

Bang, bang . . .

At first I assumed it was Grams, although I couldn't imagine what she could possibly be up to that was making so much noise. But I quickly realized that the sound I was hearing could only be someone pounding on the front door.

As in, "Let me in." And, "I mean it."

"Ugh!" I groaned, dragging myself out of bed. As I pulled on the robe I'd left piled up in a chair, I glanced at my clock and saw it was eight-fifteen. Early enough to indicate some sense of urgency, but not late enough to feel guilty that whoever was on the other side of that door was catching me still fast asleep.

I peered through the least-wavy part of the stained glass door and was surprised to see a face I recognized on the other side. Granted, it was a face I hadn't seen in fifteen years, a face that had matured. But it was completely recognizable.

Pete Bonano.

Still the same chocolate brown eyes, the same curly dark brown hair, the same chubby cheeks, and, I suspected, the same friendly smile, even though he looked dead earnest at the moment. I'd know that face anywhere.

Pete and I hadn't traveled in the same social circles. He was a star athlete back at Modderplaatz High. In fact, I seemed to remember something about him being a possible candidate for some professional football team.

But while Pete spent most of his time in the gym or out on the football field, he and I both ended up in the same English class a few times. So ever since middle school, I'd seen his big grin pretty regularly, even though it wasn't usually directed at me.

I decided to do a bit of flirting.

"Why, if it isn't Pete Bonano, the best quarterback Modderplaatz High ever saw!" I cried as I swung open the door.

I was so busy doing my Scarlett O'Hara act that it took me a few seconds to realize that not only wasn't Pete wearing a football uniform these days, he was wearing a police uniform.

Naturally, my first thought was, *Oh no, something bad has happened!*

I did a quick inventory. Grams was safe, standing just a few feet behind me. Even her two beloved sidekicks, Chloe and Digger, were fine. Not lost, not missing, not in any trouble of the sort felines and canines can sometimes get into.

I was hoping he was simply here to ask for a contribution to some worthy cause when he said, "Katherine McKay?"

"Of course it's me," I replied. Based on his tone of voice, I'd completely dropped the flirtatiousness. In fact, I was growing increasingly puzzled. Sure Pete recognized me, as sure as I recognized him. I hadn't aged that much.

Besides, he'd come to my house, the one I'd lived in since I was five years old. While Pete and I weren't best buds, Modderplaatz—Wolfert's Roost—was a small enough town that most of us knew where the other kids in our grade lived.

"I'm Officer Bonano—"

"I know who you are, Pete," I interrupted.

He cleared his throat. "I figured you did, Kate. But it's what I'm supposed to say."

"Okay, then, Officer Bonano."

"Ms. McKay, I'm afraid something terrible has happened. There's been a murder."

I was more confused than ever. "That's horrible," I replied, still not quite processing what he was saying. "Was it someone we knew? Someone from high school?"

"Yes," he said, his tone flat. "Ashley Winthrop. She was killed at her bakery last night."

I gasped. "Ashley? Oh, no! But—but I just saw her yesterday!"

His face remained a blank slate. If anything, he was looking increasingly earnest.

"Thank you for telling me," I said. "I'll try to think of whomever else I should notify. Willow Baines, of course. She and I are still friends. But there aren't that many people from school that I'm still in touch with. You see, I've been living in New York City for the past ten years, and I've only been back here for a few months. . . ."

Pete still wasn't saying anything. He just stood in the same spot, looking as if he had no intention of inviting himself in—or of going away, for that matter.

"Pete," I asked, trying to ignore the alarm bells that were going off in my head, "why did you come to my house to tell me this?"

"Ms. McKay," he replied, still as stiff as a robot, "we need you to come down to the station for questioning."

Chapter 4

Ben Cohen, co-founder of Ben & Jerry's ice cream,
has anosmia, or no sense of smell, and nearly
no sense of taste. To compensate, he insisted
on adding bigger and bigger chunks to the
ice cream he made because he needed it to
have more texture.

—*Anosmia Foundation (anosmiafoundation.com)*

I was in a daze as I shuffled through the parking lot outside the Wolfert's Roost Police Department. I was struck with the fleeting thought that my feet felt as if they weighed as much as a five-gallon container of cream. *Heavy* cream.

Ordinarily, comparing my life to an ice cream ingredient would have made me feel better. At the moment, however, not so much.

Even though I'd driven past this building hundreds of times, I'd never actually been inside it. Or given it more than a passing glance. The local police headquarters was housed in a dignified brick building with concrete steps leading up to double doors, painted a nondescript shade of green; a few columns added to its no-nonsense appearance. Frankly, it looked more like a bank that an official government institution.

At the moment, it felt very much like an institution. An intimidating one.

It didn't help that Pete Bonano insisted on walking so close to me that he practically crunched down on my foot every time he took a step. I figured he wanted to be near enough to grab me if I decided to break for freedom.

"Let me get the door," Pete said politely once we'd trudged up the few steps and reached the main entrance. "It's pretty heavy."

Chivalry, at a time like this? I thought. But I was willing to accept any kindness that was offered.

Aside from movies and TV, I'd never seen the inside of a police station. And probably because those were actually sets and not the real thing, the ones I was used to seeing were much nicer than the real-life version. I blinked, taking in the cracked gray linoleum, a few framed photos of cops forcing smiles hanging on the fake wood-paneled walls, and a high counter with a uniformed officer sitting behind it, gazing down at us with a neutral expression.

After nodding at his coworker, Pete began leading me down a short hallway. "This way, Ms. McKay," he mumbled.

"It's *Kate*!" I wanted to scream. "You know, Kate, who you used to tease because I was the only kid in English who used to actually *read* the books that were assigned? Who sat in the same school cafeteria with you every day? Who you asked to the sixth-grade Halloween Dance?

I'd actually forgotten all about that Halloween Dance thing until this moment. Somehow, having a personal history with Pete Bonano was making all this feel even worse. I even found myself wishing I'd said yes.

Pete led me to a small room that had the same linoleum and the same fake wood paneling. It had no windows, however. And while there wasn't exactly a single lightbulb dangling from the ceiling, the simple fixture that lit the room wasn't much better.

Even on a tight budget, I thought, someone from the police department could make an occasional trip to Ikea. The same went for the table. Metal, ugly, stark. As for the metal chairs, they looked as if they'd been specifically designed to be uncomfortable.

Creating a warm, welcoming atmosphere clearly wasn't a priority.

"Take a seat," Pete said. He was having trouble looking me in the eye.

I'd been assuming that good ol' Pete would be the one asking the questions. So I was surprised when a second man, one I didn't know, strode into the room. His dark blond hair was clipped extremely short, giving him the look of a military officer. His suit fit him badly, as if he purposely wanted to avoid looking like someone who cared about his appearance. The same went for his dark blue tie, which was askew.

"Good morning, Ms. McKay," the newcomer said brusquely. "I'm Detective Stoltz."

I immediately got the sense that if Pete had been the Good Cop, this guy was definitely the Bad Cop. My sense of doom worsened.

Detective Stoltz sat down opposite me. He was now close enough that I could smell his breakfast coffee on his breath.

"Ms. McKay," he began, "I know you've heard that Ashley Winthrop was murdered last night at her bakery on Hudson Street, right across the street from your shop."

I just nodded. "I'm—I'm—I don't know what to think."

"She was stabbed repeatedly with a large knife, the kind professional chefs use."

"That's horrible!" I cried.

He didn't react. "I understand you've known Ms. Winthrop for quite some time."

"That's right." My voice came out sounding like a frog's.

A frog with laryngitis. I resolved to do better. "Ashley and I went through school together, starting with kindergarten."

"Since kindergarten," he repeated, making it sound as if kindergarten was some kind of breeding ground for terrorists. "That's a long time."

"I guess." This time, I sounded like a frog that had been given a cough drop. Better, but still not quite where I wanted to be.

"That was when you two started having difficulties, am I right?" he went on. "Back from the very beginning?"

"It's not that we had difficulties, exactly." At least I sounded like myself again. "We did have a few ups and downs, I suppose." That jar of daffodil-yellow paint suddenly felt like the proverbial elephant in the room. At least, to me.

"I see," Detective Stoltz said. "So in other words, you two have been enemies for quite some time—"

"I wouldn't say enemies, exactly," I corrected him. I realized I kept shifting around in my seat. I forced myself to sit still. "I mean, that's an awfully strong word. Ashley and I may have had our differences, but really, it was nothing."

Detective Stoltz's eyes bored into mine. "Isn't it true that in high school, you and Ashley Winthrop were known to be rivals?"

I started squirming again. "Not rivals, exactly," I said, trying to sound matter-of-fact. "It was more like we traveled in different circles. It was just teenage stuff. Nothing that amounted to very much."

"I see." The way he said those words made it clear that he didn't see at all. "And then, after years and years of having 'differences' and 'traveling in different circles,' Ms. Winthrop suddenly decided to go head to head with you on your brand new ice cream business. That could well have been the last straw, couldn't it?"

"Yes. I mean no. I mean . . ." I stopped to take a deep breath, meanwhile trying to figure out what I did mean. "Look, we weren't enemies. We were just two businesspeople who happened to be living in the same town. And sure, I wasn't happy about it. But it was . . . well, something I would have figured out how to handle. It was really nothing."

" 'Nothing,' " Detective Stoltz repeated, his voice practically a hiss. " 'Nothing.' "

He stood up and placed both hands flat on the desk, then leaned over so that his face was no more than twelve inches away from mine. "It sounds to me like all those 'nothings' could very possibly add up to 'something.' "

"Look," I said meekly, "this is coming out all wrong, and I can see how it could sound—"

"Ms. McKay," he interrupted, "according to several witnesses, you and Ms. Winthrop had quite an argument on Thursday afternoon, just a few hours before she was murdered."

I gulped. "It was more like a . . . discussion."

A few more seconds of eye boring. Then Detective Stoltz finally sat down again. "More than half a dozen people have come forth and said they heard the two of you have a screaming fight out on the street at approximately three-thirty p.m."

My head was buzzing.

"Like I said, it was a discussion," I insisted. "Maybe a loud discussion, but really, just a discussion."

"And exactly what was the subject of this . . . 'discussion'?"

"I, uh, was a bit concerned that Ashley's bakery had just put up that sign, saying it was now selling ice cream. You see, I just opened my ice cream shop a few days ago. Monday, in fact."

"We are aware of that."

Of course they would know that. "Anyway," I said, "I was a little surprised to find that Ashley was suddenly in the ice cream business, too."

Detective Stoltz's face remained as blank as a clean paper towel.

"Do you think it would be fair to say that you were quite jealous of Ms. Winthrop?" he said evenly.

My mouth dropped open so wide you could have lobbed a basketball into it.

"In fact, isn't it possible that Ashley Winthrop's decision to go head to head with your new business was enough to push your lifelong rivalry over the edge?"

"But I—I—"

"*Don't* say another word!"

Those four words, spoken in a loud, assertive, male voice, made me jump. Instinctively I whipped my head around.

Standing in the doorway was Jake Pratt.

I simply stared at him in total confusion.

He was dressed in a jacket and tie, holding an expensive-looking leather briefcase. His light brown hair was slicked back, as if it had recently made contact with some sort of gel. Somehow, his demeanor matched the rest of his look. He was carrying himself as if *he* were the man in charge here.

Detective Stoltz, meanwhile, was a step ahead of me.

"Who are you?" he demanded, twisting his mouth into a most unattractive sneer.

"Jake Pratt," Jake replied in that same confident tone. He stepped over to the table and set his briefcase down on it with a loud bang. "I'm Ms. McKay's attorney."

My eyebrows shot up toward the ceiling. Part of me wanted to protest, to insist that Jake get the heck out immediately so that Detective Stoltz could continue giving me the third degree without any unwelcome intruders in the room.

But another part wanted to throw my arms around Jake in gratitude.

"And as her attorney," Jake continued with that same breeziness, "I am advising her not to answer any more questions. In fact, I'm wondering what right you had to drag her into the station in the first place."

Detective Stoltz took a few seconds to study Jake coolly. "No dragging was involved," he finally said, his tone at about the same temperature as my giant walk-in freezer. "Ms. McKay came in on her own volition."

"I see," Jake returned, his voice just as icy. "Then she will also be leaving on her own volition."

By that point, there was so much testosterone in the room that I half expected it to peel the finish off the fake wood paneling. I was glad that a good portion of it was coming from someone who was on my side.

But I guess Detective Stoltz decided that it was time to try another tactic. "Mr. Pratt," he said, sounding much friendlier, "I'm just trying to find out whatever I can. A young woman was murdered last night, and—"

"We'll be leaving now," Jake said. He picked up his briefcase and nodded in my direction. "Ms. McKay?"

"We were pretty much done here anyway," Detective Stoltz said, as if he just had to get in the last word. He pushed his chair back hard, its metal legs making eardrum-shattering shrieks. "But I promise you, Ms. McKay, that we will be in touch should the need arise."

I jumped to my feet, more than ready to get out of there. I struggled to keep my expression neutral, resisting the urge to stick my tongue out at Detective Stoltz as I hurried out of there, lickety split. No pun intended, believe me.

Jake walked down the short hallway at a brisk pace, as if he, too, was anxious to get out of the station. I trotted after him, a couple of paces behind. "Jake, I want to thank you for—"

"Don't say anything," he said, holding up one hand. "Not until we're out of here."

It wasn't until we were outside the building that I realized I hadn't been breathing normally the whole time I'd been in there. For the first time in my life I understood what the term "hyperventilating" referred to.

I took a few normal breaths, really appreciating what doing such a simple thing could feel like. Then I took some deep ones. Fresh air had never felt better, just as the warmth of the sun on my face had never seemed quite as glorious.

"Well," I said, turning to Jake, "I guess I owe you a big thank-you."

"You're welcome."

"So what happens now?"

He looked at me for a few seconds, then said, "How about breakfast? I don't know about you, but I'm starving."

As everyone in Wolfert's Roost knew, the best place for breakfast was Toastie's. It was a good old-fashioned diner, but a real one, not one of those fake ones that pretends it's a set for the musical *Grease*. No jukeboxes at each booth, no bright chrome trim on the counter, no cheerful red leatherette on the seats.

Actually, it was kind of a dump. But an authentic dump. The permanent grease stains on the Formica tables and counter were the genuine article. The same went for the eternally sticky menus. All that was missing was a gum-snapping waitress named Flo, wearing a tight pink uniform and a frilly white apron.

"Two?" the owner, Big Moe, greeted us sullenly as soon as we walked in.

He walked us over to a booth, tossed a couple of those sticky menus on the table, and disappeared.

It wasn't until then that I realized that I, too, was starving. I opened the menu greedily, anxious to see which particular carbohydrate-loaded entrée would catch my fancy. Miraculously, Big Moe resurfaced, this time with two white mugs of steaming coffee. Big Moe didn't even have to ask. He just *knew*.

It was that kind of place.

"So," I said, leaning back in my seat after doctoring up my blast of caffeine with enough sugar and half-and-half to make the finished product palatable to a three-year-old. "Once again, thanks for rescuing me."

"I've never in my life thought of you as someone who needs rescuing, Kate," Jake said.

I wasn't sure if that was a compliment or not. I decided not to try to find out.

I was glad that a waitress came by just then—wearing jeans, not a pink uniform—and took our order. Jake was having an omelet, but I went for waffles with Nutella. It was that kind of day.

Once we were alone again, I leaned across the table, not wanting anyone to overhear us.

"I don't mean to be the voice of doom or anything," I said, "especially since you're obviously trying to help me, but isn't it kind of . . . shall we say, illegal to pretend to be a lawyer? Especially if you're doing it in a police station, with real live cops around?"

Jake shrugged. "I'm not pretending."

It took a few seconds for the meaning of his words to register. "Wait. You're not *pretending* to be a lawyer? Which means you *are* a lawyer?"

"That's right."

"Since when?"

"Since I went to law school and then, after a couple of

months of mind-boggling cramming, passed the New York State bar exam."

"Oh." I leaned back in my seat again, taking a few seconds to digest that interesting little tidbit. "So you practiced and everything?"

"Yup. I worked for a big law firm in Manhattan. Not one of the fancy ones, but a pretty good one."

Manhattan? I was thinking. As in New York City? The same Manhattan I had lived in? Jake had lived there too?

This was getting more and more surreal.

I decided to keep my reactions to myself.

"What kind of law?" I asked, pulling at the paper tab of my now empty half-and-half container. There was absolutely no purpose in what I was doing other than giving my fidgety fingers something to do.

"Criminal law," he replied. "I was a defense attorney."

This kept getting better and better. "So not only do I have a lawyer, I have a high-powered lawyer from a big New York City law firm."

Jake laughed. "Something like that. The only thing is, I don't understand why you *need* a lawyer."

I sighed. "Me either." By now the last bit of paper was torn off the plastic thimble. I turned to the sugar packet, also empty. "How did you hear about what happened to Ashley?"

"Your grandmother," Jake replied. "She called me at the dairy this morning, right after you left for the station."

"*Grams?* She did that?"

"That's right. She said something about you mentioning that you'd run into me, and that you'd told her where I worked. She just wanted someone who knew you to be with you and asked me if I'd do whatever I could. So I threw on a jacket and tie, picked up my impressive-looking briefcase, and hightailed it over to the police station."

"What's in that thing, anyway?" I asked, gesturing toward the briefcase resting on the seat beside him.

"In here? Socks."

"Socks?"

For the first time since he'd shown up at the police station, Jake smiled. "I'm always losing socks. So I figured out that stashing them in my briefcase was a good way to keep track of them."

I stared at him for a couple of seconds, not sure if he was serious. The expression on his face told me he was dead serious.

"Want to see?" he asked, his blue eyes twinkling like St. Nick's on Christmas Eve, right after digging in to some of those homemade cookies that had been left out for him.

"That's okay. I believe you."

Big Moe appeared with two platters the size of pizzas. Jake's omelet was as big as a Frisbee, accompanied by a mountain of hash browns and two buttermilk biscuits so humongous they kept falling off the plate. I found myself wondering if I could come up with an ice cream flavor that incorporated some of those well-loved flavors. Hash Brown Heaven, with bits of real fried potato? Buttermilk Biscuit, a fluffy ice cream with a buttery flavor and maybe real pieces of biscuit?

My waffles with Nutella were similarly inspiring. It would be so easy to whip up a rich chocolate-hazelnut ice cream and add in small pieces of waffle. . . .

I took the fact that I was thinking about ice cream again as a good sign.

"So how do you feel about all this?" Jake asked, pulling one of the Volkswagen-sized biscuits apart and slathering it with butter. It melted immediately. "About what happened to Ashley, I mean? You've known her practically your whole life, after all. Then there's the fact that the horrible thing that happened took place right across the street from your shop."

"To be honest, I'm not sure how I feel," I said thoughtfully. "I guess I'm still in shock. I don't understand it. I guess I don't really believe it, either."

"Yeah, I know what you mean," Jake agreed. "I kind of feel the same way. It's going to take a while for all this to sink in."

"So what do you think will happen next?" I asked Jake. "In terms of the investigation." I hesitated before adding, "I guess what I really mean is, are the police going to keep bugging me?"

"Probably not," he said. "At least, not once they realize you had nothing to do with the crime. But let me give you my cell phone number, just in case you need to get in touch with me. For some free legal advice, I mean. And let me get yours."

We did the usual punching in letters and numbers routine, then lapsed into silence.

"I didn't, you know," I finally said. "Have anything to do with it, I mean. I was at home all evening. Grams can vouch for me."

Jake looked startled. "Kate, it never would have even occurred to me that you had anything to do with it!"

I just nodded, glad about his unqualified belief in my innocence. But I was thinking about what I'd just said.

My alibi was Grams. My closest relative, the one person in the world who loved me the most. A woman who would do anything to protect me, her granddaughter, a fact that was well known by anyone who knew either her or me. Grams would swear on a mile-high stack of Bibles that I was with her from four o'clock in the afternoon until the next morning when the police showed up at our door.

The question was, would anyone believe my own grandmother?

Chapter 5

Brain freeze, also known as ice-cream headache
or sphenopalatine ganglioneuralgia, is a short-
term headache caused when something very cold
makes contact with the roof of the mouth. It
occurs most often when the weather is hot and the
cold substance is eaten too fast.

—*MedicalNewsToday.com*

My anxiety over being called in to the police station stuck
with me for the rest of the day. When Willow stopped
into Lickety Splits to tell me that Ashley's funeral was scheduled for the next day, I wasn't even sure if I would go.

After all, if the police thought I might have had something
to do with Ashley's death, wasn't it possible that other people
might think so, too?

Yet I felt that *not* going would be worse.

"You have to come with me," I told Willow, not even trying to hide the desperation in my voice. "I know Saturday
morning is a busy time for you, but this isn't just any day. I
can't go alone, and I can't ask Grams to go with me. She's
just not good with stairs anymore, not to mention getting in
and out of a car. . . ."

"Of course I'll come," she said. And she gave my arm a
squeeze.

Good old Willow. I was glad that she and I had remained friends, even when I'd gone to New York straight from college and she'd returned to Wolfert's Roost to open her yoga studio. I'd cheered her on from afar, genuinely pleased at how quickly her new business took off. And knowing she was still here in our hometown had made it that much easier to come back.

Ever since we were kids, she had been my rock, a source of strength that I could always count on one hundred percent.

I'd met Willow the very first week of middle school. She and I had gone to different elementary schools, but middle school brought together kids from three different districts.

The first day of sixth grade, in Ms. Bender's fourth-period history class, she happened to sit down at the desk next to mine. But as Ms. Bender talked about what kind of notebook she wanted us to buy, this delicate, graceful girl with long blond hair streaming down her back seemed much more interested in a ring she was wearing.

"What *is* that?" I finally whispered, curious about why she kept staring at her hand.

"It's a zodiac ring," she said, holding up her hand proudly. "See? This little silver band has the symbols for all twelve signs. I'm a Gemini. That's the twins, this symbol here. What sign are you?"

Right from the start, I admired her interest in learning about things outside our day-to-day life. I'd never heard of astrology before that day, and she was so excited about it that it made it fun to learn what she knew about it.

But as we became better friends, I found out more about the reason behind it. Despite her calm facade, Willow came from a troubled household. Her mother struggled with addictions that went far beyond my addiction to ice cream. With Willow's two older brothers spending as little time at home as possible, she was left to find a way to cope with being left pretty much on her own. And astrology was just one of many different areas she explored as a means of creating a sense of order in her world.

Still, it wasn't until college that Willow discovered yoga. While she was at the State University at Binghamton, majoring in art, she signed up for it as a gym class. She took to it immediately. Yoga was catching on with the population in general, and she soon realized that making it a career would offer her a chance to spread the word about something she loved. It also allowed her to focus on her need for order, which never quite went away.

Yet on this particular day, even with Willow at my side, I was pretty jittery as the two of us walked into the Evans Funeral Home. I'd been there twice before, once when a teacher in my elementary school passed away, and another time when a friend's aunt died.

But this time, it felt very different.

"Do you believe how crowded it is?" Willow whispered.

"I sure didn't expect anything like this," I agreed. "I had no idea Ashley had so many friends."

"Or enemies," Willow said wryly.

As we elbowed our way into the entryway, I was amazed at how many people were there. Ashley was a hometown girl, after all. And in more recent years, she'd also become a local business owner.

But I had a feeling that the sensational aspect of her death had something to do with the large turnout, too.

I glanced around, clutching Willow's arm as I tried to get my bearings. I was curious about whether I'd still know very many of the people there. On the one hand, Ashley and I had spent the first eighteen years of our lives traveling in the same circles—kids from school, teachers, even the adults who had been part of our life as children, from the man who ran the candy store in town to the local dentist who was pretty much the one everybody went to. But I also knew that a lot had happened since then. Another fifteen years had gone by, almost half our lives.

As we shuffled into the main room, I continued to scan the faces. I was struck by how few of them I recognized.

I found myself growing increasingly curious about how Ashley's life had unfolded since then. What had been going on in her life, aside from running a bakery? Had she married? Had children? Developed strong friendships?

Obviously, she'd made at least one enemy somewhere along the way.

I jumped when my eyes finally zeroed in on a face I recognized. Still, I wasn't that surprised to spot Detective Stoltz in the crowd. He appeared to be doing his best to blend in. He was wearing a dark jacket and a nondescript tie, along with a solemn expression.

I wondered if anyone else noticed how carefully he was watching the crowd, studying every face, easing around the room as he briefly listened in to one conversation after another.

When he spotted me, he simply nodded, his head barely moving in a gesture that seemed to say, "Okay, I see you."

"Let's sit over there," Willow suggested. "I see a couple of seats in the back."

Willow and I were making our way across the room when I let out a little gasp. There was Jake, standing in a corner. For some reason, it hadn't occurred to me that he would be here.

I wasn't sure whether I was happy to see him or not. And that ambivalence had nothing to do with Ashley's murder.

It was the simple act of being in the same room with him. This just kept getting harder and harder.

I decided to ignore Jake, largely because I was so embarrassed about what had happened the day before. Having someone I knew see me in that position, sitting in the tiny, windowless room, being given the third degree . . . this was a new level of humiliation that I never dreamed I'd be subjected to. And our awkward coffee klatch right afterward had only added to my embarrassment.

Whenever I'd thought about the possibility of seeing Jake again, whenever I'd fantasized about sitting down and talking to him after all these years, it hadn't exactly been under these circumstances.

When he tried to catch my eye, I made a point of looking away.

As I sat through the service with my hands folded primly in my lap, I had a hard time tuning in. From what I could tell, the minister who conducted it hadn't even known Ashley. All I heard was an impersonal speech about life and death and making a difference in the lives of others.

Frankly, I couldn't wait for it to be over.

Once it was and we were filing out of the main room, I was thinking, now we can get out of here.

But Willow turned to me and said, "I'm going to get some coffee. Want some?"

"I'm fine," I replied.

But I immediately realized I should have taken her up on her offer and trotted after her. As soon as we made it to the large room in back that allowed people to gather after the service, Willow headed over to the refreshments table, leaving me standing alone.

I studied the crowd anxiously, hoping I'd find at least one person to talk to. So I literally sighed with relief when among the sea of unrecognizable faces, I finally spotted one that looked familiar. Even though it had been fifteen years since I'd last seen it, there was no mistaking that that face—still pretty, but with sharp features that gave her a pinched look—belonged to Hayley Nielsen.

Back in high school, Hayley had been Ashley Winthrop's best friend. In fact, Hayley was the number two girl, someone who played the questionable role of the next best thing to Ashley.

While it was a role that not everyone would embrace, Hayley had appeared to relish it. She dressed like Ashley, she wore her hair like Ashley, and she pretty much adopted every single opinion Ashley had ever expressed. More than once, I'd overheard her in the hallway, responding to a question someone had just asked her, with, "You know, let me talk to Ashley about that." I used to think that if we'd been born in medieval times, Hayley's official title would have been lady-in-waiting.

Yet even though Hayley was part of the popular crowd back in high school, she was always friendlier toward me than some of the others in that group. Maybe it was because through some glitch in scheduling, she and I always seemed to end up in the same gym class. We both figured out right away that we shared a hatred of both field hockey and gymnastics. That enabled us to bond on some level that went far beyond social structure.

I caught up with her just as she was ending a conversation with someone I didn't know.

"Hayley?" I said.

She turned and studied me for a couple of seconds. Then her confused expression melted into one of recognition.

"Kate," she said. "It's nice that you came."

I wondered if she and Ashley had remained best friends. Even more, I wondered if Hayley had heard anything about the police questioning me . . . or the argument Ashley and I had had a few hours before she was murdered.

"Of course I came," I replied. "I've known Ashley ever since we were both in kindergarten."

I didn't add anything about the nature of our relationship. I was pretty sure Hayley already knew enough about that.

"Isn't this the saddest thing?" I continued. "I guess I'm still in shock."

Hayley nodded, her eyes filling with tears. "I simply don't believe it. I feel like I'm just going through the motions."

"Were you two still close?"

She nodded again. "Very close. The best of friends. After high school, we stayed in touch, even when we went away to different colleges. And then, when we both ended up coming back to the area, we simply picked up where we left off."

You mean tormenting everyone who wasn't as pretty and as popular as the two of you? I thought. But then I remembered all the good times Hayley and I had had standing on the sidelines, complaining about how unnatural it was to twist your body into pretzel shapes for no good reason.

"I'm sure you're devastated," I said. And I meant it.

"It's tough," she agreed, swiping at her eyes. She took a deep breath. "But I know that what Ashley would have wanted for me would be to carry on and have a good life."

One that included the best haircut possible and plenty of designer accessories, I thought.

Now who's the Mean Girl? I immediately reprimanded myself.

"So what have you been up to?" I asked.

Hayley brightened. "Believe it or not, I'm now an interior designer!"

"That's great!" I told her. "I seem to recall that you had an interest in art in high school."

She grinned, as if pleased I'd remembered. "That's right. I took every art class that was offered, if you recall."

I did remember. But I'd always thought it was because they were easy.

"I took a few art classes in college," she went on, "but I never took it very seriously because I figured that being a starving artist wasn't for me. Instead, I majored in communications."

"That sounds interesting," I commented.

"In theory." Hayley sighed. "It turns out it's not a very useful degree. At least not around here. Maybe if I lived in the city or something. But I married my college boyfriend, who also grew up in the Hudson Valley, and we moved back here. The only decent job I could get around here was working in a law office.

"Then I got divorced. With no warning whatsoever." She laughed coldly, making a sharp sound that reminded me of Digger's bark. "Here I'd thought everything was all planned out for me for the rest of my life, that David and I would live happily after with two kids and a nice house and my job at the law firm. But then one day, completely out of the blue, the creep announced that he was running off to Paris to find himself. And then, like two days later, the lawyer I worked for told me he was getting out of law and buying a winery in Napa instead. . . .

"It was like everything went crazy, all at once. And I decided that since everybody else I knew had decided to do whatever they pleased, maybe I should, too. So I took some classes and switched careers."

"Do you enjoy it?" I asked.

"I love it," she replied sincerely. "It turned out to be the best decision I ever made." Another bark. "Certainly better than the 'I Love David' tattoo I got on my . . . well, never mind about that."

She suddenly looked at me more intently, as if a lightbulb had just gone off in her head. "You just opened a new shop in town, didn't you? An ice cream parlor?"

"That's right," I said. "It's called Lickety Splits. It's—well, it's right across from Ashley's bakery."

Hayley nodded. "I know. She told me all about it."

Did she tell you she was doing her best to drive me out of business, too? I was tempted to ask. But I banished the very thought from my head, reminding myself that it wasn't nice to speak ill of the dead. Especially when you were an individual the cops had their eyes on as someone who might have had a hand in getting her that way.

"Maybe I could be of help with that new shop of yours," Hayley said. She reached into her purse and pulled out a business card. "Give me a call sometime. The first consultation is free. You can even call me on a weekend. I see a lot of my clients Saturdays and Sundays, since most of them work seven days a week anyway."

"Thanks," I said, tucking it into my pocket. "I just may do that."

Glancing around, I asked, "Do you know many people here? I've been away for so long that I don't think I'd recognize anyone even if I'd sat next to them in math class for two years."

"Let's see." Frowning, Hayley surveyed the room. She was clearly taking her newly assigned task of social coordinator seriously. "Look over there, by that huge bouquet of flowers. That's Billy Duffy, Ashley's ex-husband. He lives in Fishkill."

My eyebrows shot up. I hadn't known there was an ex-husband.

I looked over in his direction, just in time to see him stuff a handful of cookies into his pocket. He'd wrapped them up in a napkin, as if he'd learned the hard way just how many crumbs a bunch of stolen cookies could generate.

I wondered if he had eating issues, or if, like me, he was a slave to desserts. But then I noticed that the sports jacket he wore was threadbare. Studying him more carefully, I saw that his shoes looked as if they were about to rip open at the seams.

And his face looked haggard. Maybe it was just grief, I figured. But it struck me as more likely that this was a man who was being beaten down by life.

He was actually pretty nice-looking, with green eyes and exceptionally long, thick eyelashes. He had an impressively thick head of straight light brown hair, too. Despite his drawn face, I could imagine someone like Ashley, who prized such superficialities as good looks, falling for him, back in the day.

"And look over there," Hayley said, grabbing my arm. "There's Tad."

Was it my imagination, or did she suddenly stand up a little straighter and stick out her chest a little farther? I could practically feel the hormones flying as a man in his late thirties walked into our midst, parting the crowd in a very Moses-like way. But I, too, was mesmerized. This man, whom Hayley had identified as Tad, emanated charisma, even across the room. He was tall, for one thing, probably six foot four, with a well-proportioned body that said he regularly went to the gym but didn't overdo it.

He was also handsome. The way Greek gods are handsome, I mean, with dark brown eyes, chiseled cheekbones, and an elegant nose. His perfectly symmetrical facial features were brought into sharp focus by his thick mane of dark brown hair, pulled back into a ponytail that screamed "artsy." Even his clothes conveyed that he was not your average Joe: a crisp, pale pink shirt, dark pants with funny European styling, and equally exotic forest green loafers that you could just tell had cost more than most people's monthly car payments.

"Who is he?" I asked, doing my best to subdue my own hormones.

"You don't know?"

Hayley looked at me as if I'd just spent three years at Modderplaatz High without being able to identify the captain of the Modderplaatz Monsters. Which was probably something I was capable of, back in the olden days.

"That's Tad Patrick, the famous chef," she said, sounding awestruck. "He opened Greenleaf right here in Wolfert's Roost last year. The *New York Times* immediately gave it—I don't know, however many stars that are the most they can give. Thanks to that review, his restaurant was an instant success and the man became the darling of the food world. And isn't he the handsomest, sexiest thing you've ever seen in your life?"

I couldn't exactly disagree.

"Was he friends with Ashley?" I asked.

Hayley stiffened. "He was Ashley's boyfriend."

So many red flags instantly began popping up inside my brain that you would have thought today was Chairman Mao's birthday. Given the fact that drool had practically been dripping out of Hayley's mouth as she spoke about him, I suspected that she may have entertained, at least once or twice, the fantasy that someday handsome, sexy Tad might become *her* boyfriend, instead.

"In fact," she said, "I should go over and give him my condolences. The poor man must be as distraught as I am."

Making you the perfect antidote to his sadness, I thought cynically.

"But seriously, Kate," Hayley called over her shoulder as she made a beeline for Tad, "call me about me giving you some decorating tips for your little shop. I'm just full of great ideas!"

Once I was standing by myself, I felt a wave of relief wash over me. This hadn't exactly been easy, but at least I'd gotten through this ordeal without anyone giving me so much as a funny look.

Of course, most people probably hadn't even recognized me, I realized, thanks to the passage of time, a different hairstyle, and no doubt those extra ten pounds I'd put on since high school. There were plenty of people who weren't thinking about me at all and hadn't even realized that Kate McKay was back in town. So even if they'd heard something, it wouldn't have occurred to them that I'd had anything at all to do with Ashley or her demise.

As I stood there all alone, chastising myself for having made too big a deal about the police questioning me, I suddenly spotted another face that looked vaguely familiar. Someone from my past, someone from high school . . .

It took me a few seconds to place her. But once I did, there was no mistaking Sue Prinzer. She'd been in my third-grade class, then popped up in a few of my classes in high school. I seemed to recall that she'd been class secretary at some point, too, not exactly one of the popular crowd but someone outgoing enough to nudge her way into the inner circle.

Sue was hardly a bosom buddy, but at least she was someone I could go over and talk to.

I made my way through the crowd. But when I was only a couple of feet away from her, I stopped.

The words coming out of her mouth made me freeze.

"You heard about Katy McKay, didn't you?" she said, her eyes widening to the size of saucers.

"No," replied the person she was talking to, someone I didn't recognize. "What happened?"

Sue glanced around, as if wanting to make sure no one was listening. Fortunately, since by that point I was standing with my back to her, she didn't realize that I was doing exactly that.

Lowering her voice, she said, "The police called her in for questioning."

Her companion gasped. "Really? You mean they think she's guilty?"

Sue didn't respond, but she must have nodded.

"Oh, my!" her friend cried. "You know, it wouldn't surprise me a bit if Katy did have something to do with it. She hated poor Ashley from day one. As if Ashley ever did anything bad to anybody!"

That last comment set my teeth on edge. It took every last ounce of control I possessed to keep from whirling around and setting her straight.

I quickly reminded myself that I was at the woman's funeral. And that I was in the position of having to convince everyone I came into contact with that my relationship with Ashley had been as smooth as a dish of melting vanilla ice cream.

So instead, I moved away as quickly as I could. They're only two people out of an entire town, I told myself. Who cares what they think?

But I'd barely walked ten feet before I caught another snippet of conversation. Three people I didn't recognize were huddled together in a corner, their faces close together.

"At the very least, they think she knows something," I heard one of them say.

They could be talking about anyone, I told myself. But I paused, leaning over in their direction so I could hear them better.

"I wouldn't be surprised," one of the others said. "That new ice cream shop she just opened is right across the street from the bakery. Kind of makes you wonder if it's simply a coincidence."

"From what I've heard," the third one said, "the two of them have been enemies since elementary school. Somebody told me she even stole one of poor Ashley's boyfriends away in high school!"

As if! I wanted to scream.

But I knew better than to get involved in the pointless task of trying to defend myself. Instead, I needed to get out of there. The sooner, the better.

I scanned the room, desperately searching for Willow. I was relieved when I spotted her standing near the door. She was involved in a conversation with someone I didn't know.

"Willow, we have to get out of here," I told her in a hoarse whisper.

"Give me a couple more minutes," she replied. "I'm explaining some of the controversies about hot yoga to Marilou."

But I want to leave now! I thought, glancing at the door as if somehow I could will myself onto the other side of it.

I jumped when I felt someone's hand on my shoulder.

I turned and saw that Jake was standing right behind me, his face inches away from mine.

"Hey," he whispered in my ear. "How are you holding up?"

My first instinct was to shoot back, "Fine, just fine."

Instead, tears immediately filled my eyes and my throat was instantly coated with some thick substance that reminded me of peanut butter.

He grabbed my hand and led me into the back hallway, away from everyone else.

"What's going on, Kate?" he asked earnestly.

"This is really hard," I replied in a hoarse voice. "I feel terrible about what happened to Ashley. But I also feel bad—maybe even worse—that there are people in this town who actually believe I may have had something to do with it. Some of the comments I've overheard today . . ."

Jake nodded. "This whole thing is pretty surreal. Maybe you'd like to go somewhere else?"

Do you mean . . . go somewhere else with you? I thought.

Then hated myself for the fact that when it came to Jake Pratt, I still harbored such a confusing jumble of feelings.

"I think what I'd like to do right now is just go off somewhere and be by myself," I told him.

What I really felt like doing was going back to Lickety Splits and reverting back to my childhood self by stuffing my face with as much Chocolate Mint Chip ice cream as I possibly could without feeling sick. Although on second thought, feeling sick wouldn't exactly mean I had to stop.

But one thing had become crystal clear to me. I was going to do everything I could to find out who had *really* killed Ashley Winthrop.

I didn't sleep much that night. I was busy picturing the faces of the people I'd seen at Ashley's funeral.

I flailed around in my bed, wrestling with the sheets and checking the clock every two minutes.

I kept picturing Ashley and me, screaming at each other as we stood outside on Hudson Street, and how we must have looked to the people watching. I kept hearing the two conversations I'd overheard at her funeral, juxtaposed with the questions Detective Stoltz had fired at me the day before.

I couldn't stop imagining what my life was going to be like until Ashley's killer had been caught. And I couldn't stop yearning to be just another shopkeeper, selling ice cream and trying to make people happy.

I finally got out of bed around five. I figured that if I wasn't going to get any rest, I might as well put my sleeplessness to good use. Today was Sunday, which was bound to be a busy day at the shop. Wolfert's Roost would be crawling with day-trippers, and I hoped they'd be anxious to try my irresistible offerings.

Besides, I was looking forward to spending the day in the company of strangers, people who would never even dream that the person scooping out their Toasted Coconut with Maui Macadamia Nuts was someone her neighbors thought might be a murderer.

I threw on jeans and a pink shirt that I knew would complement the pink lettering on the Lickety Splits aprons. Then I made a big pot of coffee, figuring Grams would appreciate waking up to a full pot of immediately available caffeine.

Once I'd had my own hit, I drove into town. I loved being out at that hour of the day. The air felt so clean and so pure at that hour that my head felt equally clean and pure.

Usually, I would have used that time to decide what new flavors to tackle that morning. I figured the Sunday crowd would appreciate the chance to try something inventive.

But I quickly decided on two new flavors I'd been thinking about for the past few days, Brown Sugar-Bourbon with Pralines ice cream and Cannoli ice cream, made with real ricotta and pieces of broken cannoli shell.

Then I focused on Ashley.

Who was she, really? I wondered. I mean, I knew who she was in high school. At least I thought I did. But that was a long time ago. A decade and a half, to be exact.

A lot had happened since then. I thought about all the things that had gone on in my life. Spending four years at college, moving to New York and getting my own apartment, finding a job I was excited about, doing some serious travel . . .

And of course, meeting lots of new people. People I worked with. New friends I made. And of course, men.

Suffering setbacks, too. Not getting a promotion I wanted, running into a few dicey situations while globe-trotting, having one relationship after another not work out the way I'd hoped.

It had changed me. And chances were good that whatever had happened in Ashley's life had changed her, too.

As I turned onto Hudson Street, I jumped. Sweet Things Pastry Palace was now cordoned off with yellow crime-scene tape. The darkened windows looked bleak, like the windows in a haunted house. The eerie look of the place made me shudder.

But a second later, I took a deep breath and told myself I needed to put aside all thoughts of Ashley Winthrop—as least, as much as was possible. I wanted to get back to focusing on the one thing that always brought me happiness and peace: ice cream. Besides, I had a business to run.

I found a fabulous parking space, since I was practically the only person out at that hour. But as I strode along the sidewalk, toward Lickety Splits, I suddenly froze.

From where I stood, a hundred feet away, I could see a dark shadow in the doorway, something that didn't make sense.

Shadows? I wondered. Or garbage bags? Had I been so spaced out yesterday that I left some out front? Or maybe Willow had . . . ?

But I knew that wasn't it. Even from where I stood, I could tell that the dark shape on my doorway wasn't something as innocent as shadows or trash.

My heart pounding and my throat dry, I took a few more steps.

When I got closer and finally realized what it was, I let out a scream.

Chapter 6

In 1984, President Ronald Reagan designated
July as National Ice Cream Month
and the third Sunday of the month as National
Ice Cream Day. President Reagan called for all
people of the United States to observe these events
with "appropriate ceremonies and activities."

—*International Dairy Foods Association (idfa.org)*

That wasn't a trash bag that was lying in the doorway of Lickety Splits.

It was a *person*.

For the first time, a terrifying thought occurred to me: there's a killer running around Wolfert's Roost. Somebody dangerous is in town.

And then, a second thought: I really need to start carrying an ice cream scoop with me wherever I go. A big one. Made of heavy metal.

But that was a longer term plan. At the moment, I had a situation to deal with.

I was debating what to do—Do some more screaming? Call the police? Offer this poor street urchin a double scoop of White Chocolate Raspberry Swirl?—when I realized in a flash that this wasn't just any street urchin curled up before me. I could see just enough of the face protruding from a mop of ridiculously curly black hair to recognize whom it belonged to.

"Emma?" I cried. "Is that *you*?"

My niece instantly snapped awake. Blinking, she raised herself up on one elbow, looking surprisingly alert. I could tell she was instantly on guard, as if even as she'd slept she'd been aware she wasn't exactly in the safest place imaginable.

"Hi, Aunt Kate! What time is it?"

"What time is it? It's like five-thirty in the morning. But I think a much more relevant question is, what on earth are you doing here?"

And why are you dressed like that? I wanted to ask as soon as I got a better look at her. Why do you look so disheveled?

And why on earth is your hair streaked with *blue*?

Still lying on the ground, Emma glanced up at me uncertainly. "I, um, just came for a friendly visit?"

I let out a snort that showed exactly what I thought of her answer.

"Come inside, Emma," I said, wondering if I should sound sympathetic or angry. Sleeping out on the street, even in a relatively safe town like Wolfert's Roost, was not a wise thing for a young woman to do. Especially since she had other, *safer* options.

As I took my key out of my purse, Emma picked up the shabby backpack that had been serving as her pillow and scuttled aside to let me open the door.

"If this is just a friendly visit," I asked as I unlocked the door, "why didn't you come to the house?"

"The bus got in so late," Emma said, sounding a little too whiny for an eighteen-year-old. "I took the train up from Washington to New York, then got on a Greyhound bus at around ten. Coming up we hit traffic on the George Washington Bridge. By the time we got to Poughkeepsie, it was past midnight." She shrugged. "I was afraid that if I started banging on the door at that hour, it would freak Grams out. So I Googled Lickety Splits and told the cab driver to leave me here."

I snapped on the lights, which immediately created a warmer feeling than standing on a concrete sidewalk at dawn. Even though I still wasn't sure what was up, or how, as a responsible aunt of an eighteen-year-old, I should be reacting, I couldn't help watching Emma to see her reaction.

I was instantly rewarded. Her entire face lit up, her dark brown eyes growing round and her mouth opening into a big round O the size of an Oreo.

"Wow! Aunt Kate, this is amazing!" Emma dropped her backpack on the floor and began walking around, studying each detail. Her mouth remained open the whole time.

"Wow, I love the black-and-white floor, and the pink accents like the chairs really make it pop. It feels so bright! So appealing! It's absolutely perfect—like an ice cream fantasy!"

"Thanks," I said, truly grateful for her enthusiasm.

"You must be so thrilled, having your own business," Emma said. "And an ice cream shop, of all things. I know how much you've always adored ice cream!"

"It is pretty cool," I told her. "No pun intended. But I'm more excited about Lickety Splits than I've ever been about anything my entire life. It's all mine, for one thing. I've never had that before. Working for someone else is fine, and I enjoyed a lot of what I did when I was in public relations. But this—this is all under my control. The way this place looks, the hours I keep, the flavors I serve . . . it's all whatever I want it to be."

Of course, the one thing that *wasn't* under my control was keeping out the competition. But that wasn't something I was about to bring up.

"I love everything about it. And look at these awesome paintings!" Emma had stopped in front of the three giant pictures Willow had created for me, the triumvirate of an ice cream cone, a banana split, and an ice cream sandwich. "Who made these?"

"My friend Willow," I told her. "I think you've met her a few times."

"The willowy one, right?" she replied. "Easy to remember."

"There's one more painting of Willow's in the back," I told her. "Unfortunately, the public doesn't get a chance to enjoy it. But this one has a higher mission to fulfill. Come, I'll show you."

I led Emma to the work space in the back of the shop, pausing in front of the huge, colorful rendering of an ice cream sundae. It was hanging on the wall above the counter, the place where I did some of my most creative and enjoyable work.

There was a good reason Willow's fun painting was hidden away behind the scenes. When I'd rented the storefront, one of its few flaws was a huge hole in that particular wall. Somehow the drywall had been pulled away in an area about one foot by one foot, revealing the wooden slats behind it. It was quite an eyesore, especially given its prominent location.

I'd decided that as an Empress of Ice Cream, I deserved a better view while I was playing around with my raw materials. And what better view was there than a giant ice cream sundae? Especially since this one happened to be composed of three scoops of colorful ice cream, smothered in dark brown chocolate syrup and doused with a tremendous glob of whipped cream.

The only thing missing was the cherry on top.

I had teased Willow about it from the moment she first showed it to me.

"It's gorgeous," I'd told her sincerely. "But you forgot something."

"What did I forget?" she'd asked. Anxiously she studied her work, meanwhile tapping her bottom lip with one finger. "A spoon? A napkin? A few drips from melting ice cream?"

"A cherry!" I cried. "The classic ice cream sundae always has a cherry on top!"

"Oh, my goodness," she wailed. "You're absolutely right. How could I have forgotten something so basic? I'll tell you what: I'll come back sometime when the shop is closed with a tube of red paint and a brush. I'll just add on a giant red cherry. . . ."

Laughing, I leaned over and gave her a hug. "Willow, it's perfect just the way it is. I love it. And every time I look at it, I'll think about how unique it is. I'm actually lucky to have an ice cream sundae that makes its own statement about our expectations of the way things should be!"

And it was true. I admired Willow's painting every time I went into the back. Just looking at it filled me with joy.

"I love this one, too!" Emma exclaimed. Then she frowned. "But something seems off, somehow. . . ."

"You'll figure it out," I told her with a grin.

"Willow's a really good artist," Emma said as we walked back into the shop. Casting me a shy glance, she added, "But maybe I could help you by making some more artwork for your store. I'm pretty good at that, you know."

I knew perfectly well what a talented artist Emma was. She always had been, ever since she was tiny. When the other kids were gluing pieces of macaroni onto construction paper, my genius niece was building 3-D abstract sculptures out of ziti and strips of fettuccini. By the time she was eight, she was winning prizes at school with her papier-mâché puppet heads and her animals made of soda cans. By fifteen, her paintings were winning prizes at community art exhibitions.

"Have you had breakfast?" I asked her.

She shook her head.

"I can take care of that. What do you usually have?"

"Just coffee, with lots of milk and tons of sugar. And something with serious protein in it, like an egg or some cheese."

I nodded. "Then I have just the thing."

I went into the back and headed straight for the stainless steel walk-in freezer tucked away there, directly opposite Willow's painting. The one I'd gotten was six feet by six feet, with a single door. It was practically a small room, no doubt much bigger than what I needed. But I'd wanted to keep my options open. Maybe I'd end up renting the storefront next door and expanding. . . . Even though Lickety Splits was still a brand-new venture, you never knew what the future might hold.

Besides, I felt so cool—again, no pun intended—as I walked inside and pulled down a giant container of ice cream, handmade by *moi*. I thought of my lovely freezer as a kind of temple, a shrine to ice cream. And if there was one thing on this planet that deserved a shrine, it was ice cream.

I lugged the tub over to the display case and began scooping a large mound of Cappuccino Crunch ice cream into a glass tulip dish.

As I handed it to Emma, she asked, "What's this?"

"Cappuccino Crunch ice cream. It might as well be a cup of coffee, since it's made with real espresso, cream, and enough sugar to give you a buzz that should last all morning. It also has nuts in it, so between those and the milk you'll get a major hit of protein."

She accepted it gratefully. "Perfect. Why didn't I ever think of having ice cream for breakfast before?"

Maybe I should start publicizing that concept, I thought. I was half serious. Why should Starbucks get all the customers?

I scooped out a smaller serving for myself, then sat down opposite her at one of the round marble-topped tables along the wall.

"Okay, but let's go back to how you even knew about Lickety Splits in the first place," I said. "It just opened, and I haven't talked to you—well, certainly since before I decided to go into the ice cream business."

"Are you kidding? I heard about it from Mom, of course." Emma was shoveling in spoonful after spoonful of Cappuccino Crunch as if she hadn't eaten in days. Either that or she simply loved ice cream as much as I did. "She talks about it all the time."

"In a good way or a bad way?"

Emma grimaced. "You know Mom."

I did know Mom. Or, as I usually called her, Julie.

In fact, I could hear my sister Julie's voice in my head: "It's not crazy enough that that wacko sister of mine left an amazing career in the most exciting city in the world—not to mention a salary that I can't even begin to imagine. Now she's nutty enough to open an ice cream stand . . . ? Ice cream! Can you imagine?"

I cringed. Not only could I hear Julie saying those exact words, I could picture her rolling her eyes, waving her arms, and practically acting out what she was saying.

"I hear you," I replied. "Welcome to my world."

My whole life I'd played the role of Little Sister in the McKay clan. Julie was seven years older than I was, and Nina was five years older. So since the day I was born the two of them were telling me what to do—and voicing their disapproval if every aspect of my life wasn't going exactly the way they thought it should.

As an adult, I'd done a fairly good job of getting out of the habit of looking over my shoulder to see if Julie and Nina approved or disapproved of whatever I was doing.

But Emma's sudden arrival on the scene instantly threw me back into playing the role of someone who had to take what my sister wanted into consideration. After all, this was obviously a lot more than just a "friendly visit." There had to be an important reason why a levelheaded young woman like Emma had suddenly appeared on my doorstep—literally.

"But enough about me," I insisted. To show how serious I was, I put my spoon down. "Tell me what's going on, Em."

"See, here's the thing," Emma said earnestly. She, too, put down her spoon. The thought of ice cream melting caused me pain. Then again, it was so good when it was a little soupy that maybe pausing for some serious conversation wouldn't turn out to be such a bad thing. "I love art, and I think I'm pretty good at it."

"No argument there," I said.

"But I'm also really into computers," she went on. "Computer art, but also computers in general." With a little shrug, she added, "I just think they're cool, you know?"

I nodded, even though the truth was that I personally had a love-hate relationship with computers. I loved what they could do. But I also hated the way they acted sometimes. Too much of the time, actually. They were kind of arrogant, as if they surely must know what you were trying to do but for some malevolent reason insisted on making it difficult for you. Like, "I know you want to load all your photos onto your laptop from your phone. But certainly you didn't have any intention of ever being able to *find* them again, did you?"

"So what's the problem?" I asked, sincerely not understanding where she was going with this.

"The problem," Emma said, exasperated, "is my parents."

"How do they fit in to this?" I said. "You mean they're not supporting you in your interests?"

"Oh, they're supporting me, all right," she replied. "It's just that their answer to everything is, 'Go to college.'"

"Okay," I said, still puzzled. "And that's a problem because . . . ?"

"Because I don't know what I want to do!" Emma cried. "Art or computers. And until I can decide, I don't see the point in going off to an expensive college that may or may not have the best classes in whatever it is I decide to do . . . whenever I finally do decide, which I hope will be soon but just hasn't happened yet, okay?"

"I got it," I said.

"So here it is, June already," Emma went on. "I just graduated from high school, like ten minutes ago, and they're both like, 'Okay, so you're going off to college in September. End of discussion.' I got into a pretty good school, and that's what they're expecting me to do.

"But I want to take a year off. Maybe two years. Or however long it takes for me to figure out a couple of things. Is that the end of the world?"

I thought for a few seconds. "It all sounds pretty sensible to me."

"Yeah, but not to them," Emma said, spitting out the words. "They're like, 'Oh, you can figure it out while you're taking courses. You're not the only eighteen-year-old who's confused. Everybody needs time.' But I want to spend the time that I'm figuring things out doing real-life stuff, not just sitting in a classroom. And maybe, after I have a chance to stop being a student twenty-four/seven, I'll decide that it makes sense for me to go to art school. Or maybe to some two-year computer programming school that turns me into the best geek in the world so I can move to Silicon Valley and make a zillion bucks. Or maybe I'll just end up going to college, after all, the way they want me to. But it'll be a decision I've made, instead of me just following some . . . some *formula*!"

Everything Emma was saying continued to make perfect sense to me. But I could see how Julie and her husband, Greg, could feel threatened by it. After all, they were pretty much by-the-book people. Formula folks, to borrow Emma's word.

I'd always figured that in Julie's case, her approach to life was the result of having had the formulas work so well for her. After all, she had been the queen bee in high school, picked to be prom queen, class president, head cheerleader, and everything else that had as its main requirement being the most popular girl at school. She was kind of like Ashley that way.

But the main difference was that she wasn't mean like Ashley. Julie was someone who wore her prettiness and her popularity with grace. It was as if these were gifts that had simply been bestowed upon her, and she was so comfortable enjoying them that she didn't need to show off to anyone else.

Still, I could only imagine how difficult it would be to be Julie's daughter. Especially if you were into Picasso and computers instead of school dances and pom-poms.

"Sounds tough," I said, resting my chin in my hand. "So you're taking a little vacation from your parents? Is that what this is about?"

Emma squirmed in her chair. "Sort of. But it's actually a little more than that."

"Meaning . . . ?"

She took a deep breath, meanwhile fixing her gaze on the edge of the table instead of on me. "Meaning I was hoping you and Grams would let me live with the two of you for a while."

"A while?" I repeated.

"Like . . . like a year, maybe . . . ? Until I can figure out where I want to go from here . . . ?"

My immediate reaction to her proposition was sheer joy. What fun it would be to have Emma live with Grams and me! I'd always loved her spiritedness. She was warm, funny, and one of those people who always came up with the best ideas.

Like the Christmas all three McKay sisters had gotten together at Grams's house, along with the rest of my sisters' families. We had just sat down to Christmas Eve dinner when Chloe, then barely out of kittenhood, suddenly raced up the Christmas tree, knocking it down in the process. As if that bit of chaos wasn't enough, somehow the stand got broken when the tree toppled over. So there we all were on Christmas Eve without a tree.

Emma, who was probably only eight or nine, immediately came up with a brainstorm. She found this huge piece of green felt that Grams had stashed in her closet, something that was left over from one of her craft projects. She draped it over a coat rack and stuck it in the middle of the living room, right where the real tree had been. Then we all had a grand time safety-pinning ornaments to it, meanwhile singing every Christmas carol we could think of. We even made popcorn to string, then pinned that onto the pretend tree, too. The whole thing was so much fun that it ended up being one of the best Christmas Eves ever.

Glancing around the shop, Emma added, "I was thinking that maybe I could even work for you. Here in the store, I mean." She picked up her spoon and, with a sly little grin, added, "I even promise not to eat up all the inventory. Unless you need help getting rid of extra stuff, of course." She stuck a huge glob of Cappuccino Crunch into her mouth, raising her eyes upward to show how much she was enjoying it.

"I could help out with Grams, too," she went on. "I know she still hasn't completely recovered from her fall, and I'd be happy to do some of the cooking and cleaning and whatever else needs to be done. Besides, it would be so great to be able to hang out with her, and I'm sure she'd appreciate having the company. She's been promising to teach me how to knit for ages, but somehow we never find the time. There are all kinds of things we could do together."

"Emma, it all sounds fabulous," I said sincerely. "I'd adore it if you came to live with Grams and me. But this isn't up to me. Or Grams, for that matter. It's up to your parents."

"I know," Emma replied, her enthusiasm instantly flagging. "But I am eighteen, after all. Doesn't that count for anything?"

"Sure," I said. "But you don't want to do anything your parents are totally against, do you?"

She hung her head. "I guess not."

I reached over and squeezed her shoulder. "You're at a tough age, Em. Technically you're all grown up. You're old enough to vote or join the army or get married . . . but like you've been saying, there's still so much you haven't yet had a chance to figure out. Heck, I'm still figuring out a lot of that stuff myself, and I'm thirty-three!

"I mean look at me," I continued. "Look at this place. An ice cream shop! If you'd told me a year ago—three months ago—that I'd end up running a place like this, I'd have said you were suffering from brain freeze!"

"But you love it, right?" Emma asked anxiously. "It's your dream come true, isn't it?"

I could feel a slow smile creeping across my face, one I couldn't have controlled even if I'd wanted to. "It is. I am living out a dream, even though it's one I didn't even realize I had until very recently. So I understand completely all that stuff about making your way through life, getting to know yourself better and better so you can make good decisions about what moves to make next."

"So does that mean you'll talk Mom and Dad into letting me live with you and Grams?" Emma asked, her face bright with hope.

"Emma, I'll do my best," I told her. "But I can't promise, of course—"

"Thank you, Aunt Kate!" Emma jumped out of her chair and leaned over to give me a big bear hug. "I knew you were the reasonable one in this family!"

Emma's opinion of me being the reasonable one—and her implication that the rest of our family was, shall we say, less than reasonable—was born out by the phone conversation I ended up having with her mother as soon as we'd both had enough so-called breakfast to be able to face calling her.

"Jules, it's me, Kate," I said as soon as my sister answered. Knowing how frantic she must be, I quickly added, "Emma is fine. She's with me."

"Emma is with *you*?" Julie shot back. "What are you talking about? She's upstairs in her room. And why on earth are you calling me at this ungodly hour? Kate, it's six-thirty a.m. On a *Sunday*!"

So my big sister hadn't even realized that her daughter was missing. So much for the drama of running away from home.

"I guess you haven't noticed that Emma isn't in bed," I said dryly. "Or that she didn't come home last night."

"Honestly, it's not as if I have that girl tied to a leash," Julie said. "She's always off doing her own thing, especially on the weekends. She is eighteen, after all."

Old enough not to be checked up on, I thought, but still not old enough for her to decide how she wants to spend the next year or two of her life.

"You know, Jules, maybe I should give you a little time to wake up before we have this conversation," I said, suddenly losing patience. "Maybe after you've had a cup of coffee."

Or two or three, I thought.

It wasn't that Julie was difficult; it was just that she was a linear thinker. She was one of those people who needed to have things laid out for her. Otherwise, she didn't always connect the dots.

"Katy, you've just called me practically in the middle of the night to tell me my daughter has basically run away from home, gotten herself to the hinterlands of New York, and shown up on your doorstep. I think I'd better hear about this now."

I glanced over at Emma, who was sitting right across the table from me, rolling her eyes. No doubt she could hear every word her mother was saying.

I took a deep breath. "Okay. Basically, Emma has asked me if she can come live with Grams and me while she decides what she wants to do about her education."

I held the phone away from my ear, expecting a tirade. Instead, all I heard was a sigh.

"Emma and her father and I have been over this a hundred times," Julie said, sounding exasperated. "Frankly, he and I are both getting a little tired of it." Another sigh. And then: "You know, Kate, maybe it's not such a bad idea. Let me talk to Greg and see what he thinks. But after the three of us having the same argument for almost a year now, I'm beginning to realize it's not one we're going to win. Maybe once Emma is out on her own for a while, she'll get some sense knocked into her."

She won't exactly be on her own, I thought grimly. *Living with Grams and me isn't exactly the same thing as putting in time at a halfway house.*

But even though talking to Julie was, as usual, a bit of a

downer, suddenly having Emma in my life was an upper that was even more powerful than a large scoop of Cappuccino Crunch ice cream and the sugar and caffeine rush that came along with it.

My life had just gotten a little bit sweeter.

Chapter 7

The world's tallest ice cream cone was created in
Kristiansand, Norway, on July 26, 2015. It stood
10 feet 1.26 inches high and consisted of a wafer
cone weighing about 211 pounds, a chocolate
lining that weighed about 132 pounds, 285
gallons of ice cream and 88 pounds of jam.

—*GuinnessWorldRecords.com*

"Should I take you back to the house so we can tell Grams
the good news?" I suggested to Emma as soon as our
dishes of ice cream were nothing but the last smears of cream
that even experts like us couldn't manage to extract from the
dish.

Emma nodded. "I can't wait to see her. Oh, Aunt Kate,
thank you so much! You have no idea how happy I am that
you've agreed to let me come stay with you and Grams!"

"First of all, I'm sure I'm even happier about this arrangement than you are," I told her. "And there's no doubt in my
mind that Grams will be thrilled, too. Second, from now on,
it's just Kate. Let's drop the 'aunt' part. Too many syllables."

Emma just grinned.

We stashed her backpack in the back of my truck and
headed home. All the while, she chattered away about her
plans for the new life she'd just found herself in.

"I thought that if nobody minded, I'd take the bedroom in back, the one that overlooks the garden," she chirped away happily. "And if you and Grams don't object, I thought maybe I'd plant a little vegetable garden in that space that gets the most sunlight. I've never had a chance to do that, since Mom has every inch of our property manicured so that it looks like Disneyland. . . ."

Even as she spoke, her eyes were fixed on the streets of Wolfert's Roost. Though she'd been coming here all her life, visiting Grams, I suspected that she was looking at it differently, considering all the possibilities. After all, this was her home now, too.

It was also the place in which she'd have her first taste of independence. It reminded me of going off to college and experiencing the thrill of living on my own for the very first time. Being able to make the simplest decisions, things as simple as what time to eat dinner—or exactly what that dinner would be.

It meant a lot to me that I'd be there to experience it with her. *Think of it*, I thought with a smile. *Three generations of us, living together.*

I couldn't imagine anything better.

When we reached the house, I opened the door as quietly as I could, not wanting to wake Grams. Of course, Digger undid all of my good intentions the moment we stepped inside. He began barking his welcome, skittering around the floor as if he, and not us, had just had his morning dose of caffeine.

"Hey, Digger!" Emma cried in a hoarse whisper. She crouched down to give him a hug, at least as much as that's possible with a whirling dervish of a terrier. That creature just didn't know the meaning of the words "stand still." "Sh-h-h-h! Digger, don't make so much noise! You'll wake Grams!"

"I'm already awake," Grams said, suddenly appearing at

the doorway that led to the kitchen, wearing the pink chenille bathrobe I'd given her for Christmas two years before. "At least, I think I am. Part of me thinks I must be dreaming!"

Emma laughed, then ran over to give her a big hug. "You're not dreaming, Grams. It's really me!"

"Emma, what a lovely surprise!" Grams said, hugging her back. "I didn't know you were coming for a visit."

"It's not exactly a visit," I said, watching the two of them. The three of them, if you counted Digger, who was jumping up on the two women as if he simply refused to be left out of this happy reunion. "Grams, Emma is going to stay with us for a while, if that's okay. I figured you wouldn't mind—"

"Of course I don't mind!" Grams replied. "I'm absolutely ecstatic! Now, stand back a bit so I can get a good look at you."

It didn't take long for Emma to settle in. Grams agreed that the back bedroom was perfect for her, and she immediately got busy pulling an extra blanket out of the linen closet and emptying a drawer full of fabric to make room for Emma's things. We all had a cup of real coffee, sitting together at the kitchen table, while Emma told Grams everything she'd told me about her reasons for wanting some time to think—time she felt was best spent with us.

Finally, I said, "I'm afraid I have to go back to the shop. I've got to make up a couple of batches of ice cream before we open."

Emma jumped out of her chair. "I'll come with you, Aunt Kate—I mean Kate. If you don't mind, that is. But I'm ready to get to work, so I'd love it if you'd take me back to the shop and put me to work."

It took about an hour for Emma to learn everything there is to know about running an ice cream shop. At least, everything I knew about running an ice cream shop.

And scooping ice cream was the least of it. That morning, the first thing I did was teach her how to make ice cream from scratch. Not surprisingly, she picked it up easily. And she was already letting her imagination run wild as she thought up possible flavors.

"How about Lemon Meringue Pie?" she suggested, her eyes bright. "Lemon-flavored ice cream, dotted with bits of meringue and little pieces of graham cracker?"

"That could work," I replied.

"And . . . and Cannoli!" she exclaimed. "You know, like the Italian pastry? Let's see: ricotta-flavored ice cream with crumbs from a cannoli shell, crispy but not too sweet . . . and little chocolate chips, like they sometimes dip them in!"

"That's funny," I told her. "I thought up that one, too. I guess great minds really do think alike."

Emma beamed. "How about sweet potato? With sugared walnuts!"

The girl was a gem.

And that was just the early part of the morning. When we opened at eleven and the ice cream cravers started drifting in, Emma quickly learned how to concoct all the specialties of the house. It took her about a half hour to master everything on the Lickety Splits menu, from the Rootin'-Tootin' Root Beer Float to the Hudson's Hottest Hot Fudge Sundae. She looked like an absolute pro, standing behind the counter, her blue hair tied back with a hot pink headband and her black jeans and T-shirt covered by a black-and-white checked Lickety Splits apron.

She was also turning out to be a master at chatting up the customers. She encouraged them to try new flavors, cheerfully insisting that they take advantage of our free samples policy to see if cardamom was a flavor they liked. She made sure no one walked away without a couple of paper napkins or the straw they needed. And whenever there was a lull, she hurried over to the tables to wipe them down and neatly arrange the napkin dispenser and the little vase of flowers in the middle of each one.

Emma was turning out to be even more of an asset than I'd originally thought. I was relieved to know that whenever I needed to leave the shop for some reason, I'd be leaving it in good hands. *Really* good hands.

Even though Sunday afternoons were one of my busiest times, I decided to take advantage of her ice-cream-shop-running abilities that very day.

As euphoric as I was over Emma's sudden appearance, Ashley's murder was a dark, ugly cloud that continued to hover over me. Even with the distraction of having my niece suddenly move in with Grams and me, my determination to do whatever I could to find Ashley's killer never wavered.

For the past forty-eight hours, ever since Pete Bonano had hauled me into the police station—well, maybe he didn't exactly *haul* me—I hadn't been able to stop thinking about the fact that there lurked in some people's mind even the vaguest possibility that I could have had something to do with the crime. Overhearing the town gossip at Ashley's funeral had made me feel even more uncomfortable.

I wanted to find out everything about Ashley's world I could.

True, I'd never done anything even remotely like this before. But the way I saw it, I'd figured out how to open up my own ice cream shop. I'd rented space and decorated it so that it was unimaginably cute and learned how to make big batches of ice cream and come up with fun names for flavors and irresistible ice cream concoctions.

So stretching myself a little wasn't exactly something I was incapable of.

I reminded myself of that as I pulled Hayley Nielsen's business card out of my purse and called her.

"Hi, Hayley!" I said brightly. "It's Kate McKay. I'm following up on your offer to talk about improving the look of my ice cream shop. I hope it's okay that I called so soon, but I thought it might be a good distraction for you."

"It's the perfect distraction," Hayley replied. "I'm really glad you called."

I was sincerely glad she felt that way. "Great," I said. "Maybe we can set something up for this week. . . ."

"Let me check my calendar. . . . Well, will you look at that! It turns out I just had a cancellation for this very afternoon. Would that work?"

"That would work just fine," I said. I couldn't help wondering if there was a lot of blank space in that calendar of hers.

"I can stop by at, say . . . three o'clock?" she suggested.

"Three is perfect."

I could hardly wait.

At one minute before three, Hayley strode into the shop, holding a large, heavy-looking tote bag in one hand and a clipboard in the other.

I realized that she actually looked a lot like Ashley. Only she was a slightly less impressive, less . . . *shiny* version. She, too, was tall and slim, only not quite as tall and slim. She dressed just as stylishly as Ashley, but instead of looking as if she had just stepped out of the pages of *Vogue*, looked merely like one of the mannequins at Bloomingdale's.

Today, for example, she was dressed in tailored white linen pants and a bright pink-and-green print tunic. Lilly Pulitzer, or at least some designer who was good at imitating Lilly's style. On her feet were delicate sandals, thin strips of pink leather studded with bling.

It was as if Ashley Winthrop had taught her everything she knew about how to dress.

"Thanks for coming in," I greeted her, pulling off my apron and leaving Emma to deal with the short line of customers who were awaiting ice cream bliss.

"No problem," Hayley replied. She plopped down at the

one empty table and pulled out an off-white leather folder. She flipped it open to a blank white pad.

"This is a charming little place you've got here, Kate," she said.

"Thanks," I replied, even though I had a feeling that was her opening line wherever she went. "I'm pretty happy with the way it turned out. I put it all together myself. But I'm sure it could use some improvement."

Hayley nodded. "It's great that you're open to new ideas. Not everyone is."

She glanced around, squinting a bit, as if that might help her pick out any flaws. "One thing I noticed right away is that you could improve the lighting," she commented. "It's a little bright in here, don't you think?"

I hadn't noticed. But now that she'd mentioned it, I could see her point.

"You might think about replacing these hanging light fixtures with overhead lighting that's set into the ceiling," she continued. "Installing what's called high hats. You could even get some retro ones that would look totally cool. I've seen these round plastic ones, white, of course. . . . Anyway, that's one idea.

"Another thing you might consider is changing the way the tables are placed. If it were up to me . . ."

As she spoke, I nodded and murmured "Um-hmm" every once in a while, doing my best to pretend I was interested in what she was saying. But while part of me was actually listening, even considering her ideas, most of my mind was focused on how to bring Ashley into the conversation.

I decided to use the direct approach.

"Great ideas," I said crisply, leaning back in my chair. I hoped my tone and my body language would communicate that we were done.

And then, I abruptly leaned forward. "So tell me, Hayley,"

I said in a much softer voice, "how are you doing? I know what close friends you and Ashley were."

Her eyes immediately filled with tears. "I'm still in shock," she said. "Ashley and I have been best friends since, like, second grade. I haven't yet realized what it means that she's gone."

I nodded, fighting back the tears that were now welling up in my eyes.

Somehow, I felt I could trust her.

"Hayley," I said slowly, "you're probably going to think I'm crazy, but I'm going to do everything I can to find out who killed Ashley."

She cast me a look that said that she did, indeed, think I was crazy. "You?" she said. "Why?"

"Because I've known her forever. Because she had a shop right across from mine. Because Ashley Winthrop is—was—as much a part of this town as the Hudson River."

She continued to look skeptical.

"Because," I finally said, "Ashley and I had a huge fight out on the street just a few hours before she was killed. And it seems that some people, including, uh, the police, think there's a teensy-weensy possibility I had something to do with it."

"You? *You?*" Hayley started to laugh. "As if."

I wasn't sure whether or not to be insulted.

"I mean, let's face it, Kate. You just don't have it in you to do something like that. You're much too . . . too nice!"

Somehow, Hayley managed to make that word sound like an even worse insult than the crudest obscenity she could have ever come out with.

"You don't have it in you," she went on, still chuckling. "Anyone who knows you knows there's no way you could *ever*—"

"Okay, got it," I interrupted. "Thank you, Hayley. I'm glad you have so much confidence in my innocence."

"Of course I do!" Hayley said. Suddenly, she grew serious. "If you plan to help the police with the investigation, maybe there's some way I can help."

"Anything," I said breathlessly. "Any piece of information, anything you can tell me about Ashley or what was going on in her personal life or her business . . ."

She shook her head. "I know so much about her that I wouldn't know where to start."

"In that case," I suggested, "let's start with Sweet Things. What do you know about her bakery?"

"Let's see." She frowned. "She started it about five years ago because she'd just gotten divorced from that lowlife husband of hers, Billy. She needed money, of course, but she also needed something meaningful in her life. A new project that she could be excited about. So she came up with the idea of a baking co-op—"

"Wait a second," I interrupted. "Sweet Things was a baking cooperative?"

"That's right."

"What does that mean, exactly? I mean, how did it work?"

Hayley shrugged. "It's simple, really. Ashley found local women who were good at baking, and they supplied her with the pastries she sold."

"Interesting," I said. "How come she didn't advertise that? It's really a fun idea."

"Maybe, but it's not exactly legal, either," Hayley said. "The health laws are very strict about the kitchens you can use to make food that's sold to the public. You can't use a kitchen that's also used for personal cooking. Which means you need access to an industrial kitchen, like at a restaurant."

"I see," I said. But I was less interested in the cleanliness of the cookies and cupcakes Ashley sold than I was in the women who made them.

"Boy, if we could get hold of that list," I mused, thinking

aloud, "that might be a great place to start finding out more about what was going on in Ashley's life that could have led to what happened. . . ."

"I have a list," Hayley said matter-of-factly.

I blinked. "You do?"

"Yes. A couple of weeks ago, I told Ashley that my business wasn't doing that great. What I mean is"—she added hastily—"it wasn't doing as great as I *wanted.*

"The whole thing was kind of weird," she said, speaking more to herself than she was to me. "At first, I got the feeling she didn't really want to give me their names. But then I figured she didn't want me promoting my design business to the people who worked for her, trying to sign them up as clients. Or maybe that she was, I don't know, jealous of my career or something.

"Ashley could be that way, you know." Hayley glanced around Lickety Splits again. "You might not believe this, but she wasn't always the nicest person in the world. She could be a little . . . *competitive.*"

Y'think? I thought, resisting the urge to laugh out loud.

"In fact, I think I may even have that list here with me," she said, already rifling through her tote bag. "I'm pretty disorganized, so I try to keep everything related to my business in one place. . . . Here it is!"

She pulled out an ordinary-looking piece of paper and handed it to me. "I made a few copies. Another way to save myself from my own disorganization. You can have one, if you think it might be helpful."

I glanced at it and saw that Ashley's list consisted of twelve or fifteen names, all women's names, running down one side. Next to each name was the pastry that particular woman supplied: "Lindsey Mather, Cheesecake. Allison Chibuzo, Blackberry Tart. Brandy DiNapoli, Licorice Twist."

"I have no idea if this will be helpful," I said, "but thank you."

Hayley waved her hand in the air in a "don't mention it" motion. "Good luck, Kate. I hope you—or the police—figure out what monster is responsible for what happened to Ashley."

Her eyes welling up with tears again, she added, "I know you and Ashley were never close. But she was my best friend. I'm going to miss her every day for the rest of my life."

As soon as Hayley had gone, my eyes drifted across the street, to Sweet Things. My heart instantly grew heavy and a sick feeling came over me.

While I'd been distressed by the hot pink sign Ashley had put in her store window only three days earlier, I was even more upset by the new one, stuck on the front door.

CLOSED, it read.

No explanation, no promise of a future reopening.

"Emma," I said, suddenly getting an idea, "can I borrow your laptop for a minute?"

"Of course." Emma whipped her computer out from behind the counter, opened it, and typed in whatever magic words were required to gain entry. "Here you go."

"Thanks." I brought it over to a table, sat down, and Googled the words, "Sweet Things Pastry Palace Wolfert's Roost."

The listing came up immediately, since apparently no one had thought to shut it down. I clicked on it, holding my breath.

I was struck by the fact that it turned out to be just another Web site. No mention of what had happened to its owner, no clue about its uncertain future.

No clues about its past, either. It was perfectly ordinary: a home page with a pink-and-white striped background, the same motif as Sweet Things' awning. The swirly letters, spelling out the shop's name, along with "Home of the Mile-High Cupcake," also matched the lettering on the storefront.

No clues there. Just a perfectly ordinary Web site.

I clicked here and there, trying the tabs for "Hours" and "Directions" and "Contact Us." Again, there wasn't a word about Sweet Things being closed. I looked a little further and found only general information: possible goodies that might be available, a list of events that could be accommodated, including weddings, birthdays, showers, and corporate functions. There was nothing at all about Ashley, not even a section on "History" or "Our Story" or anything that revealed a single thing about the woman behind Sweet Things.

After only a few minutes of playing around with it, I closed the computer and let out a loud sigh.

I was already getting a sense that figuring out who had wanted Ashley permanently out of the picture was going to be tough.

But thanks to Hayley—or to her list, to be more exact—at least I had a place to start.

Chapter 8

The Edy's/Dreyer's ice cream company insured
the taste buds of their Master Ice Cream Taster,
John Harrison, for one million dollars.
(That's $100 per taste bud.)

—*CookingLight.com*

The first thing I did with the list of Ashley's home bakers
was come up with ways of getting in touch with each one
of them.

That very evening, soon after Emma and I cleaned up,
closed up, and went home, I got right to it.

Or, to be more accurate, I put Emma on it.

I waited until after dinner, when Grams and Emma and I
had finished our meal and then savored our usual dessert of
an ice cream treat—tonight, s'more ice cream sandwiches I'd
made with Chocolate Marshmallow ice cream and graham
crackers. While Grams went off to watch one of her favorite
TV shows, Emma and I cleared the table, wrapped up the
leftovers, and loaded the dishes into the dishwasher.

But as she was about to head off to her bedroom, clutching her laptop as usual, I said, "Emma, could you come sit
down with me in the dining room so I can talk to you about
something?" I was doing my best to sound casual.

Emma, being Emma, was immediately anxious. "Did I do

something wrong at Lickety Splits?" she asked. "Am I scooping out too much ice cream? Too little? Did I put too many nuts in the Cashew Brittle with Sea Salt this morning? I thought I might have gone overboard. . ."

"Nothing like that," I assured her. "Believe me, Em, you are already the Diva of the Double Dip. The Princess of the Pistachio Nut. The Queen of the . . ."

"Kumquat!" she exclaimed. "Kumquat ice cream! Why not?"

I was afraid that what I really wanted to talk to her about was going to be kind of a letdown.

In fact, I was pretty nervous about telling Emma that I planned to do whatever I could to find out who had killed Ashley Winthrop. I had already decided that I wasn't going to tell her about Pete Bonano coming to the house early in the morning or Detective Stoltz giving me the third degree . . . certainly not about Jake Pratt coming to my rescue.

In the end, of course, I told her everything.

"Kate, if there's anything I can do," she told me once I'd finished filling her in on the melodrama that my life had become, "I would love to help."

"I'm glad you said that," I said, pulling out the list Hayley had given me earlier that day.

Not surprisingly, Emma was an expert when it came to tracking down people online. With amazing speed, she came up with phone numbers or addresses or e-mail addresses— sometimes all three—for each one of the women on the list.

At least as far as we knew. I wouldn't know until I spoke with them if they were actually the same women named on Ashley's list of suppliers.

As for coming up with reasons for speaking with them, I needed assistance of a different sort.

"Emma," I told her, "I'm hoping you can help me in one more way. . . ."

This was something I'd been thinking about ever since Hayley had given me that list. I wanted to question as many of the women on it as I could about Ashley's business, their relationship with Ashley, anything personal they might have known about Ashley . . . which meant I needed to engage them in an actual conversation, one in which they'd open up to me.

And I'd decided that my best shot was to use Lickety Splits to do it.

"I'm going to need some professional-looking graphics," I explained, "and from what you've told me, it sounds like you're exactly the person I need."

Emma's face lit up as if I'd just given her a present. "I'd love to help you with that!" she exclaimed. "Just tell me what you need."

"First of all, I'd like a flyer—you know, a little pamphlet or even a one-page handout—promoting kids' parties at Lickety Splits. Here, I wrote up some information about different themes and what we'd include and what it would cost." I handed her a sheet with the notes I'd jotted down over the past few weeks, while I was still planning the details of my new business. Promoting the children's parties was something I really had intended to do, once my ice cream shop got going. Now, I needed those flyers ASAP.

"This is going to be so much fun!" Emma explained. "I can get pictures of kids in party hats, eating ice cream, of course, off one of those Web sites with free photos . . . and I have a great idea for the font to use! There's this loopy, cartoon-y one I know of that'll be perfect. . . ."

I gave her a few other projects, as well. Instead of acting overwhelmed, she looked positively thrilled.

In fact, by the end of the evening, she'd printed out multiple copies of everything I'd asked for. They looked as good as anything I'd ever seen, even in my days in public relations in the city.

The Lickety Splits Marketing Department had been launched. So had the Lickety Splits Detective Agency.

Playing detective, however, was turning out to be much scarier than selling ice cream.

The next morning, as I told my GPS app to direct me to the home of the first woman on Ashley's list, my stomach felt as if it were the training ground for the butterflies' Olympic volleyball team. While working in PR had demanded that I put on a cheerful face pretty much all the time, this new endeavor I was embarking on brought the need to pretend to a whole new level.

"Quiet down!" I commanded the butterflies as I turned off the ignition, right after the GPS voice informed me, "You have arrived at your destination."

My destination, the house at 25 Chestnut Street that belonged to Lindsey Mather, the first name on the list, was a modest bungalow. The low-slung building looked as if it had been designed by taking two shoe boxes and placing them at right angles to each other. The gray-blue shingles looked pretty shabby, as if they'd weathered a few too many New York winters. The glass on one of the windows appeared to have cracked, given the stripe of silver duct tape used to patch it.

But there were also some personal touches designed to give it a warm, homey feeling. The Mathers—presumable Lindsey—had hung a wreath of dried flowers on the front door. A somewhat scraggly row of petunias peaked out of a narrow flower bed that followed the L shape of the building, interspersed with enough weeds to indicate that these homeowners were not exactly passionate about gardening.

But the most obvious signs that a young family lived here

were in back. I spotted a plastic slide, a playhouse the size of a large doghouse, and a blue kiddie pool filled with just a few inches of water.

The butterflies were not behaving. But I did my best to ignore them as I strode up the front walk and knocked on the door.

The woman who answered was young, probably in her midtwenties. She looked tired, even though it wasn't quite eleven in the morning. Stressed out, too. Her dark blond hair was pulled back thoughtlessly into a messy bun kind of thing, with some strands sticking up in the air and others hanging down around her neck. Her green eyes weren't accented with makeup, but with red ridges that told me she hadn't gotten enough sleep.

She was dressed in sagging gray sweatpants and what looked like a men's T-shirt, emblazoned with the logo of a local brewery. Despite her baggy clothes, I could see that she was small framed, but that there were definitely curves under all those clothes. But the roundness extended to her arms and her middle, as if, like me, the last decade had added a few pounds she probably wasn't crazy about possessing.

In one arm she held a squirmy little boy wearing a Batman T-shirt, his nose running and his pale blond hair sticking up all over the place. Her other hand grasped an identical little boy by the wrist. This one, who appeared to favor the Ninja Turtles, was also moving nonstop. His face was also moist, albeit from tears rather than snot.

"I don't want to!" he whined. "Ma-a-a-m-a-a, *no-o-o-o-o!*"

She seemed amazingly calm. "Can I help you?" she asked.

"Good morning!" I said brightly, speaking a little louder than usual. "My name is Kate McKay, and I'm the owner of a new ice cream shop in town called Lickety Splits. Maybe you've seen it . . . ?"

Lindsey brightened. "I certainly have!" she exclaimed. "Your place is great!"

Bingo, I thought. An ice cream lover.

"I love the way you've transformed that boring old store-front," she went on. "The colors you used, that bright pink and green, and that bench you put outside is so useful. I've already used it a couple of times. When you've got three little kids, all under the age of five, sometimes you need a place to sit down and sort things out."

"I can imagine," I said, putting on my sympathetic voice.

"M-a-a-a-a!" the Ninja Turtle-in-training shrieked. "Lemme go-o-o-o!"

"But here I am, chattering away," she said, bouncing Boy Number One up and down a bit, even though it was his clone who was having the meltdown. "What can I do for you?"

I took a deep breath. I'd always been kind of a wimp when it came to playing the role of salesperson. That was one of the things I liked about being in the ice cream business. You didn't have to work very hard to make people want to buy what you were selling.

"One of the special services I'm offering at Lickety Splits is kids' birthday parties," I said.

I pulled out one of the promotional flyers I'd had Emma whip up the night before as a way of getting me in the door at Lindsey's. They were so good that I'd decided that I'd actually use them to promote real children's parties at my shop.

I was about to hand her one when I realized she didn't have any spare hands.

She chuckled. "As you can see, I've got my hands full at the moment. But if you have a minute, why don't you come inside and tell me about how the parties work?"

I thought you'd never ask, I thought, following her inside.

As soon as I did, I let out a gasp.

The Mathers' small but charmingly decorated bungalow

looked as if a hurricane had just struck. Toys were strewn everywhere—on the floor, all over the couch, even under the coffee table. The display of colors was positively mind blowing, every bright shade of red and blue and yellow imaginable. Some of them, like the giant-size Legos and the jigsaw puzzles, had become a form of confetti, their hundreds of pieces sprinkled about the room in random places.

On the dining room table were the remains of that morning's breakfast. Boxes of Rice Krispies, half-eaten pieces of toast sitting in a nest of crumbs, a puddle of milk that, so far, hadn't quite made it to the edge of the table. A pair of tiny pink underpants was lying in the doorway to the kitchen, and a turquoise sneaker was on the upholstered chair.

"Sorry about the mess," Lindsey said, not missing a beat. "I could make up some excuse, like my babysitter just quit, but the truth is that it's always like this. And I don't even have a babysitter."

A little girl sat cross-legged on the floor, glued to the Sesame Street characters frolicking on the TV screen. I was relieved to see that her face was dry, and that her T-shirt had a picture of Dora the Explorer, rather than some testosterone-filled action figure hell-bent on saving the world through creative violence.

"This is Violet," Lindsey said, leaning over to put Boy Number One into the playpen set up in the corner. Then she lifted his twin and put him in, too. I gave them both about three minutes before they broke free. "Say hello to our visitor, Violet. Kate, isn't it? Kate runs the new ice cream store in town, so she's an important lady to know!"

Violet checked me out for a few seconds, her blue eyes big and round. Then she went back to Big Bird.

"Can I get you anything?" Lindsey asked, turning back to me. "I have Diet Coke, iced tea . . . a glass of water?"

"Thanks, I'm fine," I assured her.

Darn, I thought. She's really nice. It's going to be hard to consider her a possible suspect in a murder.

I decided that instead, I'd look at her as a source of information.

"Let me know if you change your mind," she said. She moved a few toys off the couch, enough to make room for both of us, and sat down. "So tell me about the parties."

I realized that Lindsey was actually pleased to have a visitor. I was somebody to talk to. A grown-up. And a way to break up the day. Maybe I was going out on a limb, but I got the feeling that having one child, Violet, had been a breeze. Then came the twins—twin boys, no less—and all hell had broken loose in the Mather household.

I brought out the flyer once again and handed it to Lindsey.

"Lickety Splits can host parties of up to fifteen kids," I said, trying to sound as if I'd given this spiel a hundred times before. "The kids can play games, like the Ice Cream Memory Game, where they have to remember funny flavors. They can make basic do-it-yourself sundaes, or else they can try their hand at what we call ice cream sculptures. That means the crazier they get, the better. And we give out prizes. . . ."

I took a moment to feel grateful that Emma had stumbled into my life, along with her limitless imagination. Not only had she made up these fabulous flyers, she had come up with most of the ideas I was pitching.

"Wow, all this sounds terrific," Lindsey said, scanning the flyer. She swatted at a strand of dark blond hair that had fallen into her eyes.

"We can make up ice cream cakes with any theme you'd like," I went on. By this point, I was really getting into the sales pitch thing. In fact, I'd all but forgotten about the real reason I was here. "We could do Big Bird, Dora the Explorer, Ninja Turtles. . . ."

As long as the people who own the rights to those characters didn't sue me, I suddenly thought. I'd better ask a lawyer about that one.

Jake? I immediately thought, experiencing an annoying jolt of excitement. *No,* a saner part of me immediately shot back. Not Jake. Anyone but Jake.

"I'm definitely interested," Lindsey said. "These guys are too little to have a serious birthday party," she said. "Aside from having the family over for a barbecue or whatever. But Violet is turning five in August. I'd love to throw her a really nice party. And as you can probably imagine, doing that here at home would be kind of complicated."

Involuntarily I scanned the chaos that surrounded me. And as if on cue, the Ninja Turtle twin, who appeared to be the more vocal of the two, began wailing again.

I got the feeling this was all simply business as usual. I decided to follow Lindsey's lead and simply ignore him.

"So Violet is starting kindergarten in the fall?" I asked.

Lindsey rolled her eyes. "Thank heaven! At least I'll get a bit of a break during the day. Although with these two, that's practically impossible. Would you believe that Jason and Justin *never* take a nap at the same time? It's like they insist on doing it in shifts."

I did believe it.

"Then maybe we should see if we can find a date that works for both of us," I said. I was actually flabbergasted that not only had my kids' birthday parties ploy gotten me in the door and onto the couch, it had also gotten me a nice bit of business.

"Of course, I need to talk it over with my husband before I commit," Lindsey added. "As you can imagine, things are a little tight these days. Money-wise, I mean."

"Having three kids must cost a small fortune," I said.

She laughed, without exhibiting much levity. "More like a *large* fortune."

"Still, I think you'll find that the prices for our children's parties are quite reasonable," I said, snapping back into my sales persona. "And the location is so convenient. There's plenty of parking on the street—or that big public lot right behind Sweet Things. You know, that bakery on Hudson Street with the pink-and-white striped awning . . . ?"

I kept my eyes fixed on Lindsey's face as I said those last few words, curious to see how she'd react.

She reacted, all right.

"Oh, goodness," she said, immediately tearing up. "I'm sorry for getting upset. But I'm sure you heard about what happened to Ashley Winthrop. She is—she *was*—the owner of Sweet Things."

"Yes, I did hear," I said. I was glad we'd already gotten down to talking about the topic of conversation I'd come here for in the first place. "Did you know her?"

I held my breath, hoping she'd be honest with me. But I got the feeling Lindsey Mather had a hard time being dishonest about anything.

"Not only did I know her," she said, "I worked for her." The tears that had filled her green eyes began streaming down her cheeks.

I pretended to look surprised. "Really? Oh, my. Then you must really be devastated. Did you work at the bakery? I'm sorry I never noticed you there, but I've only been in Wolfert's Roost for a few months, and as you know I only opened my ice cream shop last week."

"I didn't actually work there," Lindsey said, sniffling. Mechanically I reached into my purse and pulled out a tissue. She accepted it gratefully and immediately put it to good use. "I was one of her suppliers. What I mean is, I made baked goods here at home and brought them to Sweet Things so she could sell them."

"Really! I had no idea Sweet Things was a bakery co-op,"

I said. I gave myself an imaginary pat on the back, commending myself for how good I was getting at this pretending thing.

Lindsey made a face. "Ashley didn't actually want anybody to know about it. You see, the laws in this state make it illegal for a commercial business like Ashley's to sell food that isn't made in a kitchen that's been inspected and approved by the health department. In other words, we were both kind of breaking the law."

"I see." Glancing over in the direction of the kitchen, I said, "So you made baked goods here at the house and brought them over to her?"

"Exactly," Lindsey said. "It was really convenient, you know? With the kids here at home and all? I didn't have to pay for babysitters or anything. I didn't even have to get out of my pajamas! I could do my baking while the kids were playing or glued to the TV. Or my husband could watch them while I did whatever needed to be done. Shopping for ingredients, doing the baking, wrapping everything up just so . . ."

"But that had to have been at night," I observed. "After your husband came home from work, I mean. That sounds really tough, because I'd think that with three small children at home all day you'd be pretty wiped out by then."

"But here's the thing," Lindsey went on. She looked around, as if wanting to make sure her children weren't listening in. Violet was still enthralled by Big Bird, not the least bit interested in anything that was going on around her. And the two little boys were miraculously quiet in their playpen, one of them pulling the ear of a teddy bear and the other turning the plastic wheel on one of those touchy-feely plastic contraptions that has all kinds of activities to get tiny fingers ready for the computer age.

"My husband, Rob, is between jobs right now," she said in a low voice.

"Ah," I said. "That's a shame."

Lindsey laughed coldly. "That's putting it mildly. Things have been really tough around here for quite a while. Financially, I mean."

"How long has your husband been out of work?" I asked.

"A little over a year."

I kept myself from gasping. That *was* tough. Especially with three kids to take care of.

As if she had read my mind, Lindsey said, "And it's not as if we actually planned to have three kids. We figured we could manage two. When we found out I was having twins . . ."

"Twice as much work, I suppose," I said.

"Yeah, and twice as expensive. Two of everything. Two car seats, two high chairs, twice as many diapers and twice as much baby food . . .

"It wasn't so bad when Rob was still working. He was making pretty good money in construction. The man is an absolute genius at putting up drywall."

I thought for a few seconds. "If your husband—Rob—is out of work, it sounds as if a birthday party at Lickety Splits might not be manageable for you this year," I said gently. "Money-wise, I mean."

"Actually," Lindsey said, "I'm hoping his parents will help out with that. They're crazy about their grandkids, of course. In fact, I don't know how we'd be managing without them. Ever since the boys were born, they've done everything they can to help."

"I guess you're lucky to have them."

Lindsey shrugged. "I guess. I'd rather we could do it on our own. Especially since they think that paying for things gives them the right to make decisions about how we're supposed to use it. Like when they offered to pay for a second bathroom to be added, guess who picked out the color scheme, the tile, even the faucets?"

I smiled sympathetically. "I see your point."

"But something like this . . ." She shrugged. "Maybe my mother-in-law won't insist on making *every* decision. Besides, I don't see any other way."

Lindsey let out a deep sigh. Speaking more to herself than to me, she said, "Boy, losing the income I made from working for Ashley is going to make things really tough around here."

"How long had you been working for her?" I asked.

"I started right after Rob lost his job," she replied. "I began looking for work right away. Most of what I found looked pretty grim. You know, receptionist in a dentist's office or light factory work, that kind of thing. That's why I was so thrilled when I found Ashley's ad online and found out she was looking for local women to work for her. Women with a flair for baking, I mean, which is definitely me.

"What Ashley was offering was perfect," she continued, brightening. "Making money by working from home . . . it was great. I didn't have to go to Rob's parents about every little thing. They could pay for the extras and I could still run my own life, and my kids' lives, the way I wanted."

Her face crumpled. "Now that Ashley's gone and the bakery gig has come to an end . . . well, we'll just have to see."

"I'm sure you two will figure something out," I said. "Maybe you'll find similar work. Baking, I mean. What kind of things did you make for Ashley's bakery?"

"Cheesecake," Lindsey replied. "That was my specialty."

"I love cheesecake," I said. This time, I didn't have to pretend. Cheesecake, after all, is pretty much the closest you can come to eating ice cream without actually, well, eating ice cream. Sweet, luscious creaminess gently sweetened and flavored with vanilla . . . Aside from using cream cheese instead of milk and cream, and aside from freezing it, cheesecake was ice cream's first cousin.

I resolved to look into creating a Cheesecake ice cream the first chance I got.

"All kinds of cheesecake?" I couldn't help asking. My mind was already racing with the possibilities. "Chocolate cheesecake? Strawberry cheesecake? Kahlua cheesecake?"

"Whatever Ashley wanted," Lindsey said vaguely, waving one hand in the air. "After all, I was working for her. She was the boss."

I was starting to get the feeling that Lindsey had had enough of playing the role of hostess to an ice cream salesperson. As if on cue, the Ninja-loving toddler had just found a new use for the hard plastic touching toy he'd been playing with: using it to bonk his brother on the shoulder. *Hard*, given the reaction he got.

"Agh-h-h-h-h!" he yelled. "Mo-o-o-m-e-e-e-e!"

His twin immediately began a screamfest of his own.

"Be *quiet*!" Violet yelled. "I'm *trying* to watch TV!"

It was definitely time for me to be on my way.

"I should be going," I said, standing up. "You've got the flyer, and I hope you'll stop into the shop sometime so we can talk more about what kind of party we can put together for Violet. Or you can always call me. My cell number is on the bottom here. Why don't you give me your number, too . . ."

Lindsey cast me a look of silent desperation, as if she was thinking, "Take me with you! Please!"

As I walked back to my car, accompanied by the screams of three unhappy children, I thought about how badly the Mathers needed Lindsey's income from baking for Ashley.

No cheesecake money translated to no income in that household at all. It also brought about more interference from in-laws who felt whoever paid the bills got to make the decisions.

Which meant it was highly unlikely that Lindsey had had anything to do with Ashley's death.

Not exactly the most encouraging start, I thought grimly as I drove away. Still, I tried to take heart in the fact that I still had a long list of other suspects to question. In fact, I reminded myself, I'd barely gotten started.

Chapter 9

Missouri designated the ice cream cone as its
Official State Dessert in 2008.

—*StateSymbolsUSA.org*

On Wednesday morning, I followed my usual routine of going into Lickety Splits early to whip up a couple of the new flavors I was so anxious to try. This time, it was Avocado and Carrot Cake, carrot-flavored ice cream made with plenty of cinnamon and swirls of cream cheese. They both came out surprisingly well, despite their unlikely ingredients. I was constantly amazed by just how versatile ice cream was.

By the time Emma showed up, right before we were scheduled to open our doors, I was ready to let her take over. With amazing speed, she had become my alter ego, doing as good a job of running the shop as I could ever do.

But for now, I left her to scoop and schmooze, spreading ice cream joy to anyone who ventured into Lickety Splits. And I took off to run some errands.

While most of them were for Grams, I had a few things of my own to pick up. I started by visiting two different farm stands, buying a normal amount of fresh strawberries and blueberries and a few other fruits for Grams—plus huge quantities of the same things for my shop.

Another luscious batch of Berry Blizzard, coming up. I could practically taste it as I piled the baskets into the back of my truck: strawberry ice cream with locally grown organic strawberries, raspberries, and blueberries at their peak, and of course that distinctive touch of cardamom and cinnamon that made it one of Lickety Splits' signature offerings.

Yum.

Next stop was the market, where I bought basics for Grams like eggs, sugar, and milk. I also stocked up on dog food and cat food, wishing I could turn Digger and Chloe on to the wonders of ice cream.

After making a few more stops, at the pharmacy, the dry cleaner, and the shoe repair shop, I dropped everything off at home and checked on Grams.

Instead of driving back into town, I decided to walk. It was a beautiful June day, with a cloudless sky, a big yellow sun that looked like something out of a kid's drawing, and a barely noticeable breeze wafting off the Hudson. But it wasn't just the perfect weather that caused me to leave my car at home.

As I strolled toward Hudson Street, I made a point of walking along River Road, the meandering side street that led from the riverbank up to Hudson Street. It also happened to go right past Greenleaf, Tad Patrick's restaurant.

I'd driven past it a few times in the months I'd been back in Wolfert's Roost. Every time I did, I told myself that I really should try it one of these days. But it was common knowledge around town that the sophisticated newcomer had a waiting list as long as the Hudson River itself, with foodies from New York City and the Hudson Valley and even beyond making reservations weeks in advance.

Somehow I never thought to plan that far ahead. Not for food that had nothing to do with ice cream.

Today, however, as I walked past the restaurant, I looked at it with new interest. It was located in a small Victorian with white shingles and green shutters. On the front porch sat a few rocking chairs, also painted green. The only indication that this wasn't just another cute house was a modest sign above the door. Written out in flowing leaves—green, of course—was the restaurant's name.

Greenleaf looked pretty sleepy this early in the day. At least, from the outside. Knowing what I did about the food service business, I was sure the kitchen was hopping, with plenty of chopping, dicing, slicing, mixing, sautéing, and every other food-related verb imaginable going on.

Still, with no one watching the front of the restaurant, I was able to step onto the porch to get a better look.

Peering through the windows, I saw that the room that had once been a parlor now had six tables in it, each one covered with a pale green linen tablecloth. Dark green linen napkins, folded like nurse's caps, were placed at each setting. The dishes were stark white, like the walls. Even so, the place looked inviting, thanks largely to the huge stone fireplace and the large gilt-framed mirrors on the walls.

I checked out the menu hanging next to the door. I figured if anyone noticed me casing the joint, I'd claim that this was the reason I was loitering on the porch at eleven o'clock in the morning. Just as I expected, it was full of flowery phrases and obscure edibles. I scanned the listings, amused by the incorporation of the ever-popular flavors of *harissa* and carambola and *mahleb* and *bondon*.

I admit, part of me wondered if there was anything there I could turn into new ice cream flavors.

The menu wasn't the only thing that was posted. In the front window was a copy of the *New York Times* article, complete with the long row of stars it had bestowed upon

Greenleaf, turning it into an instant success. There were reprints of more rave reviews from other newspapers and magazines, as well.

But the one that interested me most was a simple yellow square that read, "Member, Wolfert's Roost Chamber of Commerce."

The wheels in my head were turning. Chamber of Commerce, Greenleaf, Lickety Splits . . .

I'd just come up with another way of finding out a little bit more about Ashley.

I was strolling toward Lickety Splits, still ruminating about Wolfert's Roost's star chef and his possible role in both Ashley's life and her death, when my cell phone rang. Glancing at the screen, I saw it was Emma.

"What's up, girlfriend?" I answered cheerfully.

"Hi, Kate." She'd only uttered two words, yet I could already hear the distress in her voice.

"What's wrong?" I asked, already tensing up.

Even so, I was expecting her response to be something along the lines of, "I'm so swamped with customers that I desperately need you to come help." Or maybe, "Hot fudge sundae sales are going through the roof and I can't find the extra supply of maraschino cherries." Or worse yet, "The freezer has started making funny noises."

Instead, my niece's voice sounded similarly shaky as she said, "There was kind of a . . . thing that happened just now. A few minutes ago, actually."

I instantly felt a rush of heat course through my entire body. This sounded a lot more serious than missing fruit or even a freezer that was acting up.

"What do you mean, 'a thing'?" I asked anxiously. "What kind of 'thing'?"

Emma hesitated. "Things were kind of slow this morning, but I figured it was just the usual ups and downs of running a business. But finally a couple of little girls came running in. They were, like, eight and ten, somewhere around there. Sisters, I figured, given how similar they looked. Anyway, they came rushing over to the counter, clearly excited at the prospect of getting some ice cream. . . ."

"Go on," I prompted. I was still hoping that Emma's tale of woe would end up with a punch line about two little girls who couldn't decide between Chocolate Almond Fudge and Caramel Sea Salt.

"All of a sudden, their mother—at least, I assume it was their mother—came bursting into the shop," Emma went on. "She had this . . . this *look* on her face. I could tell she was really upset. She grabbed these little girls by the arms, and right in front of me, said, 'We don't shop in this store. The lady who owns it may have done something really, really terrible.' "

"Oh, my," I said breathlessly. "That's bad."

"It's certainly not good," Emma replied.

I had started taking those deep breaths Willow was always recommending. "First of all, are you okay? Do you want to close up the shop?"

"I'm fine, Kate. Really. And a few customers came in right after this happened, which is why it took me a while to call you. Like, three different groups came in over about ten minutes. Maybe the shop hasn't been as busy as it is sometimes, but who knows why? I'm sure this is just a case of someone overreacting to whatever rumors she's been hearing. Maybe I shouldn't have even mentioned it, but I thought you should know."

"You did the absolute right thing, Emma," I assured her. "And I'll be there in five minutes. I'm a few blocks away, about a half a block from Greenleaf—"

"Honestly, Kate, take your time," Emma insisted. "Everything else is business as usual."

Business as usual. Her words rang in my head as I ended the call and instantly turned my leisurely stroll through town into a brisk walk. I certainly hoped that was what I could expect—and that, as Emma had said with such confidence, this was likely to be one isolated incident.

As soon as I opened the door of Lickety Splits, Emma came rushing over, her eyebrows knitted and her mouth pulled into a straight line.

She was still upset about what happened earlier, I concluded.

But before I had a chance to say a word, even a consoling one, she said, "Kate, there's someone here I think you'll need to deal with. She just came in."

My heart sank. I immediately pictured the mother of the two daughters she'd told me about. So I was surprised when she added, "It's a woman with a coupon." She enunciated every syllable and gave me a strange look.

"A coupon?" I repeated. "But I didn't—"

And then I understood.

The coupon I'd mailed out first thing Monday morning, mere hours after Emma, my executive vice president of marketing, had designed it.

And it wasn't just any coupon. It was exceptionally generous, extending what was, for lack of a better description, an offer you couldn't refuse.

I had mailed it to some of the women on Ashley's list, figuring it was an easy way to get them to come into Lickety Splits so I could question them.

At least, that was my plan. Whether or not it was actually going to work remained to be seen.

The woman Emma was referring to had to be the one

standing off to the side, staring idly at the ice cream display case. She was tall and slender, probably about my age. Her skin was a rich shade of chocolate brown, and her black hair was pulled back neatly into a tight bun.

A lightbulb went on in my head. This was probably Allison Chibuzo, another name from Ashley's list of suppliers. Thanks to Emma's crackerjack online probing, we'd found a woman with that name who lived in the area. We'd also learned that there was an Allison Chibuzo who had just finished her first year at Albany Law School. I figured anyone who was a student, especially a law student, had to be on a tight budget, and an offer of free food would be hard to ignore.

Allison struck me as one of those lucky women who always managed to look well groomed and put together. She was wearing beige linen capris, a black tank top, and flip-flops, yet somehow she looked as if she could be on her way to a photo shoot for *Vogue*. The silky, brightly colored scarf draped around her neck definitely helped. The vibrant oranges and golds, tempered by a rich dark brown, complemented her skin tones perfectly. The same went for the floppy orange tote bag slung over one narrow shoulder.

"Can I help you?" I asked her. "I'm Kate McKay, the store's owner."

"I got this coupon in the mail," she said, whipping it out of her tote bag. "It says it's for a free ice cream cone and a free half gallon of ice cream. Is that really true?"

"It sure is," I replied.

"You mean there's no catch?" she asked, eyeing me suspiciously. "I can really get all that free stuff for nothing?"

I nodded. "It's our Grand Opening promotion. We're trying to introduce Lickety Splits to the neighborhood, and I figured the best way is to have people come into the shop and try our fabulous ice cream for themselves."

A huge grin lit up her face. I saw for the first time that she was extremely pretty. Beautiful, even.

"What flavor would you like in your cone?" I asked, stepping behind the counter.

I waited on her myself, scooping out an unusually generous glob of Peanut Butter on the Playground. As she contemplated the list of flavors posted high on the back wall, trying to decide which one to choose for her free half gallon, she plopped her tote bag onto one of the marble tables. Three large books slid out, thick tomes in dignified shades of burgundy and navy blue with shiny gold lettering that made them look important. Law books, no doubt.

She finally chose a half gallon of Classic Tahitian Vanilla. That told me she had a practical side that balanced out the more whimsical part of her, the one that still loved peanut butter and jelly. I already knew she'd make a great lawyer.

"Thanks!" she said, grabbing her tote bag. She started to walk out of the store, meanwhile licking her cone.

I panicked. I should have offered a free Hudson's Hottest Hot Fudge Sundae, I thought. That way, she would have had to sit down to eat it.

"Uh, can I ask you something?" I called after her.

She stopped, then looked back at me, surprised. "Sure."

"Are you, uh, a student?"

"I look a little old to be a student, right?" she said, smiling self-consciously. "But I am." Holding up her heavy book, she added, "In the fall I'll be starting my second year at Albany Law School."

Fortunately, a big blob of Peanut Butter ice cream chose that moment to drip off her cone, onto her shirt.

"Oh, no," she cried. "What a mess!"

"Here, let me help," I offered, thanking the universe for the invention of gravity. I grabbed a wad of napkins, poured some water onto it from the tap, and handed it to her. "There you go. Cold water works magic."

"Thanks," she said.

"It might be easier to eat that sitting down," I suggested, gesturing toward an empty table. "I've finally accepted the fact that I'm simply not capable of eating and walking at the same time. At least, not if I want to enjoy whatever I'm eating."

"Good idea," she said. Gracefully she lowered herself onto a chair. "I have to learn to relax every once in a while. I'm one of those type A personalities who has to be doing something every second of the day. Like today, even though school doesn't start up again until September, I'm already trying to get a head start on the classes I'll be taking."

"Albany is a pretty good distance from here," I observed, fussing with the napkin dispenser on the table and using it as an excuse to sit down opposite her. "It's about an hour and a half's drive, isn't it?"

"Almost," Allison said. "I live a few miles north of here, which saves me a few minutes each way." She paused to take a few licks. "Boy, this is good! Whoever dreamed up this crazy flavor?"

"That would be me," I replied with a broad grin.

"You, girlfriend, are a true artist."

My smile got even wider. *This*, I thought, *is what Lickety Splits is all about.*

"I sure don't envy you that commute," I commented. "One of my goals in setting up my own shop was to be able to live and work in the same place. And this is a great town, too."

I let my eyes drift across the street to Sweet Things, which was still cordoned off with yellow crime-scene tape. "Not that Wolfert's Roost is as idyllic as it looks," I continued. "I suppose you heard that the owner of the bakery across the street was murdered . . . ?"

"Oh, yes," Allison replied, her expression growing serious. "I know all about it. I actually worked for Ashley Winthrop."

"Did you!" I did my usual I'm-so-surprised act. "You mean you worked in the shop?"

"Not exactly. I was one of her suppliers. I baked things she sold in the store."

Another surprised look, only this one was considerably less dramatic. "I must say, being a baker and going to law school strikes me as kind of surprising."

Now Allison looked surprised. "Really? Why?"

"I don't know. I guess I see baking and law as incompatible."

"Not at all," she said. "Basically, it was an easy way for me to make money. I started working for her right after I began my first year of law school, back in September. I could go to classes and study all week, and then on the weekends, take time out to bake my little heart out. I could even take off time if I needed to study for exams." She shrugged. "It was also a great way to unwind from the demands of law school. All in all, it was the ideal situation for me."

"I guess I can understand that," I said. But it still struck me as surprising, mainly because I was picturing Lindsey, who had seemed like such a homebody. Imagining her turning out trays of cookies wasn't that difficult. Allison, meanwhile, looked like she should be making her money in a courtroom. If not on a runway.

"What about you?" she asked. "Did you always run an ice cream shop?"

"Well, no," I admitted.

"What did you do before?"

I could already see where this was going. "I worked in public relations, for a big firm in New York."

"There you go," Allison said. "What's the difference between being a high-powered PR rep who likes making ice cream and a law student who likes baking?"

"You got me," I said. "You must be devastated, then, by what happened to Ashley. I knew her, too. She and I grew up together. And while we weren't the best of friends, I was pretty impressed by what a success she turned out to be."

Allison nodded. "I know what you mean. I really admired Ashley for running her own business. She'd taken on a lot of responsibility. And when you've got people working for you the way she did, and they're not even doing something that requires them to show up every day, so you don't really know what they're doing . . . well, that's bound to be rough.

"But I especially admired the fact that Ashley's business gave her plenty of freedom, too," she went on, speaking between licks. "Autonomy. Despite her employees, despite her customers, she was her own person. She didn't have to report to one boss or one client. . . . She'd really figured it all out."

"It sounds as if she was kind of a role model for you," I commented.

Allison looked startled. "In terms of her career, maybe. But that sure didn't extend to her personal life."

"Why is that?" I asked.

I was genuinely surprised. After all, I'd seen Tad Patrick in the flesh. And believe me, that was some piece of flesh. Tad made Brad Pitt and Chris Hemsworth look like the guys from *Dumb and Dumber*. Not that looks were everything, of course. Neither was self-confidence. Or charisma. Or being wildly successful and in demand, thanks to owning one of the top restaurants in the Hudson Valley, one that even made the *New York Times* drool.

"Tad is a hottie, no doubt about it," Allison said. "But their relationship was, to use a diplomatic word, tempestuous."

Frankly, I didn't think the word "tempestuous" was all that diplomatic. Still, her observation made me hungry for more information.

"Maybe that was just because they were crazy in love," I suggested. "People who are passionate about each other often inject excessive emotion into every one of their interactions."

"Look," Allison said, a bit impatiently, "I didn't spend much time with the two of them. In fact, I only saw them together a couple of times. But the two of them struck me as being about as compatible as oil and water."

"You mean you saw them fighting?" I asked.

"It was more like they were needling each other," Allison replied. "Like whatever one of them said, the other one would disagree with."

"What were they talking about?" I persisted. "Money? The relationship?"

Allison cast me a strange look. I got the feeling I was acting just a little too interested.

"I guess it's none of my business," I quickly added. "It's just that I've known Ashley since kindergarten, and I'm curious about what she got herself into." I took a deep breath. "And of course the police are going to be looking at Tad closely. As a possible suspect, I mean."

"I figured they would," Allison said, distractedly stroking the folds of her scarf. "And if you ask me, that's exactly where they should be looking. Aside from what I personally observed about their relationship, when a woman is murdered, about a third of the time, it's her intimate partner who's responsible. Either current or former."

"Really?" I asked. "Where did you learn that?"

"My criminal law class," Allison replied proudly.

Suddenly she glanced at her watch. "Goodness, is it that late already? I should get going. As soon as I get home and put this luscious ice cream in the freezer, I'm hitting the books. September may sound far away, but it's going to be here before I know it. But it was nice talking to you."

"Same here," I said.

After she left, I lingered at the table, thinking about what she'd said. The statistic she'd quoted wasn't that surprising, and I was pretty sure I'd heard similar numbers before. The man in a female murder victim's life was generally the first person the police looked at.

As for Ashley, she had had two men in her life: Billy, her ex-husband, and Tad, her current boyfriend.

She'd apparently had a tempestuous relationship with her boyfriend. And her relationship with Billy obviously hadn't been that great or they'd still be married.

The two men in Ashley's life had been on my list of people to question from the very start. But I was suddenly more anxious than ever to talk to both of them.

Chapter 10

Professional ice cream tasters use gold-plated
spoons to do their job, since wood and plastic
spoons leave a slight aftertaste.

—*Tydknow.net*

O nce Allison was gone, I turned my focus back to Tad.
More importantly, to the brainstorm I'd had that morning about how to engage him in conversation without being obvious about what I was doing.

But first I called my pal Willow, wanting to run my idea by her. I hoped she wouldn't be busy teaching a class. Fortunately, she answered right away.

"Hi, Kate," she greeted me cheerfully, no doubt having seen my name pop up on her screen. "I'm about to go into a class, so I have about two minutes."

"That's all I need," I assured her. "It occurred to me that maybe I should join the Chamber of Commerce and I wanted to know what you think. I figured it might be helpful with getting Lickety Splits off the ground."

I was tempted to tell her the real reason I wanted to join: to get to know Ashley's boyfriend, Tad, better. But that would require too much explaining. And frankly, I wasn't sure how she'd respond to the idea that her best friend of twenty-five years had taken up a new hobby that wasn't exactly compatible with a serene and centered life.

"That's a great idea," Willow said. "I should have suggested it sooner. I've been involved with the C of C for ages. I've gotten quite a few new clients for Heart, Mind and Soul through the contacts I've made. I've gotten some local businesspeople who are also members, but also their family members, their friends . . . the whole word of mouth thing works really well.

"In fact, our monthly meeting is next week," she went on. "It's always held on the second Monday of the month. And different businesses take turns hosting it. I don't think we have a place picked out yet, but you can get in touch with Brian Whitman, who's the current president. . . . But I really have to go, Kate. Catch you later!"

We'd just ended our call and I was about to put my phone away when it buzzed. Probably Willow, I figured, hitting redial by accident.

But then I saw the name on the screen. "Jake." Just "Jake."

I was already flustered.

Part of me wondered if Jake was calling because he'd learned something new about the case. But I knew perfectly well that the reason I was already in a tizzy had very little to do with Ashley's murder.

"Hi, Jake," I answered, somehow managing to hide the tightness in my throat. "What's up?"

"Not much," he replied, "which is probably a good thing. I wondered if you wanted to get together to talk about what's going on with the investigation. I've found out a few things you might find interesting."

You can handle that, I told myself. It's for the good of the investigation.

"Sure," I said, by this point sounding positively nonchalant. "I'm looking for all the information I can get."

"I'm free for lunch. Want to meet at Molly McGuire's Pub in a few minutes—say, at noon? I have a thing for their Reuben."

I hadn't realized food would be involved.

Oh, for heaven's sake. It's just lunch, a voice inside my head scolded me. You can handle lunch.

"Molly's it is," I said.

Once I hung up, I tried to ignore the knot in my stomach and forget all about the plan Jake and I had just made. I tried to convince myself that the strange, heady feeling I was experiencing was the result of too much caffeine and/or not enough sleep.

What you need, I told myself, is a distraction.

So I forced myself to plunk down with Emma's laptop at one of Lickety Splits' ridiculously cute round marble tables so I could join the Chamber of Commerce. Doing it took all of five minutes. I just went to the Web site, filled out the application, and put in my credit card information.

It was that simple. The Lickety Splits Ice Cream Shoppe was now a member of the Wolfert's Roost Chamber of Commerce.

It wasn't difficult to join and I knew it could be helpful to my shop's success. And the main reason I even did it in the first place was so I'd have an excuse to talk to Ashley's boyfriend and local restauranteur, Tad.

Still, it seemed to make my ice cream shop more official, somehow. As if it was a real business. Which it was, of course. It was just that sometimes I had to remind myself that it wasn't all a dream; I really was living out a fantasy of mine.

I wasn't just playing ice cream store. This was who I was now. An ice cream entrepreneur.

I decided to celebrate with a big dish of Chocolate Marshmallow and Melty Chocolate Malt, which happened to go amazingly well together. I only hoped that, somehow, my dad was looking down and seeing all this, celebrating the creation of Lickety Splits right along with me.

A couple of hours later, as I walked along Hudson Street toward the restaurant, I found myself yanking out my ponytail band and combing my hair with my fingers. Not exactly pulling out the stops in the primping department, but enough of an effort that I got irritated with myself.

Stop that! I scolded myself. This is not a date. This is not even a *pre*-date. It's a business meeting, a chance for me to find out what Jake has learned about Ashley Winthrop.

I was tempted to put my hair back in a ponytail. A messy one, even. But in the end, vanity won. At least, I told myself that all it was was vanity.

As I strode into the pub, I tried to look as businesslike as I could, which to me meant standing up straight and wearing a stern expression. I spotted Jake right away, sitting at a corner booth, checking his phone.

I wondered how any of us managed not to look bored or lonely or even uncomfortable in public places before we all had cell phones. Maybe that was why books had been invented.

"You made it," Jake greeted me, politely turning off his phone and dropping it into his shirt pocket.

"I never turn down a chance to eat," I said glibly as I slid into the booth. As if Jake were deliberately trying to annoy me, he was wearing a robin's-egg-blue T-shirt that made his eyes look even bluer than they really were, if that were possible.

Glancing around the dimly lit pub, taking in the dark green walls and the wood paneling, I added, "Gee, I haven't been to this place since—in ages."

I'd stopped myself just in time. Bringing up our high school years, after all, probably wasn't a good idea. We were here to discuss a murder investigation, not giggle over yearbook photos.

As a way to avoid making eye contact with the man sitting about two feet in front of me, I grabbed a menu. My eyes immediately gravitated toward the fish and chips. I knew a salad would be a much more reasonable choice, especially given my unorthodox appetizer of two different varieties of chocolate ice cream. But something about being this close to Jake Pratt made an infusion of greasy fried fish and French fries, the ultimate comfort food, mandatory.

Once we'd ordered, I looked him straight in the eye and said, "So tell me: what have you learned?"

"Quite a bit, actually," Jake replied. "The police have found a couple of guys they're interested in talking to. One is Ashley's ex-husband, a guy named Billy, who still lives nearby—"

"Billy Duffy," I said. "He lives in Fishkill."

Jake looked surprised. "Right. So you've heard about the ex-husband. But maybe you didn't hear that she also had a boyfriend. Kind of a new guy in town. Tad Patrick, who opened an upscale restaurant called Greenleaf about a year ago—"

"Nine months ago," I interjected. "Last September, just as leaf-peeping season was getting under way. Good time to launch a new place."

"How do you know all this?" Jake asked, sounding genuinely confused.

"I've been doing a little snooping around," I admitted, not quite looking him in the eye. "Trying to see if I can find out anything about who killed Ashley."

I took a peek at his face and was relieved to see that he didn't look shocked.

A little surprised, maybe, but not shocked.

"What exactly have you been doing?" he asked, peering at me in a strange way.

"Just talking to a few people." I was suddenly feeling foolish about this whole thing.

But I was encouraged when he said, "That's pretty brave of you. Dangerous, maybe, foolhardy, certainly, but definitely brave. Do you mind if I ask who you've talked to?"

"So far, just a couple of women who worked for Ashley. She ran Sweet Things as a co-op, selling baked goods that these women made at home. Which is illegal, by the way, because of health laws. She kept it quiet, for obvious reasons."

"Did you find out anything?"

"Not really," I admitted. "Just that the two women I spoke to had no reason I could see to want Ashley dead. They both really needed the income they got from supplying her with their homemade cakes and pastries. Actually, I feel really bad for them."

"How far are you planning to take this?" Jake asked. "Are there other people you plan to question?"

"As a matter of fact, there are," I said. "I figured I'd see if I could find out anything from the other women who worked for her. Then there's that ex-husband of hers. And her current boyfriend."

Jake nodded. "Definitely worth considering, especially since the cops always see the men who were in a woman's life as prime suspects. But do you think it's a good idea, Kate? To go poking around in her life like this, especially when you might actually find out something incriminating? Seriously, it really could get dangerous. Or haven't you ever read any mystery novels?"

"Trust me, I'm not going to do anything dangerous," I assured him indignantly. I could feel my defenses locking into place like the archers in a *Lord of the Rings* movie. "I know what I'm doing, Jake. I'm just talking to a few people, that's all."

He thought for a few seconds, then nodded his head in that way that means "whatever."

We were silent for a few uncomfortable seconds. And then he leaned back in his seat, fixed his gaze in mine, and said, "Kate McKay, leading a high-powered life in high-powered Manhattan. What was that like?"

"It was great," I replied, already more than a little defensive. "I had a job I really enjoyed. And I loved living in New York. I had a great apartment—small, of course, but with a fabulous location. And nice friends. And there was always something exciting to do. I loved going to the theater and the ballet, seeing whatever new exhibit was at one of the museums, the Met or MOMA or the Whitney...."

"Wow," Jake interjected. "Sounds pretty glamorous."

I couldn't tell if he was teasing or if there was an edge to his tone.

"I guess parts of it were," I said, responding to his comment honestly. "But a lot of it wasn't as great as it sounds. There was a lot of pressure, for one thing. It may sound cool to run an event for two hundred fifty people at a fancy restaurant, but there are a million details to see to, a million things that can go wrong... and so many personality quirks that things you never even dreamed could be a problem can end up creating a disaster."

"And what about your . . . social life?" Jake had lowered his eyes, suddenly acting as if the fork on the table in front of him was the most fascinating thing he'd ever seen.

I could feel my cheeks burning. "Not much to tell in that department," I replied, trying to sound lighthearted. "The usual college romances. Then a couple of almosts. One that lasted three years, actually. But I never found anyone I could imagine spending the rest of my life with."

He raised his eyes to mine for a fraction of a second. "Sounds kind of lonely. Although I guess I'm not one to talk."

"I did notice that there's no ring on your finger, either," I said, once again trying to sound as if I were joking.

We were both silent for a few seconds.

"It's funny," Jake finally said. "That job you had in New York doesn't sound like what I would have imagined for you. Back when we were in high school, I mean."

I shrugged. "Me either. The problem was, I didn't really know what I wanted to do. When I was finishing up my senior year at New Paltz, a friend told me she could get me an interview at a big PR firm. . . . Believe it or not, the first question I asked her was, 'What's PR?'

"But overall it worked out pretty well," I went on. "It wasn't perfect, and sometimes the hours and the demands were overwhelming, but it was rewarding, you know? Never dull, either. Always something new, different people, different places . . ."

"And what did you do for fun?" Jake asked. "I mean, when you weren't juggling personalities and, I don't know, goodie bags?"

My first thought was, Sleep. My second thought was, Go to the dry cleaner, buy basics like bread and ice cream and toilet paper, get my hair cut and my nails done so I'd always look the part I was playing.

But I said, "I traveled as much as I could."

"Ah. Now that's something I'd like to do," Jake said. This time, I could hear the envy in his voice. "Where did you go?"

"Wherever I could," I replied. "All of Europe, of course. London and Paris and Amsterdam and Italy. But one winter I took a two-week cruise in South America, starting in Buenos Aires and going around Cape Horn and ending up in Chile. That was a really amazing trip. And another time I went to Hong Kong. . . .

"But what about you?" I said, switching gears so I wouldn't

sound so obnoxious that he'd stand up and run away. "What have you been doing for the last fifteen years?"

"Law school, then lawyering," he replied, like it was all barely worth mentioning. "Then my mother's brother passed away, and my family was suddenly facing a decision point. I guess I was facing one, too. A once-in-a-life opportunity just fell in my lap, a chance to take over a successful business in a part of the country I loved. The problem was, I was pretty happy where I was. At least, I thought I was. But once I started imagining myself back in the beautiful Hudson Valley, spending my days communing with cows . . ."

I laughed. "I can see how that would be hard to turn down."

"It required some soul searching," he admitted. "I knew it was an either-or situation. I couldn't continue to practice law and run a two-hundred-fifty-acre dairy at the same time. So I had to make a choice and, well, you know how it turned out."

"But there must be a ton of stuff to know about running something like that," I said. "How did you learn it all?"

"I didn't, at least not at first. My uncle left enough money that I was able to hire the right people, just to get things started." He shrugged. "I kept learning, and eventually I was able to pretty much handle things by myself. I still have employees, of course, but when it comes to running the place, now I know what I'm doing." With a grin, he added, "Most of the time anyway.

"And I did change things around a bit. For one thing, I changed the name. It used to be called Hudson Dairy, if you recall. I wanted something that reflected the other big change I made: turning it into an organic dairy."

"Was that hard to do?"

"It took some work. I had to switch things around so my cows can graze, and they're only fed fodder that's organically certified. They're not treated with growth hormones or any of the other drugs that are commonly used in traditional dairies.

"Another aspect of running an organic operation like mine is treating the cows humanely," he continued. "I have almost a hundred cows, and I think of them as family. Well, sort of. It's not like I invite them all over for Thanksgiving or anything."

I laughed. "I love the image of all those cows crammed inside a dining room."

"Eating turkey, no less," he added with a grin.

"Remind me never to go to your house for Thanksgiving," I joked.

He didn't respond. In fact, we were both silent for what felt like a long time. And then I said, "And how has it turned out for you, Jake? Was it the right choice?"

"I think it was," he replied thoughtfully. "Like you, I don't miss the pressure. Or the long hours. Although come to think of it, there's still plenty of pressure—and those cows sure wake up early every morning. But it's different. And I really like it."

"That's great," I said. "I'm glad it worked out so well." And I meant it.

Another silence fell over us.

"Hey, Jake?" I said softly. "Can we talk about what happened that night?"

The crease in his forehead deepened. "I know I owe you an explanation, Kate. I've owed you one for, what is it, fifteen years?"

I held my breath, afraid to say anything. I had a feeling that explanation was finally about to come.

Jake took a deep breath. "It's amazing; I still remember that night like it was yesterday. It's one of those moments that's stuck in time, you know?" He was staring off into the distance, as if he had left the time and space we were really in and was going back to that evening. "All day I'd felt like I was in a dream. Going to prom with you—it was like some crazy teenage fantasy. A night that's supposed to be one of the highlights of your entire life . . . and I was convinced it would be.

"I remember putting on the rented tux, feeling like . . . well, like a man. Like I was finally a grown-up. It seemed so symbolic, somehow. I was going to this big, fancy party, all dressed up like somebody I didn't feel like I'd ever be. I had a car, I had money in my pocket. . . . How much better could it possibly be?

"And the fact that I was going with you . . ." He glanced up at me for a fraction of a second, then lowered his eyes. "I was so crazy in love with you, Kate. The feelings I had for you were so strong that sometimes they scared me."

I was still holding my breath. But by now, it wasn't because I didn't *want* to breathe. It was because I couldn't.

"I was supposed to swing by and pick you up at seven. I remember that that was the time we'd planned. So by six-thirty, I was dressed and ready." He grinned. "Hair slicked back, smelling like a flower garden from my brother's cologne, which I'd snitched without asking him. . . .

"And then the phone rang."

I started breathing again. But my breaths were short and ragged.

If there was one thing I'd learned in life, it was that hardly anything good ever begins with the words, "And then the phone rang."

"I figured it was you, calling to check up on me," Jake went on. "To make sure I was running on time or to remind me not to forget the prom tickets. But then, as soon as I picked up the phone, I heard this background noise that made me feel sick. Voices in the background. Walkie-talkie sounds."

"The police," I said, without thinking.

Jake nodded. "I knew immediately that there was trouble. And given my family, I pretty much knew who was causing it."

"Your dad?" I asked gently.

"Yup. Good old dad." His mouth stretched into a cold smile. "His drinking had been getting worse and worse. He'd just lost his job a few weeks earlier—again. My mom had been calling my uncle like five times a day, begging him to find something for my father at the dairy. But Uncle Joe wouldn't budge. He loved his sister more than anything, but the man had a business to run. And he knew my dad would only make things tougher for him.

"So in that first split second, when I figured out the police were calling, I instantly saw my whole dream go down the drain. Going to prom, having that special night with you, something I'd be able to carry with me for the rest of my life . . . The cop at the other end of the line didn't even have to say anything and I already knew how the rest of the night was going to play out.

"I was right, of course," Jake continued. "My father had been arrested."

"Drunk driving?" I asked.

"Worse." He took a deep breath. "He'd had an accident."

"Was he hurt?"

"No, the son of a bitch got off without a scratch. But I can't say the same about the people in the other car."

I gasped. "Oh, Jake!"

"No fatalities, thank goodness. Some injuries, but fortunately nothing life threatening. All three people in the car he T-boned ended up in the hospital. A little girl broke her arm, her mother had a concussion. . . . It was really ugly, Kate.

"And my dad went to prison. Where he deserved to be." He shrugged. "I haven't seen him since. He tried contacting me a few times, but I guess my lack of a welcoming response finally clued him in to how I felt about him."

"Oh, Jake," I said, feeling like a balloon that had just been completely deflated, "I had no idea about any of this."

"Of course not," he replied. "Nobody did. All this happened far away from here, in a small town in Jersey, down by Trenton. It made the local papers around there, but the news never spread up here.

"The whole thing was so devastating that I didn't want to set foot in Wolfert's Roost ever again," he continued. "There was no way I was going to show my face at graduation. I wouldn't even go back for finals. The school was actually pretty good about that, like mailing me the math final and letting me submit a couple of essays instead of going in to take the English final."

Jake paused, as if collecting his thoughts. "And there was one thing I felt really strongly about. And that was that I wanted to make sure you never found out." Grimacing, he added, "Which is why I took it upon myself to disappear."

"But Jake!" I cried. "Don't you see how much that hurt me?"

"I do now. But at the time, I was just a scared, embarrassed kid. What my father did totally humiliated me.

"And then, as time went by, the fact that I'd just shut you out the way I had made the whole episode seem even worse. To be perfectly honest, I was too ashamed to get in touch with you." He laughed coldly. "Every time I thought about it, I also pictured the way you were likely to react. If you'd have slapped me, that would have been the easy part. I just couldn't bring myself to see that hurt look in your eyes."

Tentatively he raised his eyes to meet mine, as if he was afraid he'd finally see the look he'd been dreading for fifteen years. I couldn't promise that there wasn't anything like that for him to see. But what I was feeling at that moment was sympathy, not anger.

"But that doesn't mean I wasn't paying attention to what was going on in your life," he added.

"What do you mean? How?"

"Talking to some of my friends from high school, for one thing. The ones who still lived around here. They'd have heard things from their moms talking to your grandmother or whatever."

"So you stayed in touch with them?" I asked lightly, trying to squelch a feeling of anger. He'd remained friends with them even though in my case he'd decided to cut me off completely.

He shrugged. "They didn't know about any of this. I mean, they probably noticed you and I weren't there on prom night. But it wasn't the kind of thing they made a big deal about. And the few times it came up, I just made some vague excuse about a family thing that was going on at the time." He grinned. "So much for the intelligence level of the guys I used to hang out with in high school. Then, of course, the Internet came along, so I was able to find out where you worked and what kind of things you were up to—"

"So you knew I'd stayed in the New York area," I said, still trying not to let my irritation leak out. Somehow, it seemed that doing so would only add to the pain he was experiencing. And even now, I knew Jake Pratt well enough to see how difficult reliving all this was for him. "New Paltz, then Manhattan . . ."

Jake leaned back in his seat. "I knew, Kate. Believe me, I knew. I knew exactly how close you were. That you were only a phone call away."

"But you never called me," I said, my voice hoarse. "In fifteen years, not once did you pick up the phone."

"I told you," he said. "I was too afraid—"

"Right. The high school boy who was afraid of getting his girlfriend mad never grew up into a man who decided it was time to take responsibility for what he'd done? Who was never able to put aside his own fears to make amends for a hurtful—no, a horrible thing he'd done to someone he claims to have loved?"

"I did love you, Kate," he said softly.

"That's some kind of love." I, too, had leaned back in my seat. But it was to distance myself from him, to get as far away from him as I could.

Whatever bond we had formed for those few minutes, whatever tentative gains toward mending our broken fences we had made, it was all gone by now.

And then a new thought occurred to me.

"So if you were keeping track of me," I said, "you must have heard that I was back in town."

He hesitated, as if unsure of what the right answer to my question would be. And then: "That's right. I knew."

I swallowed hard. "So you've known for weeks."

He nodded.

"And even then, it never once occurred to you to call me or stop over—"

"Oh, it occurred to me," he said, his voice cold. "It occurred to me all the time. But do you know what stopped me?"

"Fear again?" I said, my voice dripping with sarcasm.

"Exactly. Fear," he replied. "Fear that if I saw you again, if I tried to be honest with you, finally, that you'd react exactly the way you're reacting right now. Dragging out anger from fifteen years ago—"

"From fifteen years ago!" I repeated. "What *about* those fifteen years, Jake? What about all those times you could have gotten in touch with me but didn't? If you were so darn scared of seeing my anger, why not write me a note? Why not try to make the bad feelings between us that have been sitting there for fifteen years—fifteen years, Jake!—a little better by taking some action?"

He just stared at me for a few seconds without speaking.

And then: "Because I couldn't—and still can't—bear to have you feel this way about me."

"So in the end, it's all about your feelings, not mine," I said. "That's great, just great."

Without even thinking about it, I jumped to my feet. "So at least now I know who you really are, Jake. You know, I was really in love with you, too, back in high school, just the way you claim you were with me. But maybe that's just because I didn't really know you. But now, I guess I do."

He looked at me as if I had, indeed, slapped him. He wore his devastation like a mask.

"I was hoping that maybe finally being straight with you after all this time would help make things a little better," he said, speaking so softly I could hardly hear him.

"Is that why you waited for me to bring it up before you even said anything?" I countered. "That's your version of being straight with me?"

He still looked beaten down, but now that the fury I'd been carrying for fifteen years had been unleashed, it had taken on a life of its own. It was like a hurricane, growing stronger and stronger until no one could possibly contain it.

"I am so done with you, Jake," I cried. "I only wish you told me about this years ago so I could have figured out what you're really all about and stopped wondering if . . ."

I didn't want to say it. I didn't want to give him the satisfaction of knowing that deep down, part of me kept holding on to the possibility that one day, somehow, Jake Pratt and I would find each other again.

I now knew that was never going to happen.

I reached into my pocket, pulled out some bills, and slammed them on the table. "Here," I announced. "I'm paying for my meal. I wouldn't want you to think that you and I had gone out on a date or anything."

"Kate, we can't leave it like—"

"Good-bye, Jake. We are so done here."

I stalked off, keeping my head high and my stride confident. And scrunching my eyes together so the tears that were welling up in them wouldn't streak down my cheeks.

Finally, I told myself, resolution. The explanation you've been hoping for for fifteen years.

I should have felt better. After all, now I knew. I knew what had happened that night, and I knew that Jake had never been strong enough to even try to make things right.

But I didn't feel better at all. In fact, I felt like a balloon that had not only had all the air let out of it, but had been run over by a freight train.

Chapter 11

First Lady Dolley Madison, wife of fourth United
States president, James Madison, helped popular-
ize ice cream by serving it at the White House at
the second inaugural ball, in 1813. One of her
favorite ice cream flavors was Oyster,
made with sweet oysters from the Potomac River.

—*www.pbs.org/food/features/ice-cream-founding-fathers/*

The vile mood I'd come down with the day before reminded me of a stomach virus: even though it was no
longer acute, the residual effects were still lingering the following morning as Emma and I opened the shop.

I'd been sullen all afternoon and all evening. Even making
cheerful chitchat with my customers, and then Emma and
Grams over dinner, had been a strain. And I could tell from
the looks my two housemates kept giving each other that I
wasn't doing a very good job.

Even Digger kept his distance.

But as I stepped into Lickety Splits on Thursday morning,
I gave myself a clear directive: get over it.

You have a business to run, I reminded myself, the voice in
my head sounding very much like a drill sergeant's. Whatever's going on with you, you have no right to take it out on
the people around you.

So I forced myself to snap into professional mode, which meant thinking about ice cream and very little else.

I headed straight into the work space in back, ready to whip up a fresh batch of Classic Tahitian Vanilla, which was running low. I was also anxious to tackle that rhubarb ice cream Emma had thought up. Actually, Strawberry Rhubarb, the same combination of sweet and tart that made the pie such a favorite. And of course my Strawberry Rhubarb ice cream would have bits of piecrust floating in it.

I started by opening the door of my stainless steel refrigerator to get out the necessary ingredients.

"Rats!" I cried.

"Oh no!" Emma exclaimed, rushing toward the back where I was standing. "That's terrible, Kate! Where?"

"No, no, it's just an expression," I assured her. "There are no rats here. I'm just almost out of cream, that's all." I sighed. "And believe me, the last thing I want to do is go over to Juniper Hill right now."

And see Jake, I thought, without actually saying the words out loud.

"I can go over to the dairy, if you'd like," Emma offered. "Just tell me what you need."

"That would be a lifesaver," I told her. "I have plenty to do here, anyway. And on your way out, I need you to stop at the farm stand on the edge of town and pick up some fresh strawberries and plenty of rhubarb."

As I handed Emma my car keys, along with explicit instructions about what to buy, I thanked the universe once again for sending her my way. I was also grateful that I was able to avoid telling my niece the real reason why I didn't want to go to Juniper Hill. Not today, not ever again.

Fortunately, as soon as she left, I forgot all about Jake Pratt. Instead, I got busy preparing for the day ahead.

I'd already settled into a routine. These days, my life consisted of getting up early, hitting the coffeepot, and then heading right over to Lickety Splits. I put on a Lickety Splits apron, then made a few batches of ice cream, slogged through some paperwork, checked the napkin dispensers, and did a bunch of other maintenance chores. . . .

And loved every minute.

The culmination of the morning's prep was also one of my favorite parts: flipping over the CLOSED sign that hung on the front door so that the OPEN side was displayed. And this morning, just like every other morning, I experienced a little thrill.

Another day in the ice cream business had begun.

I was about to take my place behind the counter when my cell phone rang. Glancing at it, I couldn't identify the caller. But the area code was local, so I answered.

"Ms. McKay? This is Brian Whitman, president of the Wolfert's Roost Chamber of Commerce. I own Apex Appliances, the Hudson Valley's number one supplier of gas grills and dishwashers. As our slogan goes, 'If it plugs in, we've got it!'"

"It's nice to meet you," I replied sincerely.

"I wanted to thank you for joining," he went on breezily, "and welcome you to our fine organization. I hope you'll be coming to our June meeting, which takes place this Monday night."

"I certainly will."

"Wonderful, wonderful."

As Brian droned on a bit about all the good things the Chamber did for its members, I balanced my cell between my ear and my shoulder. No reason why I couldn't fill a napkin dispenser or two while he talked.

I perked up when he said, "But there is one thing you may not be aware of."

"What's that?"

"The location of our meetings rotates every month. In other words, we meet at a different member's place of business each time. So it's important to check the Web site every month to make sure you—"

"Who's hosting it this month?" I asked.

Brian cleared his throat. "Actually, I am. We sometimes have a problem getting anyone to volunteer at this time of the year, so we'll be gathering at my appliance store. It's on Route Nine, just north of Wolfert's Roost—"

"Is it too late for me to offer to host it?" I interrupted. "I'd love to introduce all the members to my shop. And I'm sure I could come up with some pretty terrific refreshments."

Part of me, a cynical part, wondered if perhaps that was why Brian Whitman had called me in the first place. Even though, as an appliance store owner, the man had more access to refrigerators and stoves than anybody else, he probably didn't use any of them to put together much in the way of enticing munchies for the town's business owners.

My hunch felt validated when it took Brian all of two seconds to agree. "That would be wonderful!" he said heartily. "There should be twenty to twenty-five people, and our meetings always start promptly at seven-thirty."

My mind was already racing, coming up with fun ideas.

But I quickly forgot all about the upcoming Chamber of Commerce meeting and my chance to play caterer for the very first time. The first customers of the day wandered in, a young mother with two little boys.

While I relished being alone in the shop in the morning, getting ready for the day ahead, I really loved what happened as soon as Lickety Splits opened. An almost supernatural burst of energy flooded into my little piece of ice cream heaven the moment it opened. A different cast of customers came in every single day, all of them in search of an ice-cream-eating experience that would delight them.

And I did my best to fulfill their dreams. Because I loved ice cream so much, I was pretty sure I was able to pass some of my enthusiasm on to them. For at least a few seconds, these strangers and I were bonded together by a scoop of Divine Chocolate or Pistachio Almond—or equally enthralled by the very fact that something like a Bananafana Split even existed on the planet we shared.

It was also hard work. Smiling, scooping, concocting, chatting . . . after a couple of hours, I was starting to get a little tired. I glanced at my watch and was surprised to see how late it was.

It seemed to be taking Emma forever to get back. I hoped she hadn't gotten lost, especially with a few gallons of heavy cream in the back of my truck.

But just as I was about to text her, she came rushing into the store. Her cheeks were flushed and her eyes were unnaturally bright.

"You're back!" I cried. "I was about to send out a search party."

"Sorry I took so long," she said. "Juniper Hill was really busy."

I found it hard to picture a line out the door at an organic dairy, but I didn't press her any further.

"Well, you're back now," I said. "As soon as you put that cream in the refrigerator and get settled behind the counter, I'm going to take off. I have a few errands to run."

I was handing a boy about thirteen who was wearing a Yankees cap a double-dip cone with a scoop of White Chocolate Macadamia Nut Paradise and a scoop of Hawaiian Coconut—a truly magnificent combination, I might add—as Emma tied on her Lickety Splits apron. She still seemed a bit dazed, or at least preoccupied.

I was about to ask her if she was feeling okay when she casually asked me, "So who's that guy, Ethan?"

"Ethan?" I repeated, thinking, *I don't know anybody named Ethan.*

"I'm sure you've met him. He works at the Juniper Hill dairy."

Ethan, Ethan . . .

My head was suddenly filled with red flags and lightbulbs and fireworks. Emma was talking about Ethan, the noncommunicative young man I'd met at the dairy the same day I'd learned that Jake now owned it. The one with the shiny black hair that hid his eyes and the oversized earphones that hid his ears.

Was it possible that *he* was why it had taken Emma so long to get back from the dairy? Emma was into *him*?

"I don't know anything about him," I told her. "I just met him once." And then, I couldn't resist asking the $64,000 question: "Why do you ask?"

Emma shrugged. "Just wondered."

So she *was* interested in him.

I was shocked by her ability to see something in him that had certainly gone way over my head. Still, I was glad she was making new friends in Wolfert's Roost. I wanted her to be happy here. In fact, I wanted her to be happy wherever she was. So if floppy-haired, unsmiling Ethan was her idea of a good time, who was I to judge?

Besides, even their names sounded cute together. Emma and Ethan. Ethan and Emma.

I couldn't help smiling.

"Okay, so I'm going to take off," I told her.

"Take your time," she assured me with a wave of her hand. "I'm in good shape here."

And she flashed me the biggest smile I'd seen on her in a very long time.

* * *

The third name on Ashley's list of suppliers, Brandy Di-Napoli, had been one of the harder ones to track down. According to the online search Emma had so skillfully conducted, she appeared to be someone who moved around a lot.

So I wasn't even sure the address we'd found, the one that seemed to be the most recent, would turn out to be correct.

I actually hoped it wouldn't be as I got close. My GPS informed me that I was only a few hundred feet away. But what was looming up before me was a trailer park.

Not one of the nice ones, either. No clubhouse, no flower beds, no swimming pool.

Instead, the Shady Pines Mobile Home Park looked like a place to park your trailer while you sobbed over how badly your life had turned out.

Warily I climbed out of my truck, carrying a heavy cooler packed with dry ice and ice cream samples. Then I looked around, wondering how I'd ever find my way to Brandy's abode.

I was beginning to wonder if I'd just embarked upon what's commonly known as a fool's errand when I spotted a middle-aged woman trudging toward one of the trailers, lugging two plastic shopping bags filled with groceries. The bags looked heavy. She looked like she really wished she had a car.

"Excuse me," I called to her. "I'm looking for a resident here named Brandy DiNapoli . . . ?"

"Brandy?" the woman responded. Gesturing with her chin, she added, "She lives right over there, the fifth one in this row. That green one."

Sure enough, a trailer the color of crabgrass was parked a couple of hundred yards away.

"Thanks," I called over my shoulder. Then I headed in that direction.

Walking through the trailer park required serious concentration. The sidewalk, where there was one, was broken up, with weeds sticking out of the concrete. There were empty Coke bottles and candy wrappers scattered here and there.

If these residents paid a Home Owners' Association fee, they weren't getting their money's worth.

Up close, I saw that the green trailer that was supposedly Brandy's was one of the shabbier ones. I already felt bad for her and I hadn't even met her.

As I drew close, a dog inside the trailer began barking. It was a deep, loud bark, a sign that the animal inside wasn't exactly a Chihuahua.

I knocked loudly, even though it was hardly necessary, given the fact that the canine resident of this trailer had already made it pretty clear to everyone in the entire park that a visitor had come to call.

A few seconds later, a woman in her early thirties opened the door, dressed in tight jeans and a loose white T-shirt. She was very tall and very thin. Her hair, dyed a shade of red that was just a bit too bright, was long and thick but could have used some brushing. And while she was pretty, she looked haggard, as if she hadn't slept very well the night before.

I was relieved to see that she was holding her roommate by the collar. Just as his voice indicated, he was on the large side, a big, black, sleek animal who was more muscle than charm. Part rottweiler, I guessed. And part werewolf.

By this point, he wasn't only barking; he was snarling.

"Quiet, Demon!" she told him, not sounding very forceful. His response was to stop barking but to continue snarling. It wasn't making me feel much better.

"Don't worry about him," she said. "He's really a pussy cat."

Right, I thought. *So is a panther.*

"What can I do for you?" she asked hurriedly. "I don't have a lot of time, so—"

I began with the same line I'd used on Lindsey.

"My name is Kate McKay," I said cheerfully, keeping one eye on Demon, "and I'm the owner of a new ice cream shop in town called Lickety Splits. Maybe you've seen it . . . ?"

The woman in the doorway, who I'd already decided had to be Brandy, eyed me suspiciously.

"Yeah, I've seen it," she said. "It's right across the street from Sweet Things, right? The bakery?"

"That's right. And I'm—"

Demon was back to barking. Loudly.

Sighing, she said, "Let me put this guy in the back room. Just give me a second."

"Sure," I said, glad Demon wouldn't be part of this discussion.

"Okay," Brandy said a few seconds later when she returned. Demon was still barking, but at least he was doing it from behind a closed door. "So what were you saying about Sweet Things?"

Actually, she was the one who'd brought up Sweet Things, but I wasn't about to point that out.

"My ice cream shop is right across the street from Sweet Things," I said, using that as a reason to keep her interest. "And I'm going around town handing out free samples as a way of introducing my shop. Could I interest you in—"

"Thanks, but I'm not much for sweets." Glancing down, she added, "Gotta keep my girlish figure, if you know what I mean."

Really? I thought. *A woman who makes pastries for a living but doesn't like sweets?* That was just *wrong.*

My mind was racing. She looked as if she was about to close the door, and I needed an excuse to keep talking to her.

I thought of asking for some water, but I realized she could have easily brought it to the door. Fortunately, I had a better idea.

"Listen, could I please ask you for a favor?" Twisting my face into a desperate expression, I added, "Could I use your bathroom? I hate to ask, but I've been out driving around since breakfast, and—"

She only hesitated for a moment. "I guess," she said, moving aside.

I wasn't surprised. Needing a bathroom was something pretty much every woman could relate to.

"Thanks," I said breathlessly. And I went inside.

Because the exterior of the trailer was in such bad shape, I just assumed the inside would be similarly ragged. Instead, it was spotless, and everything in it looked new. Not the best quality, perhaps—more Ikea than Stickley—but the small living room area and kitchen that I could see reflected a lot of thought and care. It was really clean, for one thing. Not a crumb on the counter, not a greasy smear on the stove . . . even the dish towel hanging on a bar was neatly folded.

It was also nicely decorated: off-white walls and a plain black couch, but pops of color everywhere. Sunny yellow throw pillows, turquoise canisters on the kitchen counter, tasteful curtains with geometric shapes that gave the space a nice orderly look. It was clear that a lot of care had gone into making this place a real home.

As I walked by a table with some mail on it, I checked the name. Sure enough, this was Brandy all right. I had the right person. The woman a few steps behind me, warning me to hold down the lever until the toilet was finished flushing, was, indeed, Brandy of Licorice Twist-baking fame.

After I used the bathroom, being sure to follow Brandy's

advice about the most effective flushing routine, I was glad to
see that Brandy was sitting on her black couch. Demon, fortunately, had quieted down. Maybe he was getting a sore
throat from all that barking.

"This is a great place you've got here," I said. Gesturing at
the seat next to her, I boldly asked, "Do you mind if I sit
down?"

She hesitated, then said, "Sure, but just for a minute. Like
I said, I got someplace I've got to be. And I've got to get
dressed."

"You look fine to me," I said, trying to become her instant
best friend.

She laughed. "It's for a job interview."

It made sense. Ashley, her employer, was now gone.
Brandy needed a new source of income. My challenge was
finding a way to get her talking about all that. . . .

"What do you do?" I asked, putting on my innocent look.

Brandy hesitated again. "I'm applying for a job as a file
clerk at the hospital. Just as a temporary thing, an easy way
to make some money when there's nothing more interesting
around," she added quickly. "Unfortunately the job I had
until recently just fell through."

"That's a shame," I said. "Was that an administrative-type
job, too?"

"Not exactly," Brandy replied. "I actually worked for the
bakery that's right across the street from your ice cream
place."

Now I put on my surprised look. "Really? You worked at
Sweet Things? I don't remember seeing you there."

"I didn't work at the shop," Brandy explained. "I was one
of Ashley Winthrop's suppliers."

"I'm not sure I understand what that means," I said, even
though I understood perfectly.

"I made things for her to sell."

"Really?" I said. I put on my surprised look again. "You mean you baked things she sold in her bakery?"

"Yup."

"But you said before that you don't have a sweet tooth."

Brandy shrugged. "There are a lot of things people do for money that's not their favorite thing," she said. "It's how all of us get by."

"That's true," I replied thoughtfully. I was reflecting on how, so far, I pretty much enjoyed every aspect of running Lickety Splits. But I could understand that, at some point, doing the same thing every day could get tedious. And the cleanup part, while still a novelty, had the potential to feel more like drudgery than just another aspect of playing store.

"It's interesting," I said, desperate to keep the conversation going. "I've known Ashley practically my whole life. But I never knew anything about her bakery being a co-op."

"She was trying to help local women like me make money," Brandy said. "Not that it wasn't a win-win situation. She made plenty of money, too."

Enough for a Corvette, I thought.

"It sounds as if Ashley was doing some really good things for the community," I said. "It's hard to believe anyone could have wanted her dead."

Brandy just looked at me vacantly. "I guess that, somewhere along the line, she pissed off the wrong person."

"So it seems." Putting on my innocent look again, I asked, "Since you knew her, do you have any idea who that might have been?"

"I'm not a cop," Brandy said, sounding irritated. "It's not exactly my job to find that out. But . . ."

I held my breath.

"If you ask me, I'd start with that ex-husband of hers.

Billy, his name is." She let out a contemptuous snort. "As if the fact that a grown man still calls himself Billy doesn't already tell you everything you need to know. If you look up 'loser' in the dictionary, you'll find a picture of him. But wouldn't you know it, he also thinks he's God's gift to the entire planet."

"You think he may have killed Ashley?" I asked. Her assertion had set my heart pounding, but I did my best to sound casual.

Brandy shrugged, her strangely narrow shoulders jumping up and back down again with alarming speed. "I know he was pretty angry at her."

"So you know him?"

"I don't exactly *know* him," she replied, "but I was in the shop once when he came in. I was dropping something off—or maybe picking up a check? Anyway, I was there in the off hours, like right before closing time, and I was in back of the store with Ashley. All of a sudden, this guy Billy comes barging in, all fired up over something, stomping around and yelling and screaming like some kind of nut. . . .

"I stayed in back while Ashley went out front to deal with him. I'm not one to back down, but Ashley wanted me to keep out of it. Anyway, this nutcase Billy was in a rage because he thought she should be giving him more money. It seems that for some crazy reason, poor Ashley was paying her good-for-nothing ex alimony payments. Can you believe that? It seems that even though he's always bragging about all these million-dollar ideas he keeps having, he has yet to actually *do* anything."

Brandy shook her head in disbelief. "Anyway," she continued, "he kept insisting that since she was making so much money now—so much more than when they'd both agreed on whatever financial arrangement their divorce lawyers had worked out—that he deserved more.

"I remember he kept saying the same thing over and over again: 'I've had enough of this. I've had enough of this.' He knew about her new Corvette, of course, since everybody in Wolfert's Roost knew about that car. And maybe he'd heard about some of the other extravagant ways she was spending money. At any rate, he'd clearly had enough of feeling he wasn't getting his fare share."

Another snort. "Why that A-hole—excuse my French—thought he deserved a *penny* from her, when he was sitting on his butt all day and Ashley was working hers off . . . But that's the way a lot of men are, right? They think they're God's gift to women and nothing is too good for them."

"How did that little scene end?" I asked.

"I couldn't hear everything Ashley was saying, but I'm pretty sure she ended up writing him a check, just to make him go away," Brandy replied. "Still, I got the feeling that whatever she did, it wasn't going to be enough to shut the idiot up. He was really angry, and he sure didn't strike me as the kind of guy who was just going to go away."

I made a mental note to take extra care if and when I managed to speak to Ashley's ex. If Brandy's anecdote was accurate, he sounded like someone I'd have to be careful with.

She stood up abruptly. "Look, I've really got to get dressed for this interview."

"Oops, sorry," I said, standing up, too. "I stayed much too long. Hey, good luck!"

Of course, I wasn't sorry at all. As I walked out of the trailer park, noticing that it already felt a little less seedy and more like just a place where a bunch of people lived, I was pleased that Brandy had been so forthcoming.

And I was convinced that she'd been honest. I absolutely believed her story about the frightening interaction between Ashley and her ex-husband that day at her shop.

Billy Duffy sounded like someone I'd have to watch out

for. Brandy's use of words like "nutcase" and "rage" actually instilled something along the lines of terror in me.

In fact, as I got back in my car, I found myself wondering if, when I was ready to go looking for him, Brandy would let me borrow Demon for a few hours.

Chapter 12

One of the five main ingredients in all
ice cream is air.

—IceCreamNation.org

That evening, as I trudged up the front steps of 59 Sugar
Maple Way, my legs felt as heavy as my giant walk-in
freezer. I was *that* tired.

Still, I had the presence of mind to notice that tonight my
Hudson Valley home looked exceptionally . . . well, homey.
Compared to Brandy's place, the wonderfully dilapidated old
Victorian was so welcoming that I could hardly wait to get
inside.

Even Digger seemed more lovable than ever. I knew I had
Demon to thank for that. But the same went for Chloe. As
the two four-legged sweeties ran over to greet me, I made
sure to give them both some extra ear scratching.

I was unusually quiet during dinner. I had a lot to think
about.

And the murder investigation I'd gotten myself involved in
was only part of it. Even more absorbing was the conversation I'd had with Jake the day before. A conversation that
some people might characterize as an argument.

Fortunately, Emma and Grams kept the conversation
going, with Emma doing her best to explain the ins and outs
of computer graphics. Since I knew as little as Grams did

about that particular topic, I was happy to do little more than half listen, interjecting a question every now and then to keep from seeming completely rude.

"I'll clean up tonight," Emma offered once we were done. "You seem tired, Kate."

She began gathering up the dishes from that night's ice cream dessert: an ice cream *coupe* that she'd made. My protégée had already gotten busy with looking into ways of expanding Lickety Splits' offerings, going online to do some serious research. That was how she'd learned about *coupes*, a simpler version of an American ice cream sundae that was dreamed up by the French. A *coupe* typically consisted of ice cream topped with sauce and some fruit.

In this case, Emma had concocted a truly delicious version, made with a rich, dense chocolate ice cream smothered with brandy-soaked bing cherries, the warm liquor partially melting the ice cream and treating the tongue to rich, creamy magic. Somehow, this dessert seemed so sophisticated that you just knew the French had to be behind it.

I had a feeling we'd be offering *coupes* at Lickety Splits sometime soon.

With Emma handling the cleanup, Grams and I drifted into the living room. I curled up on the red velvet couch with Digger, who was happily gnawing on a craggy rawhide bone that seemed to give him limitless pleasure.

Grams settled into her favorite chair, the dark green upholstered one that she said gave her back the support it needed. She immediately began working on her knitting project, the purple popcorn scarf that was already more than three feet long. Chloe lay contentedly in her lap, purring loudly as Grams clicked her needles rhythmically right above her head. That cat was purring so loudly I was sure Emma could hear her, even though she was singing as she clanked pots and pans in the sink.

Grams and I remained peaceful for a minute or two, simply enjoying each other's presence. And then my eyes drifted up to a black-and-white framed photograph on the mantelpiece. Grams and Gramps, standing in front of this very house, holding hands. They were young, and according to family lore, that picture had been taken the day they moved in.

The photographer had caught them glancing at each other, each with a satisfied grin that seemed to say, "We did it! We bought our very own house! And now we can turn it into a home. We're about to start the next exciting chapter in this great adventure that's our life together."

The photo had been in that exact same spot for as along as I could remember. Yet it suddenly seemed to be calling to me.

"I wonder how many people actually manage to find the love of their life and spend the rest of their life with that person," I mused.

Grams frowned. "This concept of the 'love of your life'— well, I'm not sure it's completely true. After all, there are a lot of great people out there. And most of the time, when one relationship doesn't work, even though both parties were convinced that they'd found the person who was perfect for them, sooner or later a replacement comes along who becomes the new bearer of the title, 'love of my life.'"

Thoughtfully, she added, "But there *is* something to be said for finding a very special person and feeling that that's the one you want to spend the rest of your life with."

I sighed. "The way you did with Gramps. You're so lucky that you married someone you were so crazy about, the one person in the universe you were certain was made for you. . . ."

Grams's eyebrows shot up and she stopped knitting. "Good heavens, is that really what you believe?"

Now it was my turn to be astonished. "You mean that's not what happened?"

She just stared at me for a few seconds. And then she burst out laughing.

"My goodness. How history gets rewritten!"

"You mean—you mean—" I sputtered.

"Your grandfather—Thornton—was a lovely man," Grams said. "He adored me, he was totally devoted to his children, he worked hard all his life, he was cheerful and loyal and as reliable as they come . . . but he wasn't close to being the love of my life or my soul mate or any of those things!"

My jaw had dropped so low it was practically in my lap. "Then why did you marry him?"

"I married Thorny on the rebound," she replied. "I'd just lost the man I was convinced *was* the love of my life."

I finally remembered to snap my mouth shut. "Grams, I had no idea! I never—"

She didn't appear to have heard me. "I was absolutely crazy about him," she said. "And he was crazy about me."

Her eyes had a faraway look, as if she were drifting back in time. They also had a shine that I'd rarely seen.

"His name was Phillip," she went on in a dreamy voice. "And almost from the moment we met, there were fireworks. So much passion! So much excitement!" Her cheeks had turned bright pink. "We couldn't stand to be apart from each other. It felt as if the entire universe had shifted, and that Phillip was suddenly my focus and I was his. I'd never experienced anything like it before."

"So what happened?" I asked eagerly.

All the brightness faded. With a shrug, she said, "Life got in the way. Even though he and I both believed we were destined to spend the rest of our lives together, it just didn't work out that way."

My mind raced as I thought about all the possibilities. Disapproving parents, a sudden illness, an obligation in a distant place . . .

But Grams had drawn her mouth into a tight line. Either this was still too painful to talk about or she simply didn't want to share the whole story with me.

Nevertheless, I was still left to deal with the astonishing news that Gramps hadn't been her first choice. Maybe he was cheerful and loyal and reliable, but he wasn't the love of her life. Not even anything that came close.

"You don't have any regrets, do you?" I asked in a soft voice.

Grams shook her head hard. "No. Not a single one. Thornton and I had a wonderful marriage. And I did love him. Just not in the way you see in movies or read about in books."

I decided not to ask her any more questions. Because despite her insistence that she was perfectly satisfied with the way things had worked out, I was certain I detected sadness in her voice.

Besides, I couldn't ignore the way she'd lit up when she talked about Phillip. The way her cheeks grew flushed and her eyes grew bright and her voice became wistful.

Even now. Even after all these years.

I was still thinking about what Grams had said as I lay in bed that night, trying to fall asleep.

So she hadn't married the love of her life, the way I'd always believed. Maybe she really had been happy with her marriage. She was certainly insistent that she had been. But I couldn't help wondering if she'd been trying to send me a message.

About Jake, of course.

Was Jake the love of my life, if there even was such a thing? He was certainly someone who had once made my heart pound and my head spin, someone who had caused me to experience all those famous symptoms of real love that we always hear about in books and songs.

And maybe he still did.

It was pretty obvious that Grams thought I should give Jake another chance.

If I dug down deep, talking to myself as if I were my best friend, I had to admit that I was truly furious with him. He had hurt me. And it was a hurt that had lasted for years, one that had left scars that were still deep enough and sensitive enough to cause me pain all over again.

But what Grams had confided forced me to see everything in a different light. To wonder if, maybe, sometimes the price of happiness was forgiveness.

I could picture myself in forty years, having the same conversation I'd had with Grams with a grandchild.

And imagining that scene made me very, very sad.

When I woke up early the next morning, my ruminations about my love life seemed as remote as a dream that had seemed important while it was going on, but faded quickly as the new day began. And that was largely because I was already in the habit of focusing on ice cream from the moment I opened my eyes.

On this particular morning, I had something else important to focus on, as well.

An hour later, as my ice cream maker churned up a fresh batch of Honey Lavender that I was certain was going to be one of Lickety Splits' most popular flavors, I hauled three huge containers of ice cream out of the freezer and began making an ice cream cake.

First, I pressed a two-inch-thick layer of chocolate ice cream into the pan. I sprinkled it with a layer of chocolate cookie crumbs. Then came a layer of raspberry ice cream, followed by more crumbs. Next, a layer of Almond Chocolate Chip. This time, I slathered a generous layer of whipped cream across the top like frosting, smoothing it with a metal spatula. As a final step, I used a silicone icing bag to create a decorative white edge around the circumference with what was left of the whipped cream.

When it was done, I stood back to admire it, feeling a surge of satisfaction over my creation. To me, it was a work of art.

Maybe Ashley had her Mile-High Cupcake, I thought, allowing an ugly streak of competitiveness to come out. But I have my Mile-High Ice Cream Cake.

I realized I could also make it a brand-new offering at Lickety Splits. My shop could now become the Home of the Mile-High Ice Cream Cake.

Instead of feeling that I was competing with Ashley, it could be my way of honoring her memory. Maybe we weren't the best of friends, but that didn't mean I didn't appreciate her skill at marketing.

As I packed it up inside a pink cake box, I only hoped I didn't regret wasting all this lovely ice cream on Ashley's ex-husband. While I didn't want to make any assumptions about anyone, Brandy's story about him storming into the shop in a rage and demanding money from his ex-wife still had me more than a little nervous about meeting him.

As soon as Emma arrived at the shop, I left Lickety Splits in her capable hands and drove over to Billy's house.

My nervousness only got worse. The plan I'd come up with was going to require quite a bit of acting skill.

I only hoped I was up to it.

I also hoped the ice cream cake was up to it. The June sun was doing its best to remind us all that summer was almost officially upon us, and ice cream is famous for its dislike of sunshine.

Billy Duffy's house looked ordinary enough. It was a typical suburban house, a sprawling ranch with a two-car garage. The lawn looked like it could use mowing, and the shrubs in the flower beds were pretty scraggly, but other than that, it looked like any other house.

As I strode up the front walk, I wondered if this was the

house Billy and Ashley had lived in when they were married. Frankly, it was so nondescript that it was hard to imagine her being satisfied with it.

The house was so ordinary, in fact, that a lot of my fears vanished. Up until this point, I'd been imagining that Billy Duffy lived in something more along the lines of the *Amityville Horror* house.

But once Billy answered the door, some of those fears came back with a vengeance. He looked disheveled, as if he'd been asleep. Or at least flopped out on the couch. His straight light brown hair was unkempt, with a big piece sticking out at an odd angle. And he was wearing jeans and a wrinkled T-shirt.

No matter what I'd interrupted him doing, it certainly wasn't getting dressed for work.

"Yuh?" he greeted me, his green eyes reflecting confusion. Or maybe it was just irritation.

I took a deep breath and jumped right in.

"Mr. Duffy," I began, "my name is Kate McKay. I was friends with Ashley. At least, I used to be, when we were in school."

Once I'd delivered that introduction, the confusion in his eyes faded.

"I was so sorry to hear about Ashley," I went on. "She and I knew each other since kindergarten. Did she ever mention me to you?"

He thought for all of two seconds, then shook his head.

"Ah," I said, not letting on how relieved I was. After all, the last thing I needed was for him to know that Ashley and I had never been actual friends, that in fact we'd been the opposite.

"Anyway," I continued with the same brazenness, "given our long history, you can imagine how thrilled I was to recently find out that her bakery was right across the street from my brand-new ice cream shop in town, on Hudson Avenue. I suddenly felt like I was back in high school again. I thought I'd been given a chance to rekindle my friendship with an old friend from my childhood. . . .

"Anyway, I just wanted to tell you how sorry I am. And I wanted to give you this."

I gestured toward the big, pink, impossible-to-miss cake box in my hands. But I didn't quite hand him the box, since I didn't want to let go of it. Not until I was sure I didn't need it as a way of getting into his house.

Billy shoved his hands into his jeans pockets. "That's real nice of you, but . . . it sounds like you didn't know that Ashley and I have been divorced for five years now."

"Oh!" I pretended to be surprised. "My goodness, how embarrassing. I had no *idea*!"

It scared me, what a good liar I was turning out to be. At least I hoped I was. As far as I could tell, Billy was buying this.

"In any case, Ashley was obviously a very important person in your life at one time, and I'm sure that you're feeling her loss as much as any of us," I went on.

He didn't respond.

"So let me explain what I've brought here," I said, chattering away like someone on a caffeine high from too much Cappuccino Crunch. "This is an ice cream cake that I've named the Mile-High Ice Cream Cake. Cute, don't you think? I actually got the idea from Ashley, who was selling what she called the Mile-High Cupcake. Anyway, it's three layers of ice cream, separated by chocolate cookie crumbs. . . . Oh, boy, I hope you like chocolate, because chocolate is the star."

"I like chocolate," Billy said, looking a little puzzled by this manic ice-cream-cake-bearing woman standing at his front door.

"That's great. Because this cake is practically a tribute to chocolate. . . . But you know, I should probably wrap it up in some plastic wrap," I went on. "I didn't think of it until now, but that'll help keep it fresh, even in the freezer. It's going to take you some time to eat this gorgeous creation, given how big it is. Do you have any plastic wrap in the kitchen? If not, I think I've got some in the car. . . ."

I guess I made it pretty clear that I wasn't about to leave without making sure my ice cream masterpiece was getting the treatment it deserved.

He hesitated for another moment, then moved aside to let me in. As I breezed into his house, I remembered Brandy's words—and hoped I wasn't making a mistake.

That feeling was aggravated by the fact that Billy seemed to be looking at me with new interest. It was as if he'd just realized that a decent-looking young woman was on the premises. I knew I had to act friendly, but not *too* friendly.

"Hey, now that you're here, can I get you something?" he said. "A beer, maybe?"

Eleven a.m. was a little early for me to start drinking. Actually, I was pretty sure it was too early for most of the population.

"Thanks, but I'm good." I glanced around the living room. I didn't see a laptop, so he didn't seem to be someone who worked from home. In fact, even though this was what I thought of as the best time of the day, the television was indeed on, although the volume was turned way down. The cases from a few DVDs and some video games were scattered around the coffee table, a sign that Billy was a master at keeping himself occupied.

"It's nice that you were able to take some time off from work at this difficult time," I said, figuring I'd give him the benefit of the doubt.

"I'm not working right now," Billy said. "At least, not at a traditional job. I'm not one of those jerks who's dumb enough to get stuck at some desk job, having to show up at nine every morning to put up with some boss's never-ending bull. At the moment, I'm exploring a bunch of other really amazing options."

"Really?" I asked, genuinely curious. "Like what?"

He waved his hand in the air dismissively. "Too many to tell you about. But I've got this one idea—an invention, really—that's guaranteed to make me rich. It's one of those billion-dollar ideas that's absolutely foolproof. I just have to find the right people to back me."

Whoa. So Brandy hadn't been exaggerating. He really did believe he was destined for greatness. Yet as I looked around, taking in the messed-up hair and the beer and the video games, I had to conclude that he wasn't exactly on the verge of fulfilling that particular destiny.

"Anyway, forget about the cake," he said, plopping down on the couch. "Come sit down next to me. Let's get to know each other a little."

My cue to go anywhere *but* next to him.

"I'll just look around the kitchen until I find that plastic wrap," I said firmly, heading toward the kitchen. "Or aluminum foil would work."

I was dismayed when he pulled himself up off the couch with a loud sigh and followed me into the next room. He positioned himself in the doorway, leaning against the jamb as if he needed support just to stand up. I made a point of keeping busy with the plastic wrap and the cake, a task that should have taken about ten seconds but which I planned to make last as long as I could.

"From what I heard," I said, "the cops are having a hard time coming up with any solid leads. About who killed Ashley, I mean."

He made a face, the one that said the people we were talking about, the cops, were completely incompetent. "In that case," he said, "those dummies should follow the simplest rule around: follow the money."

I was confused. "What do you mean?"

He shrugged. "They should be looking at where her money was going."

I thought I knew what he meant. After all, I knew all about the flashy Corvette. And the expensive designer accessories.

But it turned out there was something I *didn't* know about.

"Did you know good old Ashley bankrolled her boyfriend's restaurant?" Billy said, his voice dripping with disdain. "Greensleeves, or whatever it's called?"

I froze. "Ashley financed Greenleaf? Tad Patrick's place in Wolfert's Roost?"

"That's right," he said, wearing an ugly smirk. "Me and Ash had a huge argument about it once, back when I first found out. Seemed to me she could have been doing a little better on her monthly alimony payments to her loyal, formerly loving ex-husband if she had enough cash around to go gambling on some fancy restaurant."

I wondered if that was the argument Brandy had told me about. Of course, it was just as likely that the one she had overheard was just one in an ongoing series.

"Then again," Billy continued, "Ash didn't always have the common sense you'd expect from somebody who was doing as well as she was."

"It seems to me that investing in Greenleaf was a great move," I pointed out. "The restaurant is apparently doing really well, getting great reviews and bringing in people from the city and the whole Hudson Valley. . . ."

"Maybe, but that wasn't guaranteed," Billy insisted. "She didn't know that was how it would turn out. Some huge percentage of new restaurants fail. I think I read it's something like sixty percent. But Ash wasn't in it to make money. She was in it because she had the hots for that guy with the ridiculous name. Ted or Todd or whatever it is."

"Tad," I muttered, even though that didn't seem the least bit relevant.

"Whatever. Anyway, even though she was obviously good at business, she wasn't practicing good business sense. She was making decisions with her heart. Or maybe some other part of her body."

I could feel my cheeks growing pink.

But while Ashley may not have been investing her money in the wisest way possible, it wasn't that strange, or that unusual, for her to invest in someone she cared about.

Billy didn't seem the least bit sympathetic to that point of view, probably because he clearly wanted to get his hands on as much of that money as he could. "Anyway, the point here is that Ash and Tad had a business relationship, as well as a personal relationship. Which means there was a huge potential for one or both of those to sour. I bet he was squeezing her for more money and she wouldn't give in. . . . Yeah, old Ash could be pretty tight when it came to sharing the wealth."

The more time I spent with Billy, the more I disliked him. In fact, I was trying to think of a way to extricate myself from his house as quickly as I could.

"But there's one thing I'll say about Ash," Billy went on thoughtfully. "For all her faults—and believe me, she had plenty—she was always good to Danny."

My ears pricked up the way Digger's furry ones did anytime anyone within a square mile of our house even touched some food item that was wrapped in cellophane.

"I'm sorry, who did you say Danny is?" I asked.

"I probably didn't." Billy sighed. "To tell you the truth, I try to talk about him as little as possible. Heck, I try to *think* about him as little as possible."

"Danny is . . . a friend of yours?"

Billy laughed coldly. "No-o-o-o. Danny is our son. Me and Ash, I mean. Danny is the fruit of our sacred union."

I blinked. "Ashley had a son?" I was amazed that I'd never heard a thing about him before.

"Ashley had a son," Billy repeated. "It's funny. I always think of him as *her* son, not mine. Even though he is, of course. Biologically, at least."

I was completely confused. Billy and Ashley had had a baby together, yet Billy wanted nothing to do with his own son?

"So he doesn't live with you?" I asked, trying as gracefully as I could to find out as much as I could.

"Hah. That kid doesn't live with anybody." Billy was practically sneering as he explained, "He lives in a home, as they call it. Or, to be more politically correct, a group residence. This place called Halliday House. See, he's what we called disabled." Twisting his mouth into a sneer, he added, "He's got cerebral palsy. Do you believe it? A kid of mine?"

I gulped. But somehow, I managed to utter the words, "Oh. I see."

And I was pretty sure that I did see. Billy's son hadn't turned out to be the child he'd planned on. And as a result, he'd found it difficult—impossible, even—to accept him, much less to love him.

My heart was breaking for the boy, even though I'd never even met him. And not only because of his disability. I felt sorry for him for having a father like Billy.

"How old is he—Danny?"

"Let's see, I guess he'd be about nine."

Billy wasn't sure of his own son's age. Which meant he probably didn't even visit him, much less try to choose the perfect birthday present for him every year.

Ashley had certainly had a lot more to deal with than I'd ever expected.

As I drove away, relief washed over me that I was out of

Billy's lair. But I was also pleased that I'd learned even more than I'd hoped.

As despicable as Billy was, I found it hard to believe he'd killed Ashley.

After all, by killing his ex-wife, he'd lose his meal ticket. Killing the goose that laid the golden eggs, to use an apt metaphor. After all, without Ashley and her successful bakery business, there'd be no more alimony payments.

Then again, people didn't always do things for logical reasons.

Billy Duffy wouldn't be the first person to act in the heat of the moment, only to realize right afterward that he'd just become his own worst enemy.

Chapter 13

Hawaiian Punch was originally designed to be an
ice cream topping. Originally called "Leo's
Hawaiian Punch," it was created by Tom Yates,
A. W. Leo, and Ralph Harrison in a garage
in Fullerton, California, in 1934.

—*www.TodayIFoundOut.com*

While I was learning plenty about the people in Ashley's life, I was also anxious to learn more about the dessert diva's lifestyle—and, more importantly, how she managed it on the profits from a small-town bakery.

The most likely explanation, I figured, was that she was drowning in debt. Her concern with status dated way back to our days at school. I suspected that she'd grown up to be one of those people who felt that keeping up the appearance of being wildly successful was worth juggling credit cards and car payments and whatever else she was carrying, even though she really couldn't afford any of it.

One aspect of her extravagant lifestyle that was as obvious as it was troubling was her expensive sports car. I was curious to know how much it had cost, how much she'd borrowed, and how much she had to pay each month. Or maybe she'd even leased it and it hadn't cost nearly as much as I'd assumed. I'd certainly seen plenty of TV commercials advertising low monthly payments on fancy cars.

I wanted to find out exactly what Ashley's car expense was. Which was why the first thing on my list for that day was visiting a local car dealership.

Hudson Chevrolet was the closest dealership that sold Corvettes and the one I figured Ashley was most likely to have bought her car from. As I drove onto the lot in my pickup, I wished I'd taken the time to get it washed before venturing out. Being surrounded by all those sleek, immaculate cars made me feel like I'd just shown up at a formal wedding dressed in jeans.

As I went inside the glass building, which was as sleek as the cars it contained, I noticed that the car salesman who came over to me as soon as I entered didn't seem to mind my attire. For all he knew, I'd come in to buy a brand new pickup truck, which meant both my vehicle and I had the right look.

I certainly wouldn't be mistaken for someone in the market for a Corvette like Ashley's. I could feel my eyes growing as big and round as Oreos as I noticed some of the sticker prices. $68,985 . . . $72,795 . . . $87,715 . . .

I was having trouble wrapping my head around those numbers. I knew Ashley's car had been expensive, but I hadn't really understood up until this moment *how* expensive.

I was anxious to find out how she had financed this little toy of hers.

"Nice pickup," the salesman observed, gesturing toward my chariot with his chin. He was a young man with jet black hair that was as impeccably styled as his suit. His bright red tie matched the Corvette we happened to be standing next to. The name tag on his lapel read Bao. "Looking to upgrade?"

"Not exactly," I replied. Although now that I was here, standing among all these shiny new vehicles, I was starting to think that maybe, one of these days, owning a sparkling new cherry red pickup truck might be fun. Maybe once Lickety Splits became as successful as Sweet Things seemed to have been . . .

"Actually," I went on, "I was hoping I could speak to whoever handles the financing. It's kind of a personal matter."

I could see Bao's interest in me drop like a scoop of ice cream falling out of a four-year-old's waffle cone. I realized he now assumed I'd come into the dealership in person because I was having trouble making my monthly car payments.

I hated having someone see me that way, even though it wasn't true.

"It's really about a friend," I said. Then realized immediately that sounded even worse.

"Let me see if Deenie is available," Bao said, still smiling but backing away a bit. "She's our assistant manager."

Deenie was, indeed, in. She sat behind a big desk in an office that was glassed-in on all sides. I wondered if that was so she could keep an eye on the showroom to make sure no one shoplifted any of her inventory. The middle-aged woman was the very image of efficiency: dark hair pulled back neatly and fastened with a barrette, a tailored blouse, adorned only with a simple string of pearls, a pair of glasses dangling from a chain around her neck.

"How can I help you?" Deenie asked as I sat down in the chair facing her.

"I'm here to make a car payment," I said.

"Okay . . . but you know that doesn't have to be done in person," Deenie said, looking a little confused. "You can make payments on our Web site. Or, better yet, you can have them automatically charged to your credit card every month. . . ."

"It's not for me," I explained. "It's for a friend. Someone who just passed away."

"Oh, I'm so sorry." Deenie looked flustered. But she was

already clicking keys on her computer. "What's the name on the account?"

"Ashley Winthrop," I said. "She had a Corvette."

Her expression changed immediately, and her fingers froze above the keyboard. "Ashley," she repeated, as if she knew exactly whom I was talking about.

"You sound as if you know her," I observed.

"Only from her car purchase," Deenie said. "But working with her was kind of hard to forget."

"What do you mean?" I asked, my heart pounding.

Deenie turned away from her computer and faced me, folding her hands on her desk. "Ashley didn't owe anything on her car."

I guess I still looked puzzled because a second later, she added, "She paid cash for it."

I gasped.

"That was my reaction, too," Deenie said, shaking her head slowly. "We sell a lot of nice cars here. A lot of expensive cars. And I can count on one hand the number of times someone bought a car in that price range for cash. Well, two hands, maybe, but it's still extremely rare. And the fact that it was literally cash . . ."

"You mean she had a bank check?" I asked, wanting to make sure I understood this.

Deenie glanced out at the showroom, as if wanting to make sure no one was listening. Or, since we were behind glass walls, lip-reading.

"I shouldn't be giving out this information," she went on, "but since you two were obviously close friends, and since she passed away and all . . ."

The urge to gossip is hard to resist. Probably even more than ice cream.

"Ashley showed up here knowing exactly the model she wanted, including all these extra features that drove the price up even higher," Deenie said in a soft voice. I couldn't tell if she was trying not to be overheard or if she was simply so awed by what she was saying that she couldn't help but speak in a near whisper. "And then, when it was time to pay up, she opened up her pocketbook and started pulling out wads of cash."

Almost as if she were speaking to herself, she added, "Fortunately, it was a large pocketbook. A tote bag, practically."

I knew there were hundreds of questions I should have been asking, but my head was spinning so fast that I couldn't think of any of them.

"Where did all that money come from?" I whispered. Now *I* was the one who was talking to myself.

Deenie grimaced. "Frankly, I wondered the exact same thing," she said. "But even though I didn't say anything to her about how unusual it was for someone to buy a car for cash, Ashley seemed to feel she owed me an explanation."

"She probably said her bakery in town was doing really well," I guessed.

"It was more than that," Deenie said. "She made some vague comment about her bakery becoming a franchise." She shrugged. "Whatever was going on, she sure didn't seem worried about money."

A franchise? This was the first time I'd heard anything about that.

But I immediately found myself wondering if Ashley had simply been showing off. That, after all, was something she'd always been good at.

Or what was more likely was that she was trying to come up with a viable explanation for how she came to be carrying around stacks of bills in her purse.

But something was bothering me much more than Ashley's grandiose claim about Sweet Things becoming the next Panera. And that was the point Billy had raised.

Follow the money, he'd said. But he was talking about where it was going while I was trying to find out where she'd gotten it in the first place.

And the more I learned, the more suspicious I became that she hadn't come by all that money honestly. Which meant Ashley may have been involved with some people whose names weren't on my list—people against whom even a dog like Demon wouldn't offer enough protection.

As intriguing as the new information I'd gotten at the car dealership was, I still had another important destination on my list. So the minute I got back into my truck, I Googled "Halliday House," the residential facility Billy Duffy had mentioned. The address came right up. Sure enough, it was in Catskill, less than a half hour's drive away.

Catskill, located across a bridge on the other side of the Hudson, was a charming town that rivaled Wolfert's Roost in the cuteness department. Its main street was lined with buildings from the 1800s that housed funky shops and sophisticated restaurants.

Halliday House, located on the outskirts of town, sat amid a huge piece of property overlooking the river. The freshly mown lawn, the color of a kid's green Crayola, stretched from the road to the banks, with the two-story gray stone house plopped down right in the middle.

The building was big, but not so big that it looked institutional. In fact, only a modest sign out front gave any clue that this wasn't just some wealthy person's weekend getaway.

The yard was crisscrossed with walkways, some edged with benches, others with colorful flower beds. Four or five children, presumably residents, were in wheelchairs. The men and women pushing the wheelchairs all wore big smiles and appeared to be chatting away happily, exuding warmth toward their charges.

I drove into the parking lot, hoping to get a better look without invading the residents' privacy. But as soon as I pulled off the road, a woman who'd been heading toward her car stepped over.

"Can I help you?" she asked. She was in her midforties, with a neat blond pageboy, a dark pantsuit, and an ID hanging around her neck that read, "Margaret Campbell, Human Resources."

I rolled down the window. "I'm a friend of Ashley Winthrop," I said. "I understand her son Danny lives here."

Margaret eyed me uncertainly. "We're not allowed to give out any information about our residents," she said.

"Of course not," I replied. Glancing at the building, taking in the pleasant grounds and the cheerful-looking employees, I added, "I just wanted to see where Danny lives. And I'm glad to see it's such a nice place."

"Halliday House is one of the best residential facilities for kids like Danny in the entire country," Margaret said proudly.

Partly out of sincerity and partly as a means of fishing, I added, "I'm not surprised Ashley wanted to make sure her son got the best care possible."

Margaret nodded. "I think it was the right decision. Ashley's a single mom, and she just doesn't have the time and energy to give Danny the care he needs. Deciding to have him live here is the best possible thing she could have done."

Okay, so Margaret had broken the rules by giving out that information. But I assumed she'd figured out by that point that I already knew that Ashley's son lived here.

"Does the state pay for this kind of residence?" I asked casually.

Margaret looked surprised. "Are you kidding? I wish. The state pays for big, impersonal nursing homes, but not this kind of place."

"So Ashley paid for this herself," I mused. I didn't have the courage to ask what it cost for her to ensure that her son had the best care available. But I had a feeling it didn't come cheap. "What will happen to Danny now?"

Margaret's expression grew grim. "That remains to be seen. For one thing, it depends on what kind of arrangements his mother made in her will. If she consulted a good lawyer, hopefully Danny will be able to stay on. If not . . . well, like I said, it remains to be seen."

We were both silent for a few seconds, as if we were each pondering the possible outcomes for the rest of Danny's life.

And then, Margaret said, "Look, I don't mean to be rude, but you really can't stay here. This is private property, and, well, I'm sure you understand."

"I do," I assured her. "Thanks for your time."

With that, I did a quick three-point turn and headed out of the parking lot.

As I drove away, I felt a little sheepish that I'd spent so much time concentrating on Ashley's negative side that it had never occurred to me that the woman might also possess a positive side.

No matter what else was going on in her life, no matter what else she was spending her money on, she'd been a loving mother, one who'd made sure she could provide the best possible care for her son.

But while I was touched that Ashley had done everything possible to take care of Danny, her ability to spend continued to raise the same question. And the more I learned, the more convinced I became that I wouldn't find her killer until I found out what was behind her wealth.

Chapter 14

Howard Johnson's 28 original flavors included
Vanilla, Chocolate, Strawberry, Frozen Pudding,
Orange Pineapple, Fruit Salad, Macaroon, Ginger,
Peanut Brittle, and Apple.

—FoodTimeLine.com,
quoted from "28 Flavors Head West,"
Life *(magazine), September 6, 1948 (p. 74)*

My main motivation in joining the Wolfert's Roost
Chamber of Commerce had of course been that I saw
it as a way of furthering my investigation. So I was surprised
to find that I was actually looking forward to getting to
know more local people—especially since they, like me, were
mostly small business owners.

I was also excited about having a chance to show off Lickety Splits. I was very proud of what I'd created, and hosting a
C of C meeting was really the first opportunity I'd had to
showcase it. Holding the meeting here was pretty much the
same as throwing a party.

True, I didn't know any of the guests. But I did know ice
cream.

And I decided to go all out on this occasion. As usual, fantasizing about ice cream, all the wonderful flavors and all the
magnificent things that could be done with it, had been a pleasure. But this was a specialized occasion. The people gathering

at Lickety Splits on Monday night would be there to network, not to nosh.

I had to do something extra special to get their attention.

Which was how I came up with the idea of ice cream hors d'oeuvres. Well, not actually hors d'oeuvres, since I wouldn't be serving them before dinner. I'd be serving them after.

So they'd be desserts, but tiny, easy to handle, delectable to nibble desserts. Desserts that were passed around on a tray by my best server, Emma, who as usual would be wearing a crisp black-and-white checked apron with the pink Lickety Splits logo across the front. It was kind of like she'd pretend she was passing around scallops wrapped in bacon or teensy-weensy crab cakes while she'd actually be handing out little bursts of sweet, creamy flavor.

I even came up with the perfect name. Ice Cream Incidentals.

But there would be nothing incidental about them. I developed three different types.

One type was bite-size ice cream sandwiches, made with round, rich chocolate cookies that were about the size of an Oreo. Homemade, of course, baked in small batches in Lickety Splits' kitchen. True, my work space wasn't equipped with an oven. But I took care of that minor problem by buying a brand-new toaster oven.

Whenever a new batch of cookies had cooled enough, I scooped out softened ice cream, placed it on a cookie, and squished it down with a second cookie. I stuck with Classic Tahitian Vanilla or Double-Rich Chocolate. No nuts or chocolate chips or coconut, since I wanted the cookies to lie flat without any risk of breaking.

A second variety of Ice Cream Incidentals was my own personal take on mini cupcakes. I loved cupcakes as much as anybody, but like so many other things, they could be vastly improved by incorporating ice cream. In this particular case, by actually substituting ice cream for, well, for the cupcakes themselves.

I created these little gems by inserting pretty cupcake papers in pastel colors like baby pink, pale blue, and mint green into mini cupcake pans. Then, using a melon baller, I filled each one with a small scoop of ice cream. I used every ice cream flavor I had on hand. I pressed them down to make them flat on top, which also made them fill out the entire space, including the little ridges on the edges of the cupcake papers. As a final step, I topped each one with sprinkles: colorful bar-shaped sprinkles, tiny ball-shaped sprinkles, chocolate sprinkles, or shiny silver dragées, those tiny pearls that make everything they're on look like it's dressed up for a party.

Who needs a Mile-High Cupcake? I thought as I admired my creations before popping them back into the giant freezer to harden. Teensy-weensy bite-sized cupcakes were so much more fun, especially if they were made out of ice cream.

The third idea was inspired by those oversized Asian appetizer spoons made of white ceramic, normally used for serving a small dollop of goat cheese with figs or some other variation on interesting chopped-up food combinations. But my spoons would be filled with a mini scoop of one of Lickety Splits' most unusual ice creams. It was my chance to let as many people as possible try my fun flavors, like Melty Chocolate Malt or Lemon Raspberry Swirl. Or even goat cheese ice cream. I could even mix in small pieces of fig.

To make them even more special, each one would have a cherry on top. After all, who doesn't love a cherry on top?

The hours before the Chamber of Commerce meeting were crazily busy. Thank goodness that Emma was able to do her usual expert job of running Lickety Splits pretty much single-handedly, and with her usual good cheer. She had a way of making it all look so easy.

Of course, she'd been in an especially good mood ever since that day she'd so casually mentioned Ethan.

But while things appeared to be running perfectly smoothly in the front of the house, the scene in the kitchen was one of chaos and panic.

Willow and I were crammed into the tiny space, finding out the hard way that making Ice Cream Incidentals was anything but easy. She was in charge of baking the chocolate cookies in the small toaster oven, only a dozen at a time. That meant a lot of hot cookies to juggle, finding places to lay them out so they could cool. Without falling onto the floor. Without breaking. And, I might add, without getting eaten by their two creators.

I was working on a makeshift assembly line. While I waited for each tray of cookies to cool, I scooped out little balls of ice cream from every container I had stored in my giant freezer. Then I placed it inside one of the white plastic spoons. And finally, I added a cherry on top.

For some bizarre reason, this was all insanely fun.

"These are coming out great," Willow commented. "Each one of your Ice Cream Incidentals looks like a little piece of sculpture."

"Edible sculpture," I added. "The very best kind."

"You could serve these at all kinds of parties," Willow said. "Weddings, fancy catered events at people's homes, even kids' parties."

"We could decorate these with edible flowers," I mused, studying one of the artful spoonfuls of ice cream.

"At Easter we could put two bunny ears on each one," she suggested. "Little Santa hats at Christmas . . ."

"Or little birthday hats," I said, growing excited. "I think a new industry is being born here, Willow. Either that or we're turning into Martha Stewart."

I was so excited about my new Ice Cream Incidentals that

I temporarily forgot why I'd created them in the first place. But then, at seven-fifteen, as Emma was putting up a sign on the door that read CLOSED FOR PRIVATE EVENT, I remembered.

And started getting nervous.

Aside from trying to impress my fellow businesspeople, or at least convince them that I knew what I was doing, I was hoping tonight would turn out to be my big chance to talk to Tad, the man who had been Ashley Winthrop's boyfriend.

Who was also a suspect in her murder. A very likely one, as well.

But in addition to giving him the third degree without him noticing, I also had to act like a real member of the local Chamber of Commerce. Which meant getting to know as many people as I could.

I glanced at the list of members, doing my best to learn the names and occupations of the people I'd be meeting tonight. I recognized most of the names of the local businesses they ran: an insurance company, several real estate agencies, a computer repair service, two automotive repair services, and most of the shops and other businesses in town, including Stitchin' Time, the cheese shop, the florist, and of course, Willow's yoga studio. I saw that Big Moe, the proprietor of Toastie's, was a member. I hoped he liked my cooking as much as I liked his. The list also included the managers of some chain restaurants on the outskirts, as well as the *Daily Roost*.

There were two names in particular that made my heart pound a little faster. One was Tad Patrick of Greenleaf. The other was Ashley Winthrop's name, listed next to Sweet Things Pastry Palace. Just seeing it in print was a jolt.

A few minutes after seven, a chubby man in his fifties with a ruddy complexion and a huge smile bustled into the shop. He immediately stuck his hand out to shake mine.

"You must be Kate," he said, positively bursting with joviality. "I'm Brian Whitman. Pleased to meet you!"

"I'm pleased to meet you, too," I replied. I was impressed by how firm his handshake was. This was a man who meant business.

"Thanks so much for joining—and thanks doubly for offering to host tonight's meeting!" Brian went on. "Especially since the only other volunteer we had for tonight was Nancy Role over at Clip and Dip Dog Groomers, and I'm allergic to fur!"

His eyes drifted over to the platters of Ice Cream Incidentals that Emma was bringing out. They immediately grew as big as the cookies in my mini-ice-cream sandwiches.

"Whoa!" he exclaimed. "Now I'm *really* glad you're tonight's host!"

Even though I'd liked him from the moment he walked in, I suddenly liked him even more.

"I can see what a welcome addition your shop is to Wolfert's Roost," he said, helping himself to two of the tiny ice cream cupcakes, indicating a clear preference for chocolate. He was truly a man after my own heart. "And if I didn't already say this, welcome to the group."

"I'm glad to be part of it," I told him sincerely. "Here, take a couple more."

People began showing up then, chattering away as they filed in, looked around, and almost invariably nodded their approval. Within five minutes I had a full-fledged party on my hands.

I did my best to work the room, sashaying around with my trays of ice cream treats. As I'd anticipated, handing out free ice cream was a great way to make friends fast. Glancing around, I was pleased to see that Emma was also doing a wonderful job of chatting with the other members of the organization as she handed out the frozen goodies, no doubt creating enough goodwill to get us through the entire evening.

Eyeing the crowd, I also noticed that one member of the

group was missing. And it happened to be the one person I'd specifically wanted to come.

"Let's call the meeting to order," Brian said a few minutes after seven-thirty. "We have a lot to cover tonight—starting with the parking situation."

The entire group erupted into a loud groan.

I was completely deflated by Tad Patrick's failure to appear. After all, that had been the whole point of all this.

I was trying my best to focus on the discussion about the lack of sufficient spaces, the annoying necessity of visitors having to scrounge for quarters to feed the meters, and the two-hour time limit that had the potential to cut short day-trippers' shopping sprees. Just as I had managed to convince myself it was actually interesting, the door of Lickety Splits swung open.

It was as if a burst of light had been released into the room.

In strode Tad, his knee-length trench coat swirling around him like a cape, as tall and slender as Ichabod Crane and with the same sort of low ponytail that the fictional character also probably wore.

But without any of Ichabod's geekiness, at least according to the way Washington Irving had described the nineteenth-century schoolmaster.

I'd begun to wonder if I remembered him as more handsome and charismatic than he really was. But now that he was right in front of me, I saw that the reality was as startling as the fantasy. His features were just as perfect, his dark brown eyes just as intense. The man positively radiated self-confidence, as if he knew that by having merely shown up, he'd bestowed a gift upon everyone around him.

If I could bottle that, I thought, I'd *really* have something to sell.

Tad scanned the crowd and, with a charmingly bashful

smile, mouthed the word, "Sorry!" Then he crossed the room and plopped down in the chair right next to mine.

I was instantly engulfed in a cloud of aftershave or cologne or whatever he doused himself with before coming to the meeting. And even though Nancy the dog groomer was still talking about the sorry condition of the two parking lots back behind the bank, he turned to me and stuck out his hand.

"I'm Tad Patrick," he said, flashing me a big smile. "I own a little restaurant in town called Greenleaf. Welcome to Wolfert's Roost. This town has needed a place just like yours for ages."

Was it just my imagination, or did he actually possess more teeth than most people have?

"Thanks," I replied, shaking his hand.

Up close, I could see that his dark eyes were actually speckled with hazel. I wondered if that was something you have done surgically. Or maybe Walt Disney was now creating contact lenses that could make anyone's eyes sparkle like Tinker Bell.

But I forced myself to turn back to the topic at hand. Which, instead of parking, was now weekend traffic.

During the next forty minutes, I was introduced to half a dozen problems that local businesspeople faced. I was glad I hadn't heard about any of them before I opened Lickety Splits. If I had, I might not have had the nerve.

I was relieved when Brian stood up, stretched, and said, "It's great that we're covering so much tonight. But why don't we all take a short break? Maybe Kate even has a few more of those magical ice cream thingies stashed in back somewhere."

I was afraid that Tad would shoot out of his chair and get busy with some serious networking. So I immediately turned to him, determined not to let him get away.

"Tad—that's an interesting name," I commented.

"It's short for Tadeusz," he replied, flashing me a huge smile.

"Isn't that Polish?" I asked.

"That's right," he replied, looking pleased. "My parents were born there. In fact, the name I was born with was Tadeusz Patryk Pulaski." Grinning, he added, "You can see why I go by the name Tad Patrick."

The man was certainly charming.

"And I heard through the grapevine that you're a home-town girl," he said.

"That's true," I replied, then treated him to a six-sentence summary of my entire life that ended with the grand opening of Lickety Splits.

"You know," he said, stroking his chin thoughtfully, "I just had a great idea." He moved closer, so close I could literally smell him. I was afraid I was going to choke on Eau de Testosterone.

"What's that?" I asked, not certain I should.

"How about if you and I put our heads together and do a tie-in?" he suggested. "What I mean is, I could offer a Lickety Splits dessert at Greenleaf. You and I could cook up something special together."

"That is a good idea," I told him.

And I meant it. It *was* a good idea. Still, I somehow got the feeling that Tad Patrick, aka Tadeusz Patryk, was a little light in the sincerity department.

"Let's think about it," he said with a wink. "Something flambé, maybe. With peaches or bananas . . . I'm sure you know where I'm going with this. Or, hey, here's a thought: how about rolling a cart up to the table and using liquid nitrogen to make ice cream right in front of the guests? Sure, it's theatrical. But from my experience, customers love that kind of thing."

It was a gimmick I'd heard of. And never approved of. After all, that's pretty much what it was: a gimmick.

"We definitely have to come up with something," I said. And then I grew somber. "By the way," I said, "before someone else comes along and grabs your attention, I want to extend my condolences. I can't imagine what you must be going through."

"Thanks," he said brusquely, his voice hoarse. His dark brown eyes suddenly got very, very shiny.

"I'd known Ashley since we were both in kindergarten," I went on. "Still, I spent the last fifteen years away, first at school and then living in the city. And she and I didn't stay in touch, so I didn't really know what was going on with her over the past few years."

Tad frowned. "Join the club," he said. Then, realizing he was being unclear, he added, "What I mean is that, to be perfectly honest, I feel as if I didn't know Ashley as well as I thought I did, either. I certainly don't know what was going on with her over the past few weeks. The past few months, really. She'd changed."

"Really?" I asked. "How?"

He glanced around, as if wanting to make sure no one was listening. Fortunately, people probably noticed that we were sitting with our heads together and so decided to leave us both alone.

Moving a little closer and speaking a little more softly, Tad said, "She'd gotten more materialistic, for one thing." He laughed. "If you know Ashley at all, that's saying a lot. She was always a bit of a princess, ever since I first met her. Only the best would do. Designer clothes, luxury vacations . . . Even restaurants, which is how we met."

"I don't actually know the story of how you two met," I prompted. I know that's an anecdote few people can resist telling.

"It was right after Greenleaf got that nice review from the *New York Times*," Tad said. "Ashley dropped in one afternoon, about an hour before we'd be opening for the evening. She said she wanted to meet me." He shrugged. "I must say, I was flattered that a woman as beautiful and smart and talented as Ashley was going out of her way to meet a guy like me, who cooks for a living."

Alarms immediately started going off inside my head. The story of how he and Ashley had met totally contradicted what her ex-husband had told me just a few days earlier.

Even more importantly, Billy had claimed that Ashley had been the restaurant's backer. Of course that meant she'd met Tad long before she'd sidled up to the bar to meet the handsome newcomer in town.

Either he was lying or Billy was lying.

I held my breath, wondering if Tad's version of history would include anything at all about Ashley having been his business partner. But he was already moving on.

"Anyway, there was an instant attraction between us," Tad said. "We became inseparable practically from that day on."

"That's a lovely story," I said, still not sure if a word of it was true. "And it sounds as if the two of you had real chemistry."

"It was even more than that," Tad insisted. "We both had a real respect for each other—our ambition, the businesses we both built, how hard we'd worked to get where we were. . . . We formed kind of a mutual admiration society. I admired her and her accomplishments. And she appreciated what I did, especially because of the acclaim Greenleaf garnered from the very start. She came to the restaurant all the time and was always so complimentary about the wines I chose and the presentation of the food. Loving the good things in life was something we had in common."

Speaking more to himself than to me, he added, "She was really hot, too."

I cleared my throat, hoping to redirect his focus.

"But as time went on," he continued, "she got more and more into *things*. Ashley's good taste and her appreciation of the finer things was one of the reasons I was attracted to her in the first place, but in the last few months it was as if those great qualities of hers started to go haywire. She began buying herself all kinds of luxuries, stuff I wasn't sure she could afford."

"Like the Corvette?" I asked.

"Exactly. I can't imagine what the monthly car payments are on that thing."

Aha. So Tad didn't know that Ashley had paid cash for her seventy-five-thousand-dollar toy.

"Did you ever ask her about it?" I inquired. "Where she was getting all that money?"

Tad shook his head. "I didn't think it was any of my business. But that was something else I noticed. She got kind of, I don't know, mysterious, if that's the right word. And it wasn't only the way she was spending money. She was more secretive, somehow. We'd make a plan and she'd show up late. Or she'd be at Greenleaf, sitting alone at her favorite table in the corner, and she'd spend the whole evening texting. Or going out onto the sidewalk to talk on the phone.

"Whenever I made a comment about it—teasing her, most of the time, about how much work the bakery business seemed to be—she'd just laugh and brush it off without giving me a real answer about what was occupying her time so much." He shrugged. "I was definitely getting the feeling that there was something going on with her, something she wasn't willing to talk about. Not to me, anyway."

"Okay, folks," Brian Whitman called out, instantly causing most of the conversations buzzing around the room to end. "Why don't we get back to business. We don't want this to turn into too late a night. . . ."

I turned my attention back to Tad, but our tête-à-tête was over. I'd lost him. I could tell by the way his eyes were traveling around the room. I surmised that he was checking out the other attendees, evaluating whether by allowing me to monopolize his time he had missed out on any worthwhile networking opportunities.

"Hey, you didn't get a chance to try any of my ice cream," I whispered to Tad as Brian once again became the focus of everyone else's attention.

"That's okay," he replied. With a wink, he added, "I'll come by for a private tasting some time."

Whoa! I thought, wishing I'd turned up the air-conditioning.

The dude certainly possessed more than his share of charm, charisma, and good old-fashioned sexiness. It was no surprise that Ashley had fallen for him.

But at the same time, I wondered if her entanglement with the man she had thought of as Mr. Right had, in the end, gone miserably—*fatally*—wrong.

Chapter 15

In 1997, the Ben & Jerry's factory in Waterbury,
Vermont, created a Flavor Graveyard, complete
with granite headstones and witty epitaphs
for each flavor. It began with four flavors:
Dastardly Mash, Economic Crunch, Ethan
Almond and Tuskegee Chunk. As of 2015,
it included 35 flavors.

—*BenJerry.com*

I didn't sleep very well that night. And the amount of sugar I'd consumed over the course of the evening, thanks to the magnificence of my mini cupcakes and the other Ice Cream Incidentals, had nothing to do with it.

In the past week and a half, since Ashley's murder, I had gathered together what I thought was an impressive amount of information about the woman and her life and the people around her. But I had yet to make any real sense of what it all added up to. I hadn't come close to figuring out who could have wanted Ashley dead—or why. I had a few suspects. I had plenty of loose ends and innuendos and hearsay. But I had nothing solid.

The one thought that ran through everything I'd learned, the notion that had hummed in the background during every conversation I'd had with someone who'd known her, was that there had to be something else going on in her life. And my gut feeling was that it was something that was related to her business.

Ashley may have been running a successful bakery, but my hunch was that she was running some other operation on the side.

How else would she have had all that money?

The question was, what was it—and how had it led to her murder?

Drugs were one obvious possibility, since that particular industry was well-known for its high profits and preference for cash over MasterCard or personal checks. On the one hand, it was hard to picture Ashley Winthrop as a drug lord. But on the other hand, I'd binge-watched *Weeds* on DVD, so I knew that folks in that line of business didn't always look the way you'd assume they'd look.

That theory wasn't my first choice, but I decided I couldn't rule it out completely.

Especially since I didn't have any *second* choice, much less a third or a fourth.

As I lay in bed, listening to the house creak and the occasional owl let out a spooky hooting sound, I mulled over other possible ways of getting even more information about Ashley. And I suddenly remembered having read an article about her and her business in the *Daily Roost* a few months earlier, not long after I'd moved back to town.

It wasn't much, but it was one more rock to look under.

So first thing the next morning, after opening Lickety Splits and whipping up a batch of Cinnamon Bun ice cream and making sure Emma was ready to take charge, I headed over to the Wolfert's Roost Public Library.

The library was a big, old, brick building that I'd always loved. When my mother and sisters and I had first moved in with Grams, it immediately became a refuge for me. I headed over there every chance I got. The building may have looked stately and maybe even a little forbidding on the outside, but inside I would invariably find hundreds of friends waiting for me: the beloved characters I got to know in the pages of the books I devoured.

On this particular day, however, I headed straight for the research desk. The woman stationed there reminded me of the old-fashioned image of a librarian: dark hair streaked with gray pulled back into a bun, glasses on a chain around her neck, a plain dark dress that looked like she'd borrowed it from a headmistress in a Roald Dahl novel.

"May I help you?" she asked, not coming even close to cracking a smile.

"I'm doing some research, and I'm looking for an article that appeared in the *Daily Roost* a few weeks ago." I hesitated before adding, "It's about Sweet Things, the bakery in town. And its owner."

She frowned. "The microfilm reels are sorted by date, not by subject."

"In other words," I asked, "no one ever created an index?"

"I'm afraid not."

Now it was my turn to frown. I'd just assumed I'd be able to look up "Sweet Things" or "Ashley Winthrop" in some directory and easily find the date and page number of the article I remembered seeing, as well as any other articles that had ever been written about Ashley or her shop.

Not that easy.

So when the librarian led me over to a drawer filled with boxes of microfilm reels, I grabbed the box of microfilm that included editions of the *Roost* from March. Then I went into a small room, got comfy at the microfilm machine, and followed the diagram that showed how to thread the film.

I skimmed through each edition of the *Roost* that lit up on the screen, page by page. I'd expected the process to be te-dious, but it was actually going pretty fast. It certainly helped that I remembered exactly where that annoying article about Ashley's successful business had appeared: within the first few pages, probably page three or page five, on the right-hand side.

Finally, I spotted it. March 14, page three.

How Sweet It Is! the headline cried. Local Woman Celebrates Five Years in the Bakery Biz.

I groaned at the cliché. Really? I thought. " 'How sweet it is'?" Whoever wrote this couldn't come up with anything more original?

But I wasn't there to do a literary critique. So I kept reading.

> *"It doesn't get any sweeter than this," says Ashley Winthrop, the proprietor of the Sweet Things Pastry Palace, located at 112 Hudson Street.*
>
> *Winthrop, a lifetime resident of Wolfert's Roost, just celebrated the five-year anniversary of her shop, a favorite with locals and visitors alike.*
>
> *To commemorate the occasion, Winthrop gave a free mini cupcake to every customer (minimum purchase required). Nearly three dozen cupcakes were given away.*

"Now *that's* generous," I mumbled. "A mini cupcake. Not even a mile-high one. And a minimum purchase required? Really?"

I read on. The article gushed about what a great business-woman Ashley was and what an asset to the community Sweet Things was. You would have thought she was feeding the poor instead of loading carbs into every passerby with a credit card.

The ending made me groan.

*"Running a bakery isn't something I ever thought
I'd do when I was growing up," she says. "I just
kind of fell into it."
And those of us with a sweet tooth are glad she did!*

"Doing okay in there?" the research librarian called in.

"Doing fine," I assured her.

I sat hunched over the screen, studying the photos that accompanied the article. There was one of the exterior of Sweet Things, probably taken from the sidewalk right in front of Lickety Splits. There was also a close-up of the shop, which featured the words "Home of the Mile-High Cupcake" written in swirly letters on the awning.

The third photo was an interior shot. The picture featured the bakery's Mother Teresa–esque proprietor, standing proudly in front of a display case. She was holding one arm out, gesturing toward the pastries that were neatly lined up in the case, as if to say, "Here they are. Check 'em out!"

Interestingly, she was wearing an apron, which of course was festooned with the shop's logo. But she was also wearing spindly high heels, a short skirt, and enough makeup that I'd personally worry that flakes of blush or eyeshadow would fall into the cake batter.

Still, there were no surprises there.

Yet I continued to study the photo, thinking that maybe if I stared at Ashley's picture hard enough, somehow I'd be able to see something I'd never seen before. Crazy, I knew, but I was getting desperate.

I'd barely had that thought—about being crazy—when my entire body jolted.

I suddenly felt as if I'd been struck by another one of those lightning bolts.

I blinked hard a few times, wanting to make sure I was seeing what I thought I was seeing.

I did. I absolutely did. And it wasn't Ashley that had gotten my attention. It was the display case right behind her.

The glass case was filled with humongous chocolate chip cookies, nut-studded brownies, gingerbread boys, and layered rainbow cookies. There were less sugary pastries, as well: muffins, scones, and what looked like an assortment of croissants.

The selection of goodies looked ordinary enough, exactly the kind of assortment you'd expect to find in any bakery you walked into.

Yet something was wrong. Very wrong.

Not one of the baked goods on display appeared to be one of the pastries that Ashley's suppliers claimed to bake.

And it was that fact that was making my heart pound so loudly that I was afraid the librarian would come in to check on me.

How can this be? I thought. Could this photo have been taken before any of the women I talked to started working for Ashley?

But I remembered Lindsey saying she'd been baking for Ashley for almost a year. I was positive she'd told me that she'd started working for her soon after her husband had lost his job. And Allison had definitely said she'd been working for her since last fall, right after she started law school.

I was starting to get a very strange feeling about all this.

I pulled out the list of Ashley's suppliers and checked it against the photo, my eyes darting back and forth between the two. I could clearly see a double row of chocolate chip cookies. But scanning the list from top to bottom, no one was listed as making chocolate chip cookies. The same went for gingerbread boys, brownies, and croissants.

And then I tried doing the reverse. I studied the display case in the photo, searching for cheesecake. I didn't see any.

Not slices, not entire cakes. There was nothing there that even vaguely resembled cheesecake.

Okay, so maybe Lindsey hadn't made any that day because the Ninja Turtle in her life had a cold.

So I looked for something that could be called a blackberry tart.

Nothing.

Maybe some unusual pastry that could be labeled a Licorice Twist?

I came up short once again. Nothing in the display case had any black dots on it, in it, or around it to signify licorice. And nothing was twisted, either.

I continued going down the list, looking for the other pastries that were written next to the women's names. No Sugar 'n Spice Delight. No Cherry Jubilee. No Charlotte Russe. No Whipped Cream Éclair.

And then I was struck by another lightning bolt.

Had I remembered this correctly or was I just imagining things . . . ?

My hands were trembling as I stared at the list I held, and my mouth had become uncomfortably dry. Yet I forced myself to focus on the names printed on the list. Actually, not the names as much as what was printed right after them.

"Lindsey Mather, Cheesecake."

No problem with that. But then I looked at the second name on Ashley's list of suppliers, Allison Chibuzo. Written next to it was "Blackberry Tart."

Not "Blackberry Tarts," the way I would have written it if I were making a list like that. In fact, when I'd jotted down the list of Ice Cream Incidentals, figuring out how many of each type to make, I'd written, "Mini Cupcakes—24. Ice Cream Sandwiches—30."

Plural. Not singular.

I'd have expected Ashley to do the same thing. It was like

making a shopping list. You didn't write "banana." You wrote "bananas."

I checked the list one more time, wanting to make sure I was getting this right.

Sure enough, next to Brandy DiNapoli's name, she'd written, "Licorice Twist."

The pieces of this puzzle I'd been agonizing over for almost two weeks, ever since Ashley had been murdered, were starting to snap into place.

I could be wrong about this whole thing, I told myself, trying to stay focused despite the fact that my thoughts were whirling around inside my head like the flakes inside a snow globe.

But I didn't think I was. In fact, I now had an entirely new possibility to investigate: the possibility that the kind of sweets that Ashley had been peddling didn't require a fork to enjoy.

My new theory was making my head buzz as I left the library. I needed to find out more. And I couldn't wait.

So instead of heading back to Lickety Splits, I went home. I knew that on Tuesday mornings, Grams met with her book group. That meant I'd have the house to myself.

Digger was excited to see me, as always. Chloe was in a bit of a snit, for some reason, so she chose to ignore me. But that was fine with me. I wasn't in a mood to socialize.

Instead, I sat down at the kitchen table, but not until I'd armed myself with a cup of coffee and a big dish of Cappuccino Crunch—a natural accompaniment, after all. True, the last thing I needed was a caffeine rush, given the rate at which my brain was racing. Even so, there was always a chance it would help me focus. And at the moment, that was exactly what I needed.

I opened my laptop and immediately began typing words

into the search engine: "Hudson Valley Wholesale Suppliers Baked Goods."

I was shocked when after hitting Search, a long list of wholesale bakeries popped up. I'd had no idea there was so much baking going on all around me.

I opened the Web site of a place called Huffernan's Baking Company.

"We supply restaurants, banquet halls, country clubs, and bakeries," its About Us page informed me.

Doesn't anyone ever bake from scratch anymore? I wondered.

I clicked on the Our Products page—and was astonished by all the offerings. The list of Bundt cakes alone was mind-boggling: Chocolate Bundt Cake, Vanilla Bundt Cake, Carrot Bundt Cake, Marble Bundt Cake, Walnut Bundt Cake, Blueberry Bundt Cake, Strawberry Bundt Cake. . . .

And that was just the ten-inch size.

There were also sheet cakes, cupcakes, sponge cakes, layer cakes, pounds cakes, and *babkas*.

I clicked to the Cookie page. And found that Huffernan's offered chocolate cookies, chocolate chip cookies, peanut butter cookies, gingersnaps, snickerdoodles, chocolate chocolate chip cookies, white chocolate macadamia nut cookies . . .

So much for that one supplier.

There were half a dozen more that were less than an hour's drive away. I methodically wrote down the name and phone number of each, determined to get in touch with as many of them as I needed to until I found what I was looking for.

Then I shoveled in the last of the Cappuccino Crunch in my dish, took a final few swigs of coffee, and called the first number on my handwritten list.

"Hudson Bakery," a woman with a pleasant voice answered. "This is Lena. How can I help you?"

I reminded myself of something I'd once heard: To be a good liar, stick as close to the truth as possible.

"My name is Kate McKay," I began, "and I currently run an ice cream business. But a bakery in town has recently come on the market, and I'm thinking of expanding my business." I hesitated, then added, "The bakery is called Sweet Things. It's on Hudson Street in Wolfert's Roost."

"We supply bakeries and supermarkets all over the Hudson Valley," the woman replied. "What exactly would you like to know?"

Thanks to Lena's helpfulness, I got a quick tutorial in how the wholesale bakery business worked. There was a minimum order, I could modify the details anytime I wanted, and I could pick up my order or pay a small extra fee to have it delivered.

No surprises there.

But what I'd really been looking for was something much more specific.

And it wasn't until I called the fourth supplier on my list that I got what I was looking for.

I started out my call to Blue Ribbon Wholesale Bakers with what had become my usual opening. But as soon as I said the words "Sweet Things," the woman who'd answered interrupted.

"But Sweet Things is already a customer of ours," she said.

My jaw dropped so far my chin hit my phone.

"Just give me a minute to call up that account. . . ." she went on cheerfully. "Our computers are so darned slow today. . . . Ah, here it is. Ashley Winthrop is the usual buyer. But you said you're taking over for her?"

Something like that, I thought. "Yes, that's right," I said aloud.

"In that case, this should be a breeze," the woman went

on. "I've got the usual order right here in front of me. We've got six dozen chocolate chip cookies—that's three dozen to be picked up on Saturday mornings and three dozen on Wednesdays. Then there's four dozen brownies, also split up into two batches. Then we've got carrot cake. . . ."

Sirens were going off in my head by that point.

Chocolate chip cookies, brownies, carrot cake . . . all the usual suspects in the bakery biz.

And the exact same pastries I'd seen in the photo that had been taken at Sweet Things mere weeks before Ashley was murdered.

Which meant my hunch had been correct.

Sweet Things' inventory had come from a wholesale bakery. It wasn't a baking co-op, the way she pretended.

Which meant that Ashley's "suppliers," Lindsey and Brandy and Allison and all the other women on the list, hadn't been supplying her with baked goods. They'd been in an entirely different business altogether.

"Emma, I need your help."

I sailed into Lickety Splits ten minutes later with my laptop under my arm. Fortunately, it was still early enough in the day that there weren't many ice cream aficionados out and about. Surprisingly, most people don't consider it a breakfast staple. That was something I knew I'd have to work on.

"Sure," Emma said, drying her hands on a towel and coming out from behind the counter. "What's up, Kate?"

"I'm trying to find Ashley Winthrop's Web site for Sweet Things. But not Sweet Things, the bakery. I want to see if there's a second Web site that's related, but not exactly the same. Maybe even something with the same name. If you know what I mean."

I could tell by her expression that she had no idea what I was talking about. I could also tell that she was more than willing to take on whatever challenge it was that I was offering her.

"Let me fiddle around with your computer," she offered, taking it from me. She sat down at one of the round marble tables and instantly became engrossed in the screen as her fingers clicked away, making it sound as if a troupe of flamenco dancers had just come into the shop.

I, meanwhile, began putting on an apron. Someone with this much nervous energy, I figured, should put it to good use. And I couldn't think of a more worthwhile task than creating some new, never-seen-before flavor of ice cream.

But I'd barely had a chance to think about what that new flavor might be before Emma said, "Kate? You might want to take a look at this."

I scurried over, my curiosity about what she'd found sending my entire body into overdrive. Then I looked at the screen.

And immediately did a double take.

Staring back at me was a face that looked strangely familiar. Familiar, yet different, somehow. . . .

The woman on the screen was looking out through heavy-lidded eyes. Those lids were not only smeared with shiny blue eye shadow, they were also studded with what looked like tiny blue rhinestones. Her eyelashes, as thick as Taylor Swift's bangs, were clearly false.

Her mouth was even shinier than her eyelids. Her slightly open lips were a deep, wet-looking shade of red, made larger by the unnatural but blatantly suggestive way she was puckering them.

Even her hair was different. It was shiny, long, and very, very big. It was puffed up around her like the rays of the sun, curving from the red satin pillow behind her head.

It only took me a second or two to see through the makeup and the pouty lips and the eighties hair and realize who it was.

Lindsey Mather.

But this Lindsey Mather bore little resemblance to the one I'd met. It wasn't only the lack of sweatpants or red-rimmed eyes or screaming toddlers on each hip, either.

This was a Web site that featured sweet things, all right. And Lindsey was one of them.

Any doubts I may have had about what I was seeing were banished by the swirly lettering above Lindsey's head. Lettering that spelled out "Sweet Things in the Valley."

"Oh, my heavens!" I said breathlessly. "Ashley was running an escort service!"

"I think that's being polite," Emma said. "Let's see what else we can find on this Web site."

She moved on to another page, one that was dedicated to photos of Lindsey—the alluring version, not the sweatpants version. It featured half a dozen pictures of her in which she posed in suggestive positions: draped across a couch, peering seductively over one shoulder, gazing up at the viewer through those five-pound fake eyelashes that were stuck onto her lids. In one of them she wore a clingy, low-cut evening gown, carefully arranged to show a lot of leg, complete with stiletto heels. A couple of the pictures showed off other, nonleg parts of her.

And then I saw it. Lindsey's code name, or whatever you'd call the name she was using on the Sweet Things in the Valley Web site.

"Cheesecake."

Bingo.

I was right. Ashley's bakery was a front. What she had really been running was an escort service—from the look of her Web site, one in which the escorts did a lot more than escort.

"Okay, so it looks like this 'sweet thing' has the nickname

Cheesecake," Emma said seriously as she kept clicking away and I kept studying the images on the screen. By that point, I wasn't the least bit surprised that Brandy was identified as Licorice Twist.

As her code name suggested, she owned an entire wardrobe of black leather garments. Bustiers with so many straps I couldn't imagine how she ever figured out how to put them on. Teensy-weensy miniskirts studded with silver spikes. Tight black leather pants that—well, let's just say the way they were designed would make it really easy to go to the bathroom.

And from the props and poses featured in the photographs, it appeared that her specialty was services that were on the kinky side.

Allison was next as Blackberry Tart. There was no sign of the buttoned-up law student here. Instead, she appeared to specialize in novelty looks. In one, she was dressed like a college cheerleader, her skintight sweater decorated with a big U for some unnamed university. Her skirt was short enough that even a modest leap into the air would have been treacherous for a real-life cheerleader.

In another shot, she was dressed up like a shepherdess. I found it hard to believe there could possibly be much demand for that kind of thing these days, but then again, I was hardly an expert. Besides, for all I knew, her outfit could have been a way of communicating some other special interest that was completely alien to me.

My head continued to buzz the whole time. I looked at the images of the other women pictured on the Web site, as well. They all had tons of makeup plastered on their faces. Shiny hair that swooped and swirled. Sexy clothes that communicated a bit about their specialty.

And most of all, an expression that made it pretty clear that it wasn't cookies these ladies were heating up in their ovens.

"So Ashley Winthrop's bakery on Hudson Street was just a cover," Emma said with a sigh. "Whoever would have thought something like that was going on in a little town like Wolfert's Roost?"

"I'm as surprised as you are," I replied. "It looks like the bakery served as a money laundering operation, too. After all, Ashley's shop was a completely legitimate business, one that the IRS and the vice squad and whoever else might be interested in her couldn't question. It also provided her with the means to buy herself nice things."

"Exactly," Emma said. Grinning, she added, "Her whole setup was pretty sweet. Get it? *Sweet?*"

I groaned to show that I appreciated my niece's humor. But I wasn't exactly in the mood for laughing. Not when I was still reeling from what I'd just learned about Ashley's business.

Sweet things, indeed.

Chapter 16

At the St. Louis World's Fair in 1904, an ice
cream seller named Ernest A. Hamwi,
a Syrian, had a booth that sold a kind of wafer
called Zalabia next to one of the fifty booths at
the fair that sold ice cream. Hamwi came up with
the idea of curling the wafers and making them
cone-shaped, and then suggested they be used
instead of his neighboring vendor's plates. The
idea caught on, and twenty years later, more
than 245 million ice cream cones had been
sold in the United States.

—Expo2015.org/magazine

That evening, while Emma ran Lickety Splits and Grams
read in her bedroom, I settled myself into the comfortable, overstuffed chair, wanting to be alone.

Wanting to simply *think*.

My plan was to sort through all the information I'd gathered and replay the conversations I'd had with everyone
who'd been involved in Ashley's life.

I figured that maybe, just maybe, if I thought hard enough
I could figure it all out. I was clearly missing something, and
for all I knew, the final pieces of the puzzle that I'd almost
managed to put together were right in front of me.

So I plopped Chloe into my lap and began distractedly

stroking her silky fur. Even though her ecstatic purring was soothing, I let out a deep sigh.

I feel like I'm so close to figuring out who killed Ashley, I thought, nearly overwhelmed with frustration. She appeared to be a successful businesswoman with nothing more serious to worry about than keeping her display cases stocked with pastries and her 'Vette filled up with premium gas. Yet I'd learned that her life was full of danger and intrigue. An illicit business, suitcases stuffed with cash to pay for fancy cars and her son's care, a long list of ladies who were part of her erotic empire . . .

It made total sense that Ashley's secret doings had led to her murder.

But then there were the two men she'd been involved with. He slimy ex-husband, Billy, wanted to squeeze even more money out of her than he already was. And her boyfriend, Tad, might have had some sort of financial dealings with her as well as an unusually tempestuous relationship—both of which could lead to serious trouble.

The list of people who might have wanted Ashley dead was certainly long.

And as I mulled over everything I'd learned in the past two weeks, I kept hearing Billy's voice in my head. *Follow the money,* he'd said. At the time, I hadn't understood what good advice that was likely to be.

I let out another deep sigh, this one so deep and so loud that Chloe stopped purring. Instead, she looked up at me quizzically.

I decided that what I needed to do was to go back to the beginning. After all, now that I knew what I knew, maybe I'd be able to see things differently.

I had to question the people I'd already talked to—people whom I would now have to consider suspects, rather than merely as sources of information.

I ticked them off my mental list. Tad Patrick would be the easiest to get in touch with again. In fact, he himself had provided me with the opening I'd need. His suggestion that Lickety Splits and Greenleaf do some kind of tie-in, with me supplying his restaurant with over-the-top ice cream desserts, made it a cinch for me to drop by sometime during the off hours.

In the case of Billy Duffy, I figured I'd pay him a surprise visit, too. And I'd already thought up an excuse. I'd claim that when I'd dropped off my gift of an ice cream cake, I delivered it on a cake plate that I intended to get back. My plan was to show up on his doorstep unannounced, asking for the plate and playing dumb when he told me that the cake had been sitting on a disposable disk, as of course it had been.

But it was too late to make either of those visits today.

Which left me with my main group of suspects: the women who'd worked for Ashley.

Now that I knew the true nature of the "sweet things" that had been the real focus of Ashley's business, I was a lot more nervous about approaching the women who had worked for her. After all, they had way more to hide than their secret recipes.

But if one of those women really was Ashley's killer, they'd be even more reluctant to talk to me. Which meant there was only one way to get them to talk to me again.

I'd have to make them an offer they couldn't refuse.

I whipped out my cell phone and my list, figuring I'd start at the top. That meant extending an irresistible offer to Lindsey Mather. She was actually one of the easy ones. After all, if anyone needed a freebie, it was the mother of three little kids with an unemployed husband. Especially now that she no longer had the cash that she'd previously been getting from moonlighting.

I called the number she'd given me, listened to the chirpy

recorded message about leaving a voice mail message, and turned on the charm.

"Hi, Lindsey!" I said brightly. "This is Kate McKay from the Lickety Splits Ice Cream Shoppe. I've come up with a great idea. How about me throwing a birthday party for your daughter at absolutely no cost to you? I figure it'd be a great promotional vehicle for my new store. I'd get a professional photographer to take pictures of the event and I'd try to get coverage in the local newspaper. . . . I'd put the whole thing on Facebook, too, and basically use Violet's party as a way to spread the word that Lickety Splits is the perfect place for kids to celebrate their birthday. I hope you'll think it's a win-win situation, too. Call me back as soon as you can, because I've got a few other people to try if for some reason you're not interested. Bye!"

One down, I thought.

Next, I called Allison. A lawyer in training, I decided, needed something better than free ice cream, if such a thing even existed.

"Hi, Allison!" I told her voice mail. "This is Kate McKay from Lickety Splits. You know, the new ice cream shop in Wolfert's Roost? I'm calling you because I could use some legal help. You see, I just relocated to this area recently, so I don't know any lawyers, but I realize I need somebody to go over my lease as soon as possible. It seems the landlord is suddenly claiming I'm responsible for a few things like electrical repairs that I don't believe I'm supposed to pay for. I know you're not a full-fledged lawyer yet, but I'd be willing to pay you if you'd just swing by sometime soon to take a look at this one section in the lease. . . ."

I went down the list, making more offers. I just hoped that I was as good as the Godfather had been in making them impossible to refuse.

* * *

By the time I got to Lickety Splits, it was almost closing time. I was glad I'd gotten there before Emma had started to close up the shop. Expecting her to do it all by herself was a lot to ask, especially since she'd already put in a long day.

"At last, a chance to catch my breath!" she exclaimed. "I've been scooping all day. It's hard work! At this rate, I'm going to have shoulders like an Olympic weight lifter by the Fourth of July."

She seemed more than a little relieved to turn the OPEN sign over so that it now read CLOSED.

The two of us got busy, putting everything away for the night and making Lickety Splits spic and span. We put the tubs of ice cream into the back freezer, wiped down the tables and every other surface, and swept up crumpled paper napkins and bits of broken cone out from under the tables.

We were just about finished when Emma casually asked, "So how's the investigation going, Kate?"

I guess the look on my face was enough of an answer.

Emma reached over and squeezed my shoulder. "Don't worry, Kate. You'll figure it out."

I was wishing I had as much confidence in my investigative abilities as my niece did when my cell phone rang. When I glanced at it, I saw an unfamiliar phone number flashing on the screen. Still, it had a local area code. My heartbeat quickened as I wondered if maybe, just maybe, one of the women I'd called earlier that evening was calling me back.

"Lickety Splits Ice Cream Shoppe," I answered in my usual crisp, professional voice. "Kate speaking."

"Hi, Kate!" a familiar voice greeted me. "It's Lindsey Mather. I got your message—and I'm positively thrilled! Thank you so, so much!"

"You're welcome," I told her, "but you really are doing me a favor. I don't know if I mentioned that I have a background in public relations, and this is exactly the kind of thing I used to do as my job. Doing a birthday party for Violet, getting press coverage and plastering it all over social media . . . It's going to be a great way to get tons of publicity for Lickety Splits."

And I had to admit that all that was true, even though publicizing my shop hadn't been my main intention. This really was turning out to be a win-win situation.

"It sounds like there are a million details to work out, so we should probably get together soon," Lindsey replied. "In fact, if it's okay with you, I thought maybe I'd stop over at the store tonight. I could be there in fifteen minutes." Quickly she added, "I know it's late, and maybe you're even closing up soon, but my husband is here and can babysit. These days, I don't get many chances to get out of the house."

I pictured her with those two little boys clinging to her like baby orangutans. I understood her point perfectly.

Besides, I was just as anxious to talk to her as she seemed to be to talk to me.

"Sure," I told her. "The shop is actually closed as of about fifteen minutes ago, but that just means we'll be free to talk without interruption." *The better to pump you for information, my dear,* I thought.

"Fabulous," Lindsey said. "See you soon. And, Kate? Thanks again. I can't tell you how excited I am!"

I was excited, too. Of all the women who'd worked for Ashley, Lindsey seemed to be the least guarded. Not that I believed that she was even close to the innocent, girl-next-door type she appeared to be. Not now, when I knew that it wasn't actual cheesecake that she'd used to sweeten Ashley's clients' days.

"I'm staying here a while longer," I told Emma. "I've got a customer coming in who's interested in holding her little girl's birthday party here at the shop." I didn't want to tell her the whole story because I didn't want her to worry. And I was certain that Lindsey would be more willing to be open with me if there was nobody else around.

Emma looked uneasy. "Are you sure you'll be okay, Kate? Staying here by yourself? The entire town is pretty much shut up for the night. It's actually kind of creepy downtown after hours."

"I'll be fine," I assured her.

"I could just hang out in back—"

"Emma! Go home!" I commanded.

"You've got your cell phone, right?" she asked me nervously.

"Good night, Emma," I said firmly, practically pushing her out the door.

Ten minutes later, as I was scrubbing a clump of mashed chocolate chips that had somehow become wedged between the wall and the baseboard, the front door swung open. Lindsey Mather came bustling in, dressed in a pair of gray sweatpants and a white T-shirt that looked as if they'd just been retrieved from the laundry basket. Her dark blond hair was pulled back into the same messy bun as the last time I'd seen her. I'd thought it was an afterthought, but it occurred to me that maybe that was simply how she wore her hair.

When she wasn't working, that is.

"Made it!" she announced with a grin. Her cheeks were flushed a bright shade of pink that exactly matched the Dora the Explorer backpack she was carrying. That, I assumed, had been borrowed from Violet.

"Thanks for letting me come right over like this," she went on. "But as I told you on the phone, Rob is home and the kids are all asleep, so—"

"No problem," I assured her as I abandoned my scrubbing project. "In fact, the timing is great. So, want to sit down so

we can work out the details of Violet's ice cream extravaganza?"

"Sure," Lindsey replied. "But before we do that, do you
think it'd be possible for you to give me a tour of the place?"

I looked around Lickety Splits. "This is pretty much it, actually. I mean, there's a small work area in the back where we
actually make the ice cream and store it, but there's not much
to it."

"That's what I meant," Lindsey said. She giggled nervously.
"This probably sounds crazy, but when it comes to food, I'm
kind of obsessive about cleanliness. Especially where my kids
are concerned. It'd make me feel much better if I could just get
a look at where the ice cream is made."

"Of course," I replied. While I did, indeed, think her ob-
session with cleanliness leaned toward the crazy side, I certainly had no qualms about showing off my kitchen. Not
only was it immaculate, I also happened to be quite proud of
the magic place where wonderful things happened with my
favorite substance in the universe. "Come on back."

Still clutching her pink backpack, Lindsey followed me to
the work space at the rear of the store.

"The work area isn't very big," I chattered away, "but it's
got everything I need. The mixers, the refrigerator and the
freezer, and some counter space where I make ice cream
cakes and do all the other behind-the-scenes work."

"Still, it looks very clean," she observed politely.

"Speaking of ice cream cakes," I said, "I can make any
theme cake that you and Violet want. I can do something traditional, of course, a round cake that's decorated with roses
or pictures of balloons or whatever else you can think of. But
I can also do something like a Dora the Explorer cake."

Or at least Emma can, I was thinking, glad I had an artist
in residence.

By that point, Lindsey and I were standing in the kitchen. I eyed it critically, glad I'd just finished cleaning up in here. I actually felt a burst of pride. It really was immaculate.

"So this is pretty much all there is to see," I said, making a sweeping motion with my arm. "Here's the sink, and this is where I store the ingredients that don't need refrigeration."

Lindsey nodded, meanwhile unzipping the pink backpack. "It's very nice. Very sanitary."

She reached into the bag. I expected her to pull out a notebook, or maybe a camera.

Instead, she pulled out a gun.

Chapter 17

In 1843, Nancy Johnson of Philadelphia received
the first U.S. patent for a small-scale
hand-cranked ice cream freezer.
The ice cream freezer was a pewter cylinder.

—*https://en.wikipedia.org/wiki/Ice_cream_maker*

I felt as if all the blood in my body was rushing to the floor in a sudden swoosh. For some crazy reason, the image that popped into my head was of an ice cream cone that someone had put in a microwave.

Talk about an instant meltdown.

This *is why she wanted to get me alone in back of the shop,* I thought. Even if someone walked by—highly unlikely, since as Emma had warned, Wolfert's Roost was a ghost town at this hour—that person wouldn't be able to see us through the window.

Here I'd thought I was setting a trap for Lindsey. Instead, she had set one for me.

So Lindsey is the murderer, I thought, feeling something that bordered on relief over having finally solved the case. I didn't know why Ashley had been killed, but at least I knew who had done it.

But whatever relief I felt over having finally learned the truth lasted less than a second. Almost instantly I was back to the horrifying realization that I appeared to be the next person on Lindsey's list.

My mind raced. *I can't let this happen*, I thought. *I have to take care of Grams. And Emma.*

I could picture both their faces in my mind.

And then another face appeared. Jake's face.

Stay calm, a voice inside my head commanded. At least as calm as a person can be while a gun is pointed at her.

And stall for time.

"What's going on, Lindsey?" I asked, doing my best to sound as if she and I were having a normal conversation.

"You know, don't you?" she replied, her eyes as steely as the gun she was pointing right at me. "You've known all along."

"I don't know what you're talking about," I said. I tried to keep my eyes fixed on her ice-cold gaze. But I couldn't keep them from darting down to the gun every few seconds.

"I think you do, Kate," Lindsey said coldly. "For one thing, somehow you managed to find out that Ashley's bakery was simply a front for her real business: an escort service. She used Sweet Things to make it look to the rest of the world like she was running a legitimate business, when really it was just a way to hide what she was actually doing. It was a way to launder all the cash she was raking in, too.

"But what you probably don't know is that Ashley's business didn't start out that way," she continued. "Sweet Things in the Valley was originally a legitimate escort service. The women who worked for her back at the beginning, including me, really did supply nothing more than our good looks and our company.

"All we were expected to do was act as companions. Her clients were businessmen who'd come to New York City or the Hudson Valley from out of town, from anywhere from Cleveland to Japan. Some of them actually lived around here. All they wanted was someone pretty to go to business dinners or cocktail parties with them. They wanted to walk into an important business event with the prettiest girl in the room on their arm. It was innocent, it was fun, and it paid really well. Like I could make as much as a thousand dollars in a single evening. And all I had to do was get dressed up in a slinky black dress and high heels, go to a fancy restaurant, and eat a big steak while the guys I was sitting with talked business.

"Even my husband approved," Lindsey went on. "Rob felt terrible that he'd been out of work for so long, especially with three small children to support. So he was thrilled that we had money coming in. Good money. In fact, he used to babysit while I went out on jobs. He would joke about how he had to stay home and watch *Full House* reruns and eat Cheerios that he picked up off the floor while I got to go out to glamorous restaurants and drink champagne.

"And when I came home, no matter how late it was, Rob would have waited up for me. We'd sit at the kitchen table together, and I'd tell him all about what I'd done that evening. We'd make fun of the obnoxious businessmen who'd paid good money just to have me sit next to them."

With a little shrug, she added, "Of course, every once in a while, one of them would try something. Put his hand on my knee or whisper something about coming back to his hotel with him. But I had clear instructions from Ashley about exactly what to do. 'That's not part of the service!' she told me to say. 'You didn't pay for that!' She instructed me to be very clear with the clients about the fact that in no way was there to be any funny business. The Sweet Things in the Valley Escort Service was exactly that: a service that provided escorts. Anything more was simply not on the menu."

Lindsey's expression darkened. "But then, out of the blue, the business started to change," she went on. "*Ashley* started to change. She began taking on different kinds of clients. And before I knew it she'd turned things around a hundred and eighty degrees. Instead of telling us not to go along with the clients' lewd suggestions, she started doing the opposite."

Lindsey swallowed hard, as if her mouth had gotten dry from just thinking about it. "In fact, Ashley started making these really crazy demands. She said things like, 'You've had it so easy up until now. But let's be real. These guys aren't paying the huge fees we charge them just to look at a pretty face across a dinner table. If they want a little more for their money, don't get all uptight.'"

So Billy had been right, I thought. It *was* about money. From what Lindsey was telling me, Ashley had been running a legitimate and lucrative escort service. But she wanted more money. She got greedy—at the expense of the women who worked for her.

Ashley had changed the deal.

"At first," Lindsey said, "I thought I could manage the clients. That I could find ways to discourage them and keep things going the way they had been. My plan was to be nice about it, of course. I didn't want to upset the clients and I sure didn't want to upset Ashley. But it wasn't long before I found myself in what I guess you'd call a compromising position."

By that point Lindsey had a faraway look and her voice sounded shaky. "There was this one time . . . Well, let's just say that I ended up in a situation where I had no choice but to go along with the guy's demands."

Her eyes filled with tears as, in a near whisper, she said, "I never told Rob about what happened, of course. He would have gone ballistic. Who knows what he'd have done?"

She paused. "Actually, I know exactly what he would have done." She nearly choked on her words. "He'd have blamed me. And from then on he'd have looked at me differently. That's kind of how he is. He's got this thing about people taking responsibility for what happens to them, as if there are never any factors that are out of their control. . . .

"So I didn't say a word to anybody, including Ashley. Unfortunately, this creep, this guy who'd been the client, had plenty to say. The very next day he called Ashley and told him what a great time he'd had with me. In fact, the slimeball couldn't wait to set up another 'date' with me." She paused to take a deep breath. "And when I told Ashley I refused to go out with him again, she told me point blank that if I didn't agree to keep working for her—under her new terms—she would tell Rob what I'd done."

For a few seconds, I actually felt sorry for Lindsey. She had taken on what sounded like the perfect job as a way to help her family through a tough time. Yet in the end, she'd suffered consequences that no one should ever have to experience.

"I'm so sorry this happened to you, Lindsey," I said softly. And I meant it.

"If you're really that sorry," she said crisply, "you'll understand that I was cornered. But I still thought I could get Ashley to back down. Not that I intended to hurt her. In fact, I was feeling pretty optimistic about the two of us talking it through when I went to the bakery late that night—that Thursday night—after Ashley had closed." With a shrill laugh, she added, "Guess what I found her doing? Sitting in the back room, counting her money! Stacks of bills. Big bills. Hundreds, mostly, that she'd lined up in neat little piles. The image of it made me sick."

"But even though I was furious, I still hoped I could talk her into letting me just walk away, without her telling Rob anything or expecting anything more from me. I begged her. I even offered to give her money. But do you know what she did? She laughed at me. She *laughed*. She said, 'Sorry, girlfriend. But you and I are in this together.'"

Lindsey's entire body was trembling. "The way Ashley reacted sent me into a rage. I was desperate. My entire life was on the line. And she wouldn't budge. Honestly, I hadn't intended to hurt her when I went to the bakery that night. I really thought I could change her mind. But when I saw that I wasn't going to get her to budge, I grabbed this big knife that happened to be lying on the counter and the next thing I knew . . ."

"Lindsey," I said gently, "I'm sure if you go to the police and explain—"

"Hah!" she cried. "If I were stupid enough to do that, do you know what would happen? I'll tell you: everything would come out. Even if for some reason I wasn't convicted of murder—and let's face it, I probably would be—I'd still lose everything. My husband would walk out on me. I'd lose my kids because I'd be considered an unfit mother. I'd lose my house, my friends, my whole life."

Suddenly her face crumpled and tears began streaming down her cheeks. "I was at a point in my life when I finally had everything I'd ever wanted. I don't like to complain, but I had a really tough childhood. I grew up just assuming that I'd always be alone and miserable. Then I met Rob, and then we had Violet, and then we got the house. . . . It all seemed too good to be true. I couldn't believe how lucky I was. And then when Rob lost his job and it looked as if everything might fall apart . . . Don't you see? All I was trying to do was hold on to everything I had. And now, if any of this comes out everything will vanish!"

She took a deep breath. "I can't let that happen, Kate. And when you called about that ridiculous free birthday party— as if anybody ever gets anything for free—I immediately knew that you'd figured it all out. That after sniffing around the way you did, asking too many questions, you knew that it was me who killed Ashley."

It didn't seem like the best time to explain that she was giving me more credit than I deserved—that I hadn't really figured it out until the moment she'd pulled a gun on me. Instead, I decided to try reasoning with her.

"Lindsey, there's no reason why anyone besides you and I has to know any of this," I said. I was trying to sound calm and practical. But even I could hear the desperation in my voice. "You had a terrible experience, and no one can deny that what happened to you drove you to commit a desperate act. I feel for you. I really do. And I promise you that I'm not going to say a word to anybody—"

Yet as I spoke, I sensed that she was far, far away. Her eyes glazed over, maybe because she was picturing what her life would be like without her kids, her husband, the life she'd treasured.

It seemed like the perfect time to pounce.

My eyes drifted away from Lindsey, away from the gun, to the wardrobe-size freezer she was standing next to.

More specifically, the door.

Even more specifically, the handle.

Suddenly, in a single, swift gesture, I reached over and grabbed the handle of the freezer door with my left hand and pulled it. At the same time, I used my right hand to push Lindsey as hard as I could in the direction of the open door.

"Wha-a-a-!" she cried as she lost her balance and fell toward the freezer. As she did, her ankle hit the bottom ledge, sending her crumpling to the floor in a heap.

As she fell, the gun went off.

But even the shock of the blast didn't keep me from slamming the door shut and locking it.

My heart was pounding jackhammer hard and my head was buzzing. Yet some logical part of my mind somehow remembered an important fact I'd read in the manual that had come with the freezer. And that was that there was enough air in there to keep one person breathing for at least fifteen minutes.

That didn't give me much time to get the police into my shop and Lindsey out of there—preferably, in handcuffs. Of course, the fact that she was yelling nonstop and undoubtedly using up the oxygen faster than normal didn't help.

But I'd hardly had time to pull my cell phone out of my pocket before I heard sirens.

Someone must have heard the gunshot and dialed 911. And fortunately, crime was enough of a rarity in Wolfert's Roost that the local police didn't have that much to keep them busy.

I called anyway, wanting to make sure the police knew exactly where they'd find the scene of our little town's latest crime. Or at least it's *almost* crime. As calmly as I could, I gave the dispatcher the address—and suggested strongly that the police officers on their way over move as fast as they could.

No more than three minutes later, Pete Bonano exploded into Lickety Splits, bursting through the front door with as much force as the bullet that had just been discharged.

"Kate!" he cried when he saw me standing in the middle of the shop, still clutching my cell phone. "I mean, Ms. McKay!"

"Forget the formalities, Pete," I replied impatiently. "There's a murderer locked in my freezer."

As if to verify what I'd just said, we both heard Lindsey's voice muffled by layers of stainless steel and Freon, yelling, "Get me out of here! Let me *out!*"

"I guess we should let her out," I said to Pete. "But first, I'd better tell you what just happened."

I felt strangely empty as I watched Pete Bonano and a second officer lead Lindsey away in handcuffs. The other cop, a woman, was reciting the Miranda rights. Pete was gingerly carrying the gun, which was already packed up in a clear plastic evidence bag.

It's over, I thought.

It was only then that I became aware that I was shaking. And that what I'd thought was emptiness was actually a feeling of being drained.

I lowered myself into one of the chairs, my knees suddenly incapable of supporting my weight. I realized I probably should have taken the cops up on their offer to get me home. I hadn't been aware of how shaken up I was.

Yet I also felt a germ of something resembling euphoria. I'd survived.

I admitted to myself then that it wasn't really over. In fact, something long and ugly was just beginning. No doubt I'd be seeing more of the charming Detective Stoltz. There would be questions to answer, statements to make, a trial to attend.

But at the moment, there were other things on my mind.

Still moving like a zombie, I retrieved my cell phone from my purse and called home. I was anxious to tell Grams and Emma I was fine before they heard anything about the incident at Lickety Splits.

There were other people I wanted to call, as well, especially Willow. But before I had a chance, there was one more thing I wanted to investigate. I wanted to see if any damage had been caused when Lindsey's gun had gone off.

I admit that it was a bit difficult, returning to the spot where only minutes earlier I'd come close to being shot. But I forced myself to go back to the work area, taking a few of those deep, cleansing breaths Willow was always talking about.

I studied the wall opposite the freezer for several seconds before I spotted the place where it had hit. And then, despite everything that had happened that night, despite the horrific few minutes I'd just lived through, I started to laugh.

It wasn't the laughter of someone who was relieved, either. My laughter was genuine.

The bullet had struck Willow's painting of the hot fudge sundae. To be more specific, it had hit the canvas right on the top edge of the giant scoop of ice cream—in the exact spot a cherry would have been placed.

"Wow, will you look at that!" I cried aloud. "If that isn't a new take on the concept of a cherry on top, I don't know what is!"

I was still marveling over the improbability of the bullet hitting that particular spot when I heard someone inside the shop call, "Kate? Are you here? Are you all right?"

Jake's voice.

"I'm in back," I called to him. My stupid heart was pounding again. And this time, it had nothing to do with any murder investigation.

A couple of seconds later he appeared in the doorway. His bluer-than-blue eyes were clouded, and his entire face was drawn into an expression of complete distress. He immediately walked over and threw his arms around me.

"I'm so thankful that you're okay," he mumbled into my shoulder.

He clutched me hard for a good ten seconds before he finally let me go.

"How did you hear?" I asked.

"Detective Stoltz called me," he replied. His face finally relaxed into a grin. "I *am* your lawyer, after all. He wanted me to know that the real killer had been caught."

"You didn't have to come running over here," I told him.

He stared at me for a few seconds with an intensity that made me stop breathing. "Yeah, I did," he finally said, his voice nearly a whisper.

The two of us were silent for a few seconds. Staring at his shoulder, I finally said, "Listen, Jake, about the other day . . ."

"Yeah . . . ?"

"I wanted to apologize."

"For what?"

"For wanting you to apologize."

He laughed. "In that case," he said, "I accept your apology and I also apologize for not apologizing." His smile faded. "I mean it, Kate. I'm sorry I hurt you. Ever. Back when we were in high school, last week when I finally told you about what happened that night, and every year, every day, in between that you ever even thought about it."

He looked so forlorn and so sincere it was all I could do to keep from hugging him and telling him that all was forgiven.

But I wasn't sure I was ready to go down that road yet.

So instead, I said, "Maybe it's time to put all that behind us."

"Fine with me," he said earnestly. "Which leaves us with a big question."

I screwed up my face. "And what question would that be?"

His eyes were boring into mine as he asked, "Where do we go from here, Katy McKay?"

I hesitated, but only for a moment.

"Where we go from here," I told him, "is that you tell me your favorite flavor."

"What for?"

"Because," I replied, opening the freezer so he could see the labels on the giant tubs of ice cream, "I'm about to make you the best ice cream sundae you've ever had in your life."

Chapter 18

In 1920, an Iowa store owner named Christian
Kent Nelson figured out a way
to coat an ice cream bar with chocolate. He called
his invention the Eskimo Pie.
By 1922, he was earning $2000 a day in royalties.

—*Archives Center, National Museum of
American History (Smithsonian)*

Eating ice cream, it turns out, isn't a cure for absolutely everything.

Conversation was strained as Jake and I sat alone in Lickety Splits, the bright lights inside the shop a stark contrast to the blackness of the moonless night outside. I felt as if the two of us were in our own little cocoon, completely isolated from the rest of the world, as we sat face-to-face at one of the round marble tables, gorging on a couple of Hudson's Hottest Ice Cream Sundaes made with Bananafana and Peanut Butter Cup (Jake's choices) and Chocolate Marshmallow and Honey Lavender (mine, even though it turns out that that's a terrible combination).

Yet even though the atmosphere was intimate, the things we were talking about were anything but. We talked about Ashley, Lindsey, secrets, sports cars, cupcakes, how strange it was seeing Pete Bonano in a police uniform, and whether I should have Willow patch up the hole in her painting or just leave it the way it was. That last topic of conversation sprang up after I showed him the brand new bullet-hole cherry-on-top that now decorated my work space.

But when the last drips of ice cream had been scraped out with a spoon and we finally parted, nothing had been settled.

After Jake left, claiming that he had a particularly early morning ahead of him because of a cow with some ailment with a long, unpronounceable name, I stood at the window, watching him leave. As I did, I tried desperately to figure out what I was feeling. Lingering dismay over our past? Definitely. Optimism about a possible future together? Not so much.

The bottom line, I guess, was that I still couldn't bring myself to forgive.

"Kate, you're famous!"

I was barely awake, lying in that dazed state in which dreams still seemed more real than reality, when Emma came bounding into my room. Her cheeks were flushed, her eyes were bright, and her hair stuck out all over the place, as if she hadn't yet combed it. In her hand was a copy of a newspaper—from what I gathered, that morning's edition of the *Daily Roost*.

"Look, you're on the front page!"

I groaned even before I got a chance to look at it. Sure enough, the editor or reporter or whatever other sadist at the *Roost* had tracked down my yearbook picture from Modderplaatz Memories. It was the stark photograph that had been taken one day in late March, a day I'd forgotten was Yearbook Picture day and therefore hadn't bothered to wash my hair or put on makeup or do anything else to make myself look spiffy. On top of that, I'd chosen not to smile, making me look as if I were competing with Nick Nolte for the Worst Mug Shot Ever Award.

"Ug-g-g-g-gh!" I moaned. "Why couldn't they have taken a picture of my ice cream shop instead?"

"There's a photo of Lickety Splits, too!" Emma assured me. "It's here on page four, where the article continues. But wait until you hear what they wrote! They make you sound like the biggest hero in the Hudson Valley since Henry Hudson himself."

"I can only imagine," I growled, pulling myself out of bed.

I didn't want to be "famous," as Emma put it. I wanted my ice cream to be famous, I wanted my shop to be famous, but I didn't want *me* to be the focus of attention. I was hardly Henry Hudson. Not even close. I wasn't even close to being *Kate* Hudson, despite the coincidence of us both having the same first name.

In fact, I wanted the whole thing to just go away. This entire incident had been so ugly, and then in the end so terrifying, that I wished we could all just move on.

When I turned on my phone, I found texts from twenty-seven different people. I didn't think I even *knew* twenty-seven people.

I was dreading looking at my e-mail.

In fact, I was about to turn off my phone when I caught a glimpse of one of the names on the screen. Jake. Jake had sent me a text.

I couldn't resist looking at it.

"Be ready this Saturday night at seven," he'd written.

"Ready for *what*?" I muttered, already telling myself I wasn't about to let Jake Pratt dictate when I should or shouldn't be ready, even for something that was totally mysterious.

"Well, aren't you the talk of the town!" Grams exclaimed as soon as I shuffled into the kitchen, desperate for coffee. "I suppose Emma showed you the front page of the *Roost*?"

"Not only did she do that, she also formed a committee to raise funds for a statue of me in Riverside Park." I poured myself a large mug of coffee, more than ready for the caffeine in it to work its magic.

I'd barely had a chance to sit down at the kitchen table next to Grams to do exactly that when the doorbell rang.

"Maybe there are TV reporters outside!" Emma cried from the living room.

"Ignore that!" I called to her.

But it was too late. I could already hear the door opening.

I braced myself for a crowd of men and women with cameras and notepads to swarm into the kitchen. Instead, a few seconds later, Emma appeared, carrying a large box.

"It was FedEx," she announced. Thrusting the box at me, she added, "It's for you, Kate."

I glanced at it skeptically. "I haven't ordered anything," I said. "Did you, Grams?"

"I think it has your name on it," Grams observed, craning her neck.

"So it does." I grabbed a knife from the drawer and wrestled with it until the package was opened. After fighting my way through a mound of white tissue paper, I pulled out something made of pale blue fabric.

It was a dress. A long, strapless gown, in fact. It wasn't new, though; the styling and its slightly worn look made it pretty clear it had been hiding at a vintage shop before it found its way to my front door.

My stomach felt as if somehow I'd swallowed a bowling ball.

I bet this is the work of Grams, I thought, turning to confront the most obvious suspect.

"Is this from you?" I demanded. "And is this supposed to be funny? Like a joke or something?"

Grams held up her hands, palms out. "Don't look at me!" she insisted. "I'm not the one who sent it."

"Then who—Emma? Is this something you came up with?"

Emma looked even more confused than Grams. "Not me. I promise, Kate. I have no idea what this is about." Studying the dress, she added, "That is kind of pretty, though. In an old-fashioned sort of way."

Before I had a chance to ask any more questions, another text came in, lighting up my phone. I couldn't help but notice that, once again, it was from Jake.

"Hope it's the right size," was all he'd written.

Okay, so Jake had some kind of crazy plan, I realized. He was going to take me someplace that required wearing clothes from the past. Maybe it was Oldies Night at some local dive. Or maybe someone we knew from high school was having a party and he thought it would be funny to dress up in clothes from those days.

I was willing to be a good sport.

So Saturday evening at a few minutes before six, after leaving Willow in charge of Lickety Splits, I came home and put the dress on.

"Okay, you two," I said, parading into the living room, where both Grams and Emma were sitting with Digger and Chloe. "It fits, I guess. Am I presentable?"

"Oooh, Kate, you look gorgeous!" Emma cooed.

"Yes, you do," Grams agreed. "Although a little makeup might be appropriate, given the fact that you're wearing such a dressy dress."

"I'll help you," Emma offered, leaping off the couch. "And I have a hair thingy you can use, too. It's made of pearls. Well, fake pearls, but it's still pretty. It's a barrette you can wear on one side. . . ."

"I think you might want to wear some dressier shoes, too," Grams suggested. "If you don't have anything, I may."

The way the two of them were carrying on, you'd think I was going to opening night at the Metropolitan Opera. But I let them have their fun, pretending I was a Barbie doll as they fixed my hair and held up different pieces of jewelry and put more makeup on me than I felt comfortable going out in public in.

Finally, they were satisfied.

"You look so pretty, Kate!" Emma cried.

Grams just looked on, her eyes filling with tears.

"Okay, so you two can now think of yourselves as my personal stylists," I told them. "Of course, it would be nice if I knew what I was getting all dressed up *for*."

"Jake must have something really cool planned," Emma said.

"He obviously put a lot of thought into this evening," Grams agreed, "whatever he's got lined up for the two of you."

Somehow, I felt as if one or both of them already knew. But I had no choice but to play along.

Finally, at one minute before seven, the doorbell rang.

"He's right on time!" Grams said, springing toward the front door with a lot more energy than I'd seen her exhibit since I'd moved back home.

"Maybe I should get that," I suggested.

I went over to the door, although not as quickly as Grams. After all, I was wearing heels, not to mention navigating a floor-length dress.

Even though I'd tried to prepare myself for anything, I gasped when I opened the door. Standing in front of me was Jake, dressed in a beautifully tailored tuxedo. Tucked into the lapel was a white flower that was so fragrant I could smell it from where I was standing. I'm no expert on flowers, but I suspected it was a gardenia. His hair had been neatly styled with some kind of gel that was as shiny as his shoes.

In short, he looked amazing.

A second later, I noticed that he was holding a box with the logo of our local florist. Through the clear cellophane top I saw that it was a wristlet made from a cluster of the same white flower.

It was then that I noticed that his cheeks were flushed. In fact, the expression on his face made him look as if he were posing for an ad for an antianxiety drug.

"What's going on?" I demanded. "Where are we going, Jake?"

He took a deep breath. "To the Wolfert's Roost High School Graduation Dance," he replied, looking a little sheepish. "It's not exactly the prom, but it was too late in the year for that. I figured this was the next best thing."

"But how—what—?" I sputtered.

"Remember Chip Callahan, that geeky kid who ran for class vice president junior year and got like three votes?"

"Sure. He was president of the Chess Club, too. And the Debate Club, I think."

"Probably. Well, Chip's the principal of Wolfert's Roost High School these days. And when I called him up and explained the situation to him, he gave me—us—permission to attend this year's graduation dance.

"I know I'm late," he went on, before I'd had a chance to say anything. "Fifteen years late, to be exact. But I hope you'll be my date for the dance tonight, Kate. It would mean the world to me."

I heard a gasp. Two gasps, actually. I whirled around just in time to see two faces duck behind the doorway they'd obviously been watching us from.

But when I turned back to Jake, I still hadn't made up my mind.

My thoughts were racing. "Jake, if I go to this dance with you—and I haven't yet decided if I'm going to—you need to know that it doesn't mean that—"

"It doesn't have to mean anything," he insisted. "It can just be you and me tying up a loose end. Finishing something we didn't get to finish fifteen years ago."

I understood what he was saying. But I also knew from the intense look in his eyes that while it didn't have to mean anything, it could also turn out to mean a lot.

A whole lot.

"So what do you think, Kate?" he asked anxiously. "Am I too late?"

I could feel Emma and Grams watching me from the doorway. But I didn't dare look over at them. Besides, I already knew what Emma thought my answer should be.

The same went for Grams. Especially Grams.

And suddenly, I knew what my answer should be, too.

Recipes

Salty 'n Sweet Chocolate Syrup with Bacon

When it comes to making anything chocolate, the quality of the chocolate you use makes a huge difference. If there was ever a time to splurge, this is it. Hershey's works great, but try using Ghirardelli or Droste or another premium brand. You're guaranteed to notice (and appreciate!) the richer, more chocolaty flavor.

Sugar-Glazed Bacon

1 pound of bacon (thick-cut works best)
⅓ cup brown sugar

Preheat oven to 400 degrees with the rack placed in the upper third. Line a cookie sheet that has a rim with foil and put a rack on top of it. Lay out the bacon on the rack, with each slice separate, in a single layer. Sprinkle the brown sugar over the bacon, distributing it evenly. Bake for approximately 15 minutes, until the bacon is cooked and covered with a glaze. For best results, cool before breaking it into small pieces and adding them to the syrup in the recipe below. (Trick: Use a pair of kitchen shears to cut up the bacon.)

Chocolate Syrup

1 cup water
1 cup unsweetened cocoa powder
1½ cups sugar
dash of salt
1 teaspoon vanilla

Boil the water and sugar in a medium-sized saucepan, whisking until the sugar is completely dissolved. Add the cocoa and salt, lower the heat to a simmer, and continue to whisk until the sauce begins to thicken. (This should take about 3 minutes.) Remove the mixture from the stove and stir in the vanilla. Add the crumbled bacon from the previous recipe. Serve over ice cream, either while it's still hot or after cooling. (Note: The syrup will become even thicker as it cools.)

Brown-Sugar Bourbon Ice Cream

Butter, brown sugar, and pecans . . . These are the three delicious main ingredients of luscious pralines, which were first created in New Orleans in the early 1800s. Because bourbon has a naturally nutty flavor, combining it with brown sugar and cream in this recipe recreates the scrumptious flavors of pralines, which is enhanced by the smooth texture of ice cream. Yum!

To make one quart:

¾ cup heavy cream
1 cup whole milk

½ cup (packed) dark brown sugar
6 egg yolks (preferably large)
2 tablespoons sugar
⅛ teaspoon kosher salt
1 tablespoon (or more) bourbon
½ teaspoon vanilla extract

In a medium saucepan, stir the cream, milk, and brown sugar over medium heat until the mixture boils.

Separately, whisk the egg yolks, sugar, and salt in a bowl until the mixture becomes a pale yellow and the sugar has dissolved.

Put a medium-sized metal bowl inside a large bowl of ice water, place a fine-mesh sieve over the metal bowl, and set it aside.

While whisking the yolk mixture in the bowl, add the hot cream mixture gradually. Return the mixture to the saucepan. Stir the custard over low heat for about two minutes, until it becomes thick enough to coat the back of a spoon. Immediately strain the custard into the metal bowl that's sitting in ice water. Let the custard cool completely, stirring it often.

Once it has cooled, stir the bourbon and the vanilla into the custard. Add more bourbon to taste.

Cover the mixture and chill it in the refrigerator.

Process the custard mixture in an ice cream maker. Serve immediately or freeze.

Black Raspberry Frozen Custard

What's the difference between ice cream and frozen custard? It's simple: frozen custard contains egg yolks. Even though frozen custard may contain as little as 1.4 percent egg yolk by weight, the lecithin that's present in those egg yolks gives it a creamier texture than ice cream.

This recipe may not be as good as what you'd get at Kohr's in Atlantic City, but it's more than enough to take care of your raspberry cravings!

To make one quart:

5 cups black raspberries
2½ cups heavy cream
1½ cups whole milk
1 cup sugar
pinch of salt
6 egg yolks (preferably large)
1 teaspoon vanilla extract

Puree the raspberries in a blender, then strain the pulverized fruit through a sieve to take out the seeds.

Pour the cream, milk, sugar and salt into a heavy saucepan and stir together. Heat the mixture until it just starts bubbling at the edges (do not let it get to a full boil).

Whisk the egg yolks in a bowl made of Pyrex or another heat-proof material. Temper the yolks by gradually adding about a third of the hot cream mixture and mixing it with a whisk. Next, add this mixture to the pot and whisk it all together. (You've got custard!)

Cook the custard over medium-low heat while stirring, taking care not to let it boil. After about five minutes, it should be thick enough to coat the back of a spoon.

Strain the custard through a sieve, then stir in the vanilla.

Stir the raspberry puree into the custard until well blended. Cover the custard and refrigerate it overnight or until it's completely chilled.

Process the custard mixture in an ice cream maker. Serve immediately or freeze.

Just six weeks after the grand opening of Lickety Splits Ice Cream Shoppe, owner Kate McKay has been enlisted to whip up sundaes at the most decadent soiree in the Hudson Valley. If only Kate knew how deadly sticky her sweet deal will turn out. . . .

Once Kate arrives at a glamorous gala hosted by world-famous fashion designer Omar DeVane, she's instantly intimidated by the mogul's luxurious mansion and the frosty personalities of his handlers. But the party completely loses its flavor when guests follow screams to a room that's eerily empty—except for Omar's freshly murdered body. . . .

While the headline-grabbing crime brings a steady stream of journalists to the sleepy village of Wolfert's Roost, Kate knows things won't return to normal until Omar's killer is brought to justice. And with the scandalous case driving customers away from Lickety Splits, she has no choice but to put down the ice cream scooper and expose the culprit on her own. . . .

As Kate crashes high-profile photo shoots and mingles with fashion's biggest influencers in search of clues, the puzzling truth about Omar's fame and fortune rises to the surface—and with it, the key to his killer's twisted motive. Kate will have to navigate the celebrity lifestyle to save her fledgling business, but her attempts to freeze cold-hearted criminals in their tracks could lead to a double scoop of deadly trouble. . . .

Please turn the page for an exciting sneak peek of

Hot Fudge Murder

Cynthia Baxter's next
Lickety Splits Ice Cream Shopppe Mystery
coming soon wherever print and e-books are sold!

Chapter 1

There are multiple stories about the invention of
the ice cream sundae. One is that it originated in
Ithaca, New York, in 1892 when Chester Platt,
who ran a drugstore with a soda fountain called
Platt & Colt's, created a cherry sundae. It
consisted of vanilla ice cream, cherry syrup, and a
candied cherry and sold for ten cents.

—*https://whatscookingamerica.net/History/*
IceCream/ Sundae.htm

"Six dozen mini ice cream sandwiches, three dozen
made with Classic Tahitian Vanilla and three dozen
made with Dark Chocolate . . ."

"Check."

"Six dozen ice cream cupcakes in assorted flavors . . ."

"Check."

"Four three-gallon tubs of ice cream. That's one Classic
Tahitian Vanilla, one Chocolate Almond Fudge, one Peanut
Butter on the Playground, and one Cappuccino Crunch."

"Check."

"And hot fudge," I added, lowering my clipboard. "An entire gallon of the best chocolate fudge sauce imaginable,
whipped up in my very own kitchen. We can *not* forget that!"

As I fought off the butterflies that had been break-dancing

in my stomach since early that morning, I surveyed my staff. Just looking at them had a calming effect, reminding me I wasn't alone in undertaking this terrifying, first-time venture.

I was still having trouble comprehending the fact that I was about to serve up a selection of my handmade ice cream treats at what could well turn out to be the Hudson Valley's most glamorous event of the summer.

I was glad I wasn't alone in taking on this terrifying challenge.

My personal team of Three Musketeers included my best friend since elementary school, Willow; my eighteen-year-old niece, Emma; and Emma's boyfriend for the past few weeks, Ethan.

Today I felt a surge of real pride over how professional they looked. For tonight's event, they had donned the spanking-new, bubble-gum-pink polo shirts I'd recently ordered for all four of us. The breast pockets were emblazoned in white with the name of my similarly spanking-new ice cream emporium, the Lickety Splits Ice Cream Shoppe. They were also wearing white pants—although Emma had opted for white jeans.

As the three of them looked at me expectantly, I found myself thinking about George Washington in 1776. I imagined him addressing his troops right before they climbed into a rickety boat to spend Christmas sneaking up on the British instead of chugging eggnog and merrily tossing tinsel onto an evergreen tree.

But I didn't *feel* like George Washington. In fact, I desperately hoped that my Ice Cream Team's bright, eager-to-please expressions would buoy up my confidence enough to get me through the night ahead.

Instead I could feel whatever small amount of it that I'd possessed when I'd walked into my shop that morning melting away like a chocolate ice cream cone that had been dropped on the sidewalk on a hot summer day.

"Do you think this will be enough for seventy-five guests?" I asked in a wavering, not-at-all-George-Washington-like voice.

"We definitely have enough," Willow assured me. "We've gone over this a hundred times, Kate. We'll be fine."

"I'm even expecting leftovers," Emma said.

"Are you kidding?" Ethan chimed in. "I'm counting on them! Leftover ice cream sounds dope!" He pushed aside the curtain of dead-straight black hair that permanently hung over his face long enough for me to make sure that he actually possessed eyes.

"And do you think I made good choices?" I asked, nervously smoothing back my shoulder-length brown hair, today worn in a neat ponytail. "I mean, not everyone likes peanut butter. Or at least not peanut butter as an ice cream flavor. And just because we all think the ice cream cupcakes are the cutest thing since puppies, with their different-colored sprinkles and their pastel-colored papers . . ."

"People go crazy for the mini cupcakes!" Emma insisted. "Everybody from the Chamber of Commerce loved them. And that day at the shop when you handed them out as freebies so people could try some of the more exotic flavors, everyone was over the moon about them. The entire concept is pure genius!"

"Emma's right," Willow seconded. "It's impossible not to like the ice cream cupcakes."

"I'm *definitely* hoping for leftovers on those!" Ethan exclaimed. "Those dudes are totally chill!"

"And the hot fudge?" I couldn't resist adding, even though I knew I was bordering on being truly annoying. "Do you think they'll like it? This is a pretty sophisticated crowd, after all. They're used to the very best . . ."

"Kate," Emma replied with remarkable patience, "your homemade Heavenly Hot Fudge Sauce is the best in the entire universe. It's what put your Hudson's Hottest Hot Fudge Sundae on the map!"

I let out a long, appreciative sigh. My crew. Perhaps not the most professional, at least in terms of training or even appearance. Willow Baines, for example, was about as far away from an ice cream entrepreneur as you can get. She was a yoga instructor, the owner of the Heart, Mind & Soul yoga studio a few blocks away from Lickety Splits. She also held classes in meditation and relaxation.

She even looked the part. Willow had pale blond hair she wore in a cute pixie cut, the perfect complement to her tall, slender frame. And the tailored outfit she was wearing today was completely out of character for her, since she usually wore loose, comfortable clothes. The woman owned an entire wardrobe of yoga pants.

Willow didn't just teach others how to be calm and centered; she was those things herself. I found that pretty impressive, given her rocky childhood. She had grown up with a drug-addicted mother and two brothers who took off as soon as they could. The instability of her early years had instilled in her a strong need to create order in her life, something I'd picked up on when I first met her back in middle school.

Her personal struggle to find balance had made her one of the kindest, most generous people I'd ever met. For example, she was big-hearted enough to spend her Saturday night helping out her BFF as a favor. And while she was committed to maintaining a healthy lifestyle, there were two exceptions: coffee and—fortunately—ice cream.

My niece, Emma, a computer whiz and a talented artist, was one of the most creative people I'd ever met, a personality trait that was reflected in the blue streaks she'd incorporated into her wild, curly black hair. At the beginning of the summer, she'd run away from her home in the Washington, D.C., area and appeared on my doorstep—literally. She announced that she didn't want to rush off to college in the fall, as expected by her parents, my oldest sister, Julie, and her husband, Ron. Instead, she wanted to take some time off to decide exactly what direction she wanted her life to go in. She felt that living with Grams and me would provide her with the perfect way to do that. She had instantly turned into my right-hand person, helping me run Lickety Splits and doing a first-rate job thanks to her quickness to learn, her organizational skills, and her strong sense of responsibility.

As for Ethan, I knew nothing about him except that he worked at a local organic dairy that was one of my suppliers and that he generally dressed completely in black no matter how hot the summer day was. His latest thing was carrying around a tattered paperback, usually one of the classic novels devoured by young men who are on a quest to find themselves. Last week, it had been Jack Kerouac's *On the Road.* This week, it was Dostoevsky's *The Brothers Karamazov.* Frankly, I had yet to figure out why he'd become an object of affection for my otherwise-reasonable niece, since his level of conversation was generally as far away from Kerouac and Dostoevsky as you can get. In fact, I didn't think it was even possible to translate the primary words that constituted his vocabulary—"awesome," "dope," "chill," and "dude"—into Russian.

But what my crew lacked in professional deportment and experience in the world of ice cream, they more than made up for in enthusiasm, energy, creativity, and general cheerleading abilities when it came to spurring me on. They also looked pretty cool in those pink Lickety Splits shirts. I had no doubt that they would help me carry the day.

"Then I guess we're all set." I took a deep breath. "Okay, gang. Let's get this party started!"

I must admit that a tidal wave of pride washed over me as I surveyed the spread of goodies laid out before me on the counter of my shop. And not only pride: surprise, too, bordering on shock. After all, it was still hard for me to believe that I'd really opened an ice cream shop just a few weeks earlier.

Six weeks earlier, to be exact.

During that time, I'd lived out every ice cream fantasy I could think of, creating fun, exotic, and not-always-successful flavors like Peanut Butter on the Playground, which is peanut butter ice cream made with freshly ground peanuts and dotted with plump globs of grape jelly; lusciously smooth and surprising Honey Lavender; and chunky Prune 'n' Raisin. (That last one turned out to be one of the not-so-successful ones.)

I'd forced myself to master the tedious, day-to-day aspects of running a small business, wrapping my head around tasks like routinely entering every single expense on an Excel spreadsheet and keeping all my receipts carefully sorted for when tax time came around.

I'd even gotten used to the demanding schedule that running an ice cream shop requires, pulling myself out of bed before sunrise practically every day of the week in order to have enough time to make fresh new batches of ice cream before opening at eleven, then staying at the shop as late as necessary to clean up.

But I'd never catered an event of this size before.

True, since opening Lickety Splits, I'd put on two children's parties, complete with ice cream clowns made with scoops of vanilla, chocolate, and strawberry topped with ice cream cone hats, gumdrop faces, and hair made from colored sprinkles.

I'd catered a fortieth birthday party at the home of a local art gallery owner, putting together an ice cream social for fifteen women. As soon as they surveyed the buffet-style spread

I'd set up on the hostess's dining room table, they all solemnly agreed to abandon their diets for the evening. Then they set about making the most outrageous ice cream concoctions imaginable from three flavors of ice cream, three kinds of syrup, a mound of whipped cream the size of a sand dune, and an array of mix-ins that included mini M&Ms, nuts, chocolate sprinkles, strawberries, blueberries, bananas, bacon, marshmallows, pretzels, popcorn, peanut butter chips, and, of course, classic maraschino cherries.

I'd also hosted the monthly meeting of the local Chamber of Commerce. That was when I'd invented Ice Cream Incidentals, my hors d'oeuvre-style ice cream mini treats that included the tiny ice cream cupcakes and bite-sized ice cream sandwiches I'd prepared for today. They were perfect for passing around at a gathering since people could pop them into their mouths without needing a spoon—or, in most cases, even a napkin.

But all of those events had been kid stuff compared to the gala event I was catering tonight.

And it wasn't even the fact that there would be upward of seventy-five guests at this Saturday night gala that was giving me pause. Even more nerve-wracking was the aforementioned glam factor.

The party I was catering was being held at the weekend retreat of a famous fashion designer.

I'm talking about someone so well-known that his line of expensive purses and wallets is one of the first things you see when you walk into any Macy's or Nordstrom in the country. Someone whose name is regularly mentioned at the Academy Awards when one of the interviewers asks one of the spectacularly dressed nominees, "Who are you wearing tonight?" Someone who regularly appears on TV as a judge on a weekly fashion design competition, making or breaking the careers of some monstrously talented hopefuls.

Omar DeVane was as much a household word as Mr. Clean.

And it wasn't just Omar whom I found intimidating. It was the guest list. When his assistant, Federico, had called to engage my services, he'd casually dropped a couple of names that I immediately recognized. One was Gretchen Gruen, a gorgeous blond, blue-eyed supermodel who has been featured in ads for everything from makeup to luxury cars to Greek yogurt. The other was Pippa Somers, the editor of *Flair*, a fashion magazine that's right up there with *Vogue*, *Elle*, and *W*.

And Omar DeVane wasn't even throwing this extravagant event for any particular reason, as far I could tell. It wasn't as if he was splurging because of a birthday or an anniversary or even the release of a new line of pocketbooks or evening gowns or any of the other items he was famous for putting his easily recognizable ODV logo on.

"Is tonight some sort of celebration?" I'd asked his assistant as I'd jotted down notes during our phone call.

Federico was silent for a few seconds. "I suppose we're celebrating Omar's life," he'd finally replied. "And Omar's estate, Greenaway, is the perfect venue."

Omar's house even had a name.

Yet despite the glamour factor, one simple fact had kept me grounded through the process of planning this glitzy event. And that was that Omar DeVane's favorite food was ice cream.

Hot fudge sundaes, to be specific.

So despite his fame, despite his fortune, despite his star-studded guest list, when you came right down to it, this Omar guy was pretty much the same as you and me. Maybe he was an internationally known fashion mogul, but deep down he was still a little kid who got excited by a dish of ice cream.

In an attempt at reining in those frisky butterflies, I re-

minded myself of this reality for the hundredth time. Or perhaps the thousandth.

At the same time, I tried *not* to think about the fact that
six weeks isn't a very long time to be in business. Especially a
brand-new business, one I'd actually known little about
when I decided to jump in and give it a try.

Before running my ice cream empire—or at least a nine-
hundred-square-foot ice cream parlor in a charming small
town in the Hudson Valley, just north of New York City,
called Wolfert's Roost—I'd been living in Manhattan, working in public relations. And I loved it, for the most part. The
challenges of the job, renting a shoebox-sized but fabulously
located apartment in the Big Apple, knowing that a seem-
ingly unlimited array of opportunities lay right outside my
door, everything from Broadway plays to ballet to some of
the world's best restaurants, museums, shops . . .

Then Grams fell.

The arthritis in her knees had been getting worse over the
years. And then, while she was completely alone in the house
except for her dog, Digger, and her cat, Chloe—neither of
whom possess any caretaking abilities aside from all the emo-
tional support and comic relief they both provide—she slid
down three steps at the bottom of the big wooden staircase in
the front hall.

Fortunately, she was able to get to a phone to dial 911. But
even though Grams thankfully didn't break any bones, she
was still faced with the harsh reality that taking care of herself and running her household was becoming increasingly
difficult. In some ways, impossible. The woman who'd raised
my two older sisters and me ever since our mother died the
summer I was ten years old was clearly in need of live-in
help.

That was where I came in.

I immediately decided that I would come back to the Hudson Valley. Once again, I took up residence in the riverside town I'd left fifteen years earlier, right after high school graduation. I'd moved back to the very same house, in fact, the dilapidated yet utterly charming Victorian at 59 Sugar Maple Way.

Of course, that also meant leaving behind my job in public relations. But when it came time to start thinking about what to do next job-wise, I found that the idea of going back to a schedule of working in an office from nine to five—actually, more like five AM to nine PM—held little appeal. Instead, I decided to live out a lifelong fantasy.

In June, the Lickety Splits Ice Cream Shoppe opened its doors on Hudson Street, Wolfert's Roost's main thoroughfare, less than a hundred feet from the town's busiest intersection.

And what a shop it was! Even now, every time I walked inside, I had to practically pinch myself to make myself believe this wasn't just a dream.

It was particularly thrilling that the store I'd created looked exactly the way I thought an ice cream emporium should look. I'd made sure of that. It helped that the space I was able to rent wasn't only in a great location. It also reeked of the turn-of-the-century charm that the downtown area itself possessed, with its quaint red-brick buildings, old-fashioned streetlights, and line of lush green trees.

Besides being just the right size, the storefront had a black-and-white tile floor that I'd had refinished, a tin ceiling that reflected the light, and—my favorite part—an exposed brick wall that added warmth along with a delightful old-fashioned feeling.

As soon as I signed the lease, I got busy turning the space into the perfect ice creamery. I'd had the walls painted pink and hung huge paintings of colorful, almost cartoonish ice cream concoctions—a three-foot ice cream cone, a gigantic banana split, and an ice cream sandwich the size of a crib mattress—that Willow had created. I'd outfitted the front with a long glass display case and brought in six small, marble-topped tables, three lining each wall. Each one was accompanied by two black wrought-iron chairs with pink vinyl seats.

Even the shop's exterior was cute. The building itself dated back to the Victorian era, so the shop had some delightful features, like two hand-carved wooden columns on either side of the front door and window boxes below the display window that dominated the front.

But I took its feeling of Disneyland's Main Street a few steps further by painting the façade a soft shade of pink, then making the wooden columns and the window box lime green. I'd also put a pink-and-green wooden bench in front of the display window. All summer, I'd kept the window box filled with pink-and-white petunias. The pastel-colored blossoms spilled over the front and sides so that the pink of the petals and the green of the leaves echoed the building's colors.

I'd planned on running the shop by myself, with occasional help from Willow. Then Emma showed up and turned out to be the perfect employee. She never missed a day or even showed up late. She was full of great ideas, dreaming up new flavors of ice cream that even I had never thought of. And her mastery of both computers and images had already proved invaluable. She'd designed fliers and created other graphics for the store. In addition, she was a master at surfing the Internet, which turned out to be particularly handy not only for my business but also when I'd investigated a murder a few weeks earlier.

At the moment, however, what I needed from my niece was for her to start packing up all the Ice Cream Incidentals.

"Emma, could you please—Emma?"

I glanced up to find that my niece had drifted over to the front of the shop, where she was staring out the huge window. Ethan was standing right next to her. True, it wasn't un-usual for him to glom onto her. They had been inseparable practically since that balmy evening in early July when he'd dropped over at the house soon after they'd met at the dairy. He claimed he'd stopped by to show her some sketches of Japanese animation-style cartoons he'd been working on. But the two of them ended up sitting on the front porch, talking, until three AM. From that day on, they were what in the old days was called an item.

At the moment, Ethan was also transfixed by whatever was on the other side of this window.

"Hey, Kate? Check this out," Emma called.

Even though we were on a tight schedule, I strode over to where the two gawkers were standing. Willow drifted over, too, unable to resist the temptation of finding out what Emma and Ethan were finding so fascinating.

I immediately saw what had grabbed their attention. From the looks of things, the construction crew that had been working on the store directly across the street from Lickety Splits for weeks was finally wrapping things up. The four of us watched as three burly guys struggled to affix a green can-vas awning to the front, a sure sign that their renovations were about to come to an end.

For five years, that shop had been the home of the Sweet Things Pastry Palace. Soon after I'd opened Lickety Splits, however, the bakery's owner had met with an unfortunate fate. The owner, Ashley Winthrop, had been a longtime ac-quaintance, someone I'd known ever since kindergarten.

Notice I said "acquaintance," not "friend." There's a story there. However, it's much too long to go into here. In fact, telling that tale would require writing an entire book.

But for the past few weeks, the storefront had been empty. That is, until early July, when construction crews began showing up first thing every morning.

Since my shop was directly across the street, how could I not keep careful track of what was going on right before my eyes?

So along with Emma and Ethan and Willow, every day I had watched the muscle-bound workmen in jeans and tight T-shirts who showed up at seven. First they hauled out the glass display cases and kitchen equipment that had been part of the store's former incarnation. Then came demolition and construction. Old walls went out, new walls went in . . . you get the picture.

On one especially steamy afternoon, in an act of what I thought was pure inspiration, I'd sashayed over with an armful of ice cream cones. I was so desperate for some information about who my new neighbor would be that I was attempting to bribe the workers. They just shrugged, insisting that they were only following the plans the contractor had given them. Then they proceeded to devour more ice cream than you'd think was humanly possible.

The arrival of the painters a few days later piqued my curiosity even further.

Whoever was moving in was clearly a big fan of earth tones, since he or she had chosen dark green for the walls. The construction guys also put up lots of natural wood accents, which lent a fresh, outdoorsy touch.

But I still didn't have a clue as to what kind of establishment the new shop was going to be. And the addition of an awning that simply replicated the forest green of the walls didn't help.

"I can't wait to find out what kind of shop that's going to be," Emma said, as if she'd been reading my mind.

"As long as it doesn't sell ice cream," Willow commented. She cast me a meaningful look, a reminder that Lickety Splits had had to deal with some head-to-head competition once before. And it hadn't exactly gone well.

Emma leaned forward so she could see better. "I don't think it's going to sell food," she said. "Not with those dark colors. That place looks more like the Amazon rain forest than a café."

"It could be a restaurant that specializes in healthy food," Ethan said. Brightening, he added, "It would be totally sick if it was one of those places that makes those awesome smoothies. I'm really into kale."

I immediately started fantasizing about kale ice cream, wondering if that would turn out to be another Prune 'n' Raisin fiasco. Which reminded me that I was in the ice cream business—and that I had better get busy with that business.

"Okay, 'Cream Team," I said, clapping my hands. "Let's get back to work. We've got a party to put on!"

My crew immediately turned their attention back to me. At that moment, I felt as if George Washington would have been proud.

Standing up a little straighter, I said, "Willow, take the keys and pull the truck up in front of the shop. Emma, start packing up all this ice cream in dry ice. Ethan, get ready to start loading the heavy stuff."

My heart was pounding with a combination of excitement and terror as my three assistants scurried around, helping me realize an entirely new chapter in what had once upon a time been a mere fantasy.

I still couldn't quite believe all this was really happening.

"Let's load up the truck," I said. "It's show time!"

We drove to Greenaway in two vehicles. Willow sat beside me in my ice-cream–laden pickup truck, while Emma and Ethan followed in Ethan's dilapidated Saab. And as we wove our way through the hills above Wolfert's Roost, I actually found myself looking forward to the evening ahead.

This is going to be an adventure, I told myself, only half-listening to Willow as she chattered away about a yoga conference she'd just attended.

In fact, I was starting to feel pretty excited about the evening ahead when Willow announced, "Here it is! Twenty-two-fourteen Riverview Drive. And there's a sign that says Greenaway, so we're definitely in the right place. That must be the driveway. Turn right."

I did—and all my anxieties came back in a sudden swoosh. Whatever I'd been picturing in my mind had been nothing compared to what was in front of me.

What was looming ahead of me wasn't a house. It wasn't even a mansion.

This was an estate—one that made Downton Abbey look like a rustic cabin in the woods.

Connect with U s

Visit us online at
KensingtonBooks.com
to read more from your favorite authors, see books
by series, view reading group guides, and more.

for sneak peeks, chances to win books and prize packs,
and to share your thoughts with other readers.

facebook.com/kensingtonpublishing
twitter.com/kensingtonbooks

Tell us what you think!

To share your thoughts, submit a review,
or sign up for our eNewsletters, please visit:
KensingtonBooks.com/TellUs.